Emily Brightwell is ——— OF BA———
She is the author of the M——— ———ry
series, and has also written romance no——— as Sarah
Temple and Young Adult novels as Cheryl Lanham.
She lives in Southern California.

Visit Emily Brightwell's website at
www.emilybrightwell.com

The Ghost and Mrs Jeffries

Emily Brightwell

Constable & Robinson Ltd
55–56 Russell Square
London WC1B 4HP
www.constablerobinson.com

First published in the US by The Berkley Publishing Group,
an imprint of Penguin Group (USA) Inc., 1993

Published in this paperback edition by C&R Crime,
an imprint of Constable & Robinson Ltd., 2013

A copy of the British Library Cataloguing in
Publication data is available from the British Library

ISBN 978-1-47210-888-3 (paperback)
ISBN 978-1-47210-898-2 (ebook)

Typeset by TW Typesetting, Plymouth, Devon

Printed and bound in the UK

1 3 5 7 9 10 8 6 4 2

CHAPTER ONE

Abigail Hodges slammed the door so hard the gold-leafed mirror rattled dangerously against the foyer wall. She paused long enough to fling the door key and her silver beaded purse onto a mahogany table before stalking across the polished oak floor to the bottom of the curving stairway.

'Mrs Trotter,' she bellowed for her housekeeper. 'Come here at once. At once, do you hear me!'

There was no answer.

'Mrs Trotter,' she shouted again. 'Thomasina? Thomasina! Where are you? What's going on here? Where is everybody?'

Impatiently her toe tapped against the floor. Where was the confounded woman? They'd pay for this! Abigail fumed. She'd teach the servants to ignore her summons. She'd teach them to play about while the mistress of the house stood waiting for service.

Her toe stopped tapping against the floor as she realized how very silent the house was. Ominously silent, almost as though it was empty.

A slow chill climbed her spine as she remembered

the medium's parting words. 'Darkness, death, despair,' the woman had intoned portentously.

Abigail took a deep breath and resolutely brushed Esme Popejoy's warning aside. What nonsense the woman had spouted. She'd been absolutely right to tell that so-called medium precisely what she thought of such silly twaddle. She'd certainly had the last word on that matter.

It was a deeply held principle that Abigail Hodges always had the last word.

But where was everybody? The house was deathly quiet. Too quiet, Abigail thought. She listened for the faint noises that indicated the presence of those well-trained servants whose duty it was to wait up for the mistress of the house. But she heard nothing. 'Hello. Is anyone here?'

After a moment she snorted indelicately. She wasn't going to stand here all night like some frightened ninny. 'Could that wretched husband of mine possibly have given the servants the night off?' she finally muttered, pushing the medium's theatrical warning to the back of her mind. She started slowly up the stairs, her steps encumbered by the heavy skirts of her evening dress. 'No doubt he thinks it was wrong of me to keep them all in last Sunday. Well,' she continued muttering under her breath, 'we'll just see about that. Coddling servants! When Leonard finally decides to bring himself home, I'll give him the task of sacking everyone. That'll put him in his place. That'll teach him, to try to undermine my authority.'

Abigail reached the top of the stairs and paused to take a deep breath. She glanced back over her shoulder, hoping to hear the tapping footsteps of a running maid or Mrs Trotter's breathless apologies for not being on duty to receive her.

She heard nothing.

Despite her brave words and utter fury, Abigail was frightened. She didn't like the feeling. It was unfamiliar to her and it made her even angrier than she'd been when Leonard had announced his intention of escorting that silly Mrs Popejoy to the train station. And after everything that had happened! Oh, she'd make him pay for this. She'd make him really pay.

Esme Popejoy. That stupid woman! She'd never go to her for a reading again. Just because Mrs Popejoy was the current rage and supposedly the best medium in the city didn't mean she had any genuine talent. Why just look at tonight's fiasco. Seven people had paid good money to try to contact their dear departed loved ones and they'd got nothing but some melodramatic claptrap! Darkness, death and despair, indeed.

Abigail's temper flared again. Why was she the one to have been singled out for a warning? she asked herself. Absolute rubbish. And that despicable Leonard! Instead of bringing her home and giving her comfort, her own husband had cavalierly agreed to escort that charlatan of a medium to the station!

Tonight was the first time Leonard had ever openly defied her wishes. The experience left a nasty taste in her mouth. Abigail wasn't used to anyone defying her wishes. She wasn't about to let it go unpunished either. She smiled slightly, thinking of the conversation she'd have when her husband finally had the good sense to come home. She'd have the last word about that too, she promised herself.

From below, she heard a loud creak. It sounded like a footstep. Abigail's heavy brows drew together. 'Who's there?'

But no one answered her.

Instead of calling out again, she stomped down the hall to her room. Bravado desperately trying to ward off an unwelcome curl of fear, Abigail frowned thoughtfully as she noticed all the lamps in the hallway had been lit. They'd been on in the drawing room as well, she remembered. Flinging open the door, she marched inside, noticing that every lamp in her room was blazing too. She wondered if Mrs Trotter had done that before she'd taken herself off tonight. Usually, that kind of wastefulness annoyed Abigail, but tonight she was almost grateful for the brightness. It helped keep the fear away.

There was another creak. Abigail froze. The sound had come from the staircase. For some reason, though, she couldn't bring herself to call out again.

Tilting her head towards the door, she listened hard for the noise to repeat itself. But there was nothing but silence.

After a few moments had passed, she decided she was merely being fanciful. Imagining things. This was an old house. Old houses groaned and creaked all the time, she had just never noticed it before. Abigail walked over and stood in front of her dressing table. Lifting her arm, she started undoing the buttons on the sleeve of her dress.

There is nothing outside the door, she told herself

firmly. She finished the buttons on the sleeves and then reached behind her. Her fingers couldn't quite reach the tiny ornate buttons on the back of the dress.

Suddenly the bedroom door crashed open. Abigail whirled around. Her mouth opened in shocked surprise, her eyes widened in sheer terror.

A shot rang out and then another.

She was dead before she hit the floor.

For once, Abigail Hodges didn't get the last word.

It was a miserable way to start the new year, Inspector Gerald Witherspoon thought as he trudged up the staircase of the opulent residence. Only the fifth of January and already there was a murder. Witherspoon sighed. He'd so hoped that 1887 would be a good year, one that didn't have people murdering one another every time one turned around.

He paused at the top of the landing and took a long, deep breath before turning to Constable Barnes. 'Now tell me again, Constable, who found the body?'

Actually he had no need to ask Barnes to repeat any information, he was merely trying to delay the moment when he had to examine the body. Nasty things, corpses. Witherspoon didn't much care for them.

'Her husband, sir,' Barnes replied. 'He found her early this morning when she didn't appear for breakfast. Looks like the poor woman walked in on a thief and he shot her. Twice. Once in the head and once in the chest.'

The inspector swallowed heavily. Oh dear, this was going to be a bad one. Gunshot wounds were so terribly messy. Then he realized exactly what Barnes had said. 'You mean the victim was murdered in the course of a burglary?' he exclaimed. The constable hadn't mentioned that fact before.

'So the lad that sent in the report seems to think.'

'But if it was a burglary.' Witherspoon argued, 'then what are we doing here? Why wasn't this case given to Inspector Nivens? Gracious, he's the Yard's expert on robbery. Furthermore, Nivens has been complaining for months that I'm getting all the homicides, practically accused me of "hogging" them. Seems to me it's only fair he should get a crack at one.'

Barnes cleared his throat. 'Now, sir,' he said cautiously, 'the gossip I got at the station was that the orders for you gettin' this one came down from Munro himself. Seems the victim is a bit of an important person. They want the case solved quickly. Besides, Nivens has got the measles.'

'Oh dear,' the inspector muttered. One didn't ignore or even dare to argue with orders that came from James Munro, the head of the Criminal Investigation Division himself. But drat, it wasn't fair. Why should he be the one who was always having to look at dead bodies? 'I expect we'd better get on with it then.'

Witherspoon and Barnes marched down the wide hallway, their footsteps muffled thumps against the thick carpet. The young police constable who'd been assigned to stand guard outside the door of the victim's room was sitting slumped in a chair, his eyes closed in a light sleep.

'Sleeping on duty, are you, lad?' Barnes called, startling the young man.

'Sorry, sir,' the young constable replied, leaping

up so fast he tripped over his feet. 'But I wasn't really asleep.'

'Could have fooled me,' Barnes said sternly.

'I was merely resting, sir,' he explained as his pale cheeks turned a bright pink. 'I was on duty all night, sir. We're a bit shorthanded at the moment.'

'The police are always shorthanded,' Barnes replied. 'That's no excuse for falling asleep at your post.'

'Now don't be too hard on the lad,' Witherspoon interrupted. 'We've all had to catch a catnap a time or two when we're on duty and I expect the constable won't do it again.'

'No, sir,' the young man replied gratefully. He quickly opened the door and stepped aside. 'Absolutely not, sir.'

Barnes let the inspector enter first. Witherspoon gathered his resolve and determined not to make a fool of himself. However distasteful it might be, he knew his duty.

Once inside, the inspector stepped away from the door so the constable could step around him. He stood where he was and slowly surveyed the victim's room.

The bedroom was large, with a high ceiling, and curved in a bow shape at one end. The walls were covered with a dark-green-and-gold-flowered wallpaper, heavy gold velvet curtains covered the windows and a brilliant emerald-green-and-gold-patterned carpet was on the floor. A bed with a carved mahogany headboard and a gold satin spread was in the centre of the room. Opposite the bed was a matching dressing table and tallboy. The drawers had been pulled out. He glanced at the bed again and saw that a jewellery case was lying upside down, propped against the foot-board.

On the side of the bed where he stood was a round table covered with a gold-fringed shawl. The top was cluttered with a lamp, porcelain figurines and a silver bowl. The room also contained an ornate dressing screen done in the Chinese style, a gold velvet settee and a footstool.

'Uh, sir,' Barnes said. 'The body's over there.'

'I know, Constable, I know. But it's important to take in the details of a place before one begins investigating.' Witherspoon thought that sounded quite good. He really didn't like the idea that others might catch on to his sqeamishness about corpses. That would be most embarrassing.

But he could delay no longer and he knew it. Steeling himself, he walked to the opposite side of the bed and reluctantly knelt beside the dead woman.

She'd been a tall, heavyset middle-aged woman with grey-streaked dark-brown hair, thick eyebrows, a jutting nose and a thin flat mouth. She lay on her back, with her hands behind her neck, her arms at sharp angles on each side. She was dressed in a pale lavender evening dress with long, tight sleeves and a high lace neck. He deliberately didn't look at the gaping hole in her chest. He flicked his gaze to her arms and saw that the cuffs of her dress were hanging open, revealing the pale white flesh of the inside of her arms. Witherspoon felt a wave of pity wash over him. Poor woman. Murder was dreadfully undignified.

'Did you notice her feet, sir?' Barnes asked.

'Er, yes,' the inspector replied hastily. He hoped he

wasn't blushing. But he'd deliberately looked away from the dead woman's limbs when he'd seen that her ankles were exposed. Still, Witherspoon knew that his duty required him to examine the victim with all due care. Why, even the smallest detail could help him solve this terrible crime.

'Looks like she were killed instantly, don't it, sir?' Barnes continued chattily.

Witherspoon hadn't the foggiest idea how the constable had come to that conclusion, but he wasn't going to admit it. He stared quizzically at the victim's feet. Her long voluminous skirts had ridden up, probably as she fell, and the inspector could see her feet, still clad in evening shoes, were crossed at the ankles. Suddenly it came to him. 'Why yes, Constable. That's my conclusion exactly. From the angle of her arms, we can conclude she was probably trying to unbutton her dress.' He forced himself not to stammer over those words. 'And if the killer came in and she whirled about quickly, then from the way her feet are crossed we can conclude that death must have been almost instantaneous.' He sincerely hoped he hadn't just made a fool out of himself and knew a tremendous relief when Barnes nodded.

'I'm not surprised she died quick, sir,' the constable continued. 'It were probably a double-fast shot. One to the head and one to the heart.'

Witherspoon nodded weakly and forced his gaze to the victim's wounds. There was a small dark hole in the centre of the forehead. But the worst was the woman's chest – it was covered in a round swell of dried blood with a crimson blackened pit at the centre. It was only duty that made the inspector bend closer and examine each of them in turn. He held his breath and tried not to get dizzy.

'We had a bit of luck with this one, sir,' Barnes said cheerily. 'The husband saw right off what had happened. He had the good sense not to touch anything.'

'Not even his wife's body?' Witherspoon was rather surprised by that.

'Not even her, sir. He said he could see she was dead as soon as he saw her lying there. And when he saw the jewellery case on the bed and them drawers pulled out, he figured it was probably a robbery. He thought it best just to close the door and send for the police. No one's been in the room since he found her.'

'That is a bit of luck,' Witherspoon agreed. 'Usually the relatives muck the body about so much that what little evidence there is in cases like this gets horribly muddled.'

'What do you make of it, sir?' Barnes asked.

'Too early to tell, Constable, too early to tell. When is the divisional surgeon arriving?'

'Dr Potter should be here any moment now.'

'Potter?' Witherspoon moaned. 'Oh dear, hasn't he retired yet? I'm sure I heard someone say he was going off to Bournemouth to grow roses.'

The constable sighed. 'Not yet, sir.'

Neither man held the divisional surgeon in high esteem.

'I suppose I'd better go and talk to the husband,' the inspector said. He'd learned what he could from staring at this poor woman. There was no point in prolonging this distasteful task. For the life of him, Witherspoon couldn't understand what one was supposed to learn from studying a corpse. It wasn't like they were ever going to speak up and tell you who'd done the foul deed. 'What's his name?'

'Hodges, sir. Leonard Hodges. The victim is Abigail Hodges.'

Drat, Witherspoon thought, I should have asked the identity of the victim before I examined the body. He wasn't sure why he should have done that, but he felt like he'd missed the boat. 'How many others are there in the household?'

'The victim's niece, Felicity Marsden, lives here and then of course there's the servants, sir. A housekeeper by the name of Thomasina Trotter, a cook, several maids and a footman. Considering the size of the house and the kind of neighbourhood hereabouts, it's a fairly small staff.'

'No butler?'

'No, sir.'

Leonard Hodges waited for them in the drawing room. He was a tall, distinguished gentleman with deep-set hazel eyes, dark brown hair worn straight back from a high forehead, an aquiline nose and prominent cheekbones. He would have been a handsome man save for the expression of utter despair and grief on his face. Dressed in an elegantly tailored black morning coat with grey trousers and a matching waistcoat, Leonard Hodges paced nervously in front of the wide marble fireplace. He also, the inspector noted, appeared to be a good deal younger than the late Mrs Hodges. But naturally one couldn't comment about such a thing.

11

'Mr Leonard Hodges,' the inspector began politely as he and Barnes advanced into the room.

'Yes.' Hodges started violently. Seeing the constable's uniform, he smiled weakly. 'I take it you're the police?'

'I'm Inspector Witherspoon and this is Constable Barnes.' They nodded courteously at one another. 'I'm sorry, sir, we didn't mean to startle you when we came in just now. Let me say I'm dreadfully sorry for your loss,' the inspector said sincerely. 'It must have been a terrible shock. I understand you're the one who found your wife?'

Hodges closed his eyes for a moment before answering. 'That's correct.'

'Could you tell us the circumstances, please,' Witherspoon asked. His heart swelled with sympathy for the poor man.

'The circumstances,' Hodges repeated blankly. 'Oh yes. Of course, you'll need to know the details. Forgive me, please, I'm not thinking too clearly.'

'That's understandable, Mr Hodges,' Witherspoon replied kindly. 'Please take your time and begin at the beginning. When did you find your wife's body?'

'When she didn't appear at breakfast this morning, I became concerned. I thought perhaps she'd taken ill during the night,' Hodges began softly. 'I went upstairs to her room and saw her lying there. I knew right away she was dead.' He paused and took a deep breath. 'So I sent Peter for the police.'

'And what time was that, sir?' the inspector asked.

'Just after seven-thirty this morning. We always breakfast at half past seven.' His voice broke.

The inspector gazed at him in dismay. 'I'm dreadfully sorry to have to put you through this, Mr Hodges,' he said gently, 'but the more you can tell us now, the faster we can catch the villains that perpetrated this evil deed.'

'Of course.' Hodges got hold of himself. 'I understand. Please, go on. Ask me anything you like.'

'May we sit down, sir?' Witherspoon enquired.

'Oh please,' Hodges said quickly, gesturing towards the wing chairs opposite the settee. 'I've forgotten my manners. Forgive me. Would you care for a cup of tea, or coffee, perhaps?'

'No, thank you,' the inspector said as he sat down. He waited until Barnes was settled in the wing chair and had taken out his notebook. Then he turned back to Mr Hodges. 'When was the last time you saw your wife alive?'

'Last night, about nine-fifteen.'

'Is that the time Mrs Hodges usually retires for the evening?' the inspector asked.

'No, no. But she didn't retire then,' Hodges explained. 'We weren't here when I last saw her. We'd been out for the evening. The last time I saw my wife alive was when I put her in a hansom cab outside Mrs Popejoy's home.' He dropped his face into his hands. 'Oh, this is all my fault.'

Witherspoon straightened. Egads, was the man going to confess? He couldn't believe his luck. 'Your fault, sir?'

'Yes,' Hodges cried passionately, lifting his head and gazing at the inspector with tear-filled eyes. 'If only I'd come home instead of going to my club to stay, this wouldn't have happened. But I was so angry. I stupidly indulged in foolish pride and my poor wife paid the price for my stubbornness. If I'd been with her, I could have protected her. If I'd only come home, she might still be alive, she might have been saved.'

'I doubt that, sir,' Barnes put in dryly. 'The way I see it, your missus was probably dead before she hit the floor.'

Witherspoon shot Barnes a frown. Really, sometimes his constable was so tactless.

'That's no comfort,' Hodges moaned. 'I'll never forgive myself. Never. I should have come straight home from the station and checked on her.'

'Could you explain that a bit further, sir?' Witherspoon asked.

'We'd gone to see a medium, a Mrs Esme Popejoy.' He shrugged. 'I know that sounds rather absurd. I'm not a believer, but my wife is, or was. Mrs Popejoy is quite well known, at least in some circles. When the séance was over, she asked me to escort her to the train station. She was going to visit a sick friend in Southend and she was rather frightened of going to the station by herself at that time of night. It was a decidedly awkward position. Well, I could hardly refuse the woman, and I thought Abigail would be perfectly safe coming home in a hansom. I didn't really feel I could say no to Mrs Popejoy's request. At the time I thought it the only decent thing to do.' He frowned uneasily and looked away. 'Abigail wasn't pleased. We had words when I put her in the cab. That's why I went to my club.'

'And what club might that be, sir?' Witherspoon asked.

Something that sounded very much like a sniffle accompanied Hodges's reply. 'Truscott's, near St James's Park.'

Before Witherspoon could ask another question, Barnes stuck his oar in. 'And what time did you arrive at your club, sir?'

Hodges sniffled again. 'It was ten-thirty. I remember because the clock was chiming the half hour when I entered the lounge.' Suddenly his shoulders slumped and he lifted his hands to cover his face. Soft, quiet sobs racked him.

Witherspoon and Barnes stared helplessly at one another. Obviously the poor man was so overcome by grief he couldn't answer any more questions.

Rising to his feet, the inspector said, 'Perhaps, sir, it would be best if we continued the questioning at a later time.'

He and Constable Barnes quietly left the room. When they were in the hall, Witherspoon said, 'Is someone taking a statement from the niece and the servants?'

'Miss Marsden isn't here, sir. One of the housemaids told me that the girl had gone to the ballet with a friend and was spending the night there. We've sent a constable round to fetch her. And as for the servants' – Barnes snorted – 'one of the lads has already told me we won't get much out of them today. The housekeeper is the only one on the premises that isn't havin' hysterics. Do you want to talk to her now?'

The inspector sighed. 'I suppose we'd better.'

'Should I have the lads start a house-to-house?'

'Wait until after Potter's seen the body,' Witherspoon

replied. 'Perhaps he'll be able to at least estimate the time of death. Asking questions is always so much easier when you can pinpoint the likely time the crime took place.'

Barnes looked doubtful. 'But what if Potter can't or won't estimate the time? You know how he is, he won't want to say a word before he does the autopsy. And you know as well as I, sir, that the longer we wait before questionin' the neighbours, the worse everyone's memory gets.'

'True,' Witherspoon admitted. 'Then go ahead with the house-to-house now, have our lads ask the neighbours if they saw anything suspicious last night. Anything at all.'

'Do you think the inspector will be home on time for his dinner?' Mrs Goodge asked. The cook cast a worried glance at the oven, where a nice bit of lamb was roasting.

'I expect so,' Mrs Jeffries, the housekeeper, replied. The servants at Upper Edmonton Gardens, home of Inspector Gerald Witherspoon, had just finished their evening meal. 'He's not involved in any important cases now, so I don't see why he shouldn't be here at his usual time.'

'More's the pity,' the maid, Betsy, added. 'He hasn't had a good case since November. I tell ya, it's right borin'.'

'I don't think it's borin',' Wiggins the footman said. A wide, cheerful grin spread across his round face. 'I think it's nice. Restful like, gives a body time for other things in life.'

'Hmmph,' Betsy said. 'You're just happy the inspector's not on a murder, so ya don't have to give up none of your courtin' time. Not that it's done ya much good. That Sarah Trippett still ain't givin' you the time of day.'

'Now, now, Betsy,' Mrs Jeffries admonished. 'Let's not tease Wiggins. He's got a right to privacy.' She smiled to take the sting out of the words. 'I wonder where Smythe is this evening? He's late.'

Smythe, the inspector's coachman, for all his independent ways, might be late for a meal, but he rarely missed one completely.

''E didn't say nothin' about bein' late this evenin',' the cook muttered. She shoved her empty plate to one side, rested her plump arms on the table and gazed thoughtfully at Betsy. 'But then again, he were a bit miffed when he left this mornin'. I could hear the two of you havin' a go at each other. What were that all about?'

Everyone looked at Betsy. She stared fixedly at her lap as a bright blush spread over her cheeks. Mrs Jeffries sighed. Really, this was becoming tiresome. For the past few months Betsy and Smythe seemed to be at odds every time one turned around. 'Oh dear. Did you and Smythe have words again this morning?'

Betsy raised her chin and tossed her head, sending one long blonde curl over her shoulder. Her blue eyes flashed defiantly. 'It weren't my fault this time,' she said. 'I don't know what's got into that man. He walks around 'ere with a long face, snarlin' and snappin' at people and stickin' 'is nose into where it don't belong. Well, this mornin' I got fed up and told him to mind his own bloomin' business.'

'Admittedly Smythe hasn't been in the best of moods

17

lately,' Mrs Jeffries agreed thoughtfully. She'd assumed that Smythe, like the rest of them, had a bad case of the winter doldrums. The weather hadn't been very good, the excitement of Christmas was over and, even worse, the inspector hadn't had a good case for them to snoop about in since November. But as she gazed at Betsy's stubborn expression she wondered if perhaps there might be more to Smythe's bad temper than a prolonged case of boredom. 'But I am surprised he actually missed his meal. He must be very annoyed with you, Betsy. Would you like to tell us why? Perhaps we can help.'

Betsy sighed. 'Oh, all right. Smythe's got a flea in 'is ear over me goin' to that spiritualist tomorrow night with Luty Belle.'

Mrs Goodge snorted. 'I don't think it's Luty Belle that he objects to,' she said. 'More like that young man who's escortin' the two of you.'

'And who might that be?' Mrs Jeffries was curious. Though most households made young female servants account for every moment of their free time, she'd always made it a policy not to interfere.

Betsy went back to staring at her lap. 'Edmund Kessler,' she mumbled. She raised her chin. 'But it's all quite respectable. Luty's goin' too. It's not like I'm goin' out and about with 'im on my own. Edmund's just a friend.'

Wiggins snickered. Mrs Goodge snorted again and even Mrs Jeffries raised an eyebrow. Edmund Kessler had been hanging about now for two months. No wonder Smythe was annoyed, the housekeeper thought. Every time one turned around, Edmund was underfoot – ever since they'd met the young man two months ago at a music hall. Luty Belle Crookshank, a rather elderly, wealthy and eccentric American, had taken them all on the outing in gratitude for the help they'd given her in finding a young friend of hers who'd gone missing. During the course of that investigation, the servants of Upper Edmonton Gardens had also helped solve a rather nasty double murder, not that one ever let on to anyone that one did such things, Mrs Jeffries thought.

Save for a few trusted friends who were privy to their investigations on the inspector's behalf, it was a decidedly well-kept secret. Their dear employer, whom they all liked and admired tremendously, was completely in the dark about their activities. And they were committed to keeping him in the dark as well.

But unfortunately one of the results of their lovely outing to the music hall had been that Mr Edmund Kessler, bank clerk, had become smitten with their Betsy. He'd also become a bit of a nuisance.

Edmund had contrived excuse after excuse for seeing the girl. He brought Mrs Goodge recipes, he kept them apprised of where the best bargains for household linens were to be had and he'd even gone so far as to help Wiggins wash the front windows. But Mrs Jeffries knew that the girl wasn't really interested in the poor lad. Why, she was actually quite surprised that Betsy had even agreed to go to a séance with him. It wasn't like the maid to lead the boy on. Betsy must really want to go to that séance.

'Well,' Mrs Jeffries said, 'I expect Smythe is over his bad temper by now. He'll come home in his own good time.'

The words were no sooner out of her mouth than

they heard the back door opening and the subject of their conversation stepped inside.

Smythe was a tall, powerfully built, dark-haired man with heavy, almost brutal features usually softened by a generous smile and a pair of twinkling deep-brown eyes fringed with long lashes.

He was not smiling tonight, nor was there a cocky grin on his face.

'It's bloomin' cold out there,' he said, shrugging off his overcoat and hanging it on the oak coat rack. 'Almost as bad as last year.'

He walked to the table, his big body moving almost silently despite his being such a large man. Under his arm he carried a folded-up newspaper. Smythe's heavy dark brows came together in a scowl when his gaze fell on Betsy. She refrained from looking at him. Instead, as he tossed the evening paper down at his place at the table, she snatched it up and opened it.

'Sorry I'm late,' he mumbled, easing himself into a chair and ignoring the fact that Betsy had pinched his newspaper.

'That's quite all right, Smythe,' Mrs Jeffries assured him, 'we've already eaten, but Mrs Goodge has your supper warming in the oven.'

The cook started to heave her considerable bulk to her feet, but the coachman stopped her. 'Don't trouble yerself gettin' up,' he told her. 'I can wait a bit fer me dinner and I can get it myself.'

'We were having a nice natter about Betsy goin' to that spiritualist,' Wiggins said innocently.

Smythe's scowl deepened, but he said nothing. The footman didn't appear to notice.

20

'I'm only goin' 'cause it might be interestin',' Betsy said. She put the paper down. 'Not like we've got much else to do.'

'I don't see what's so excitin' about wantin' to talk to a lot of dead people.' Wiggins helped himself to another currant bun. 'Let the dead rest in peace, that's what I always say. I mean, how do they know what's goin' to 'appen in the future?'

'You don't go to a spiritualist to find out about the future,' Betsy argued.

'Then why do you go?' Smythe asked quietly. He reached for the pot of tea and poured some into his mug.

'Lots of reasons,' Betsy replied. 'It's interestin'; it's different.'

'It's silly,' Smythe said, and smiled at Betsy's outraged gasp. 'For once, the lad is right. Spiritualism and séances are a right old load of rubbish. The only people who take notice of such stupid carryin's-on are gullible old ladies and stupid twits.'

'Are you calling me a twit and Luty Belle stupid!'

'If the shoe fits, wear it.'

Mrs Jeffries knew she really should intervene. This was getting out of hand. 'Now really, this must stop. Calling one another names is vulgar. And I do believe that however the rest of us feel about spiritualism, Betsy and Luty Belle have a perfect right to investigate any . . . er . . . philosophical avenue they choose.'

'I don't reckon it's the girl that's so eager to go as it is Luty Belle,' Mrs Goodge commented. 'Frightening though it is, I'm forced to agree with Wiggins. Let the dead stay dead and buried. Seems to me if you keep botherin' 'em with a lot of tomfool questions, they'll get right annoyed! Probably tell a packet of lies just so you'll leave 'em be.'

'Leave off it,' Smythe snapped. 'You're all talkin' about it like it were real. Spiritualists are nothin' but a bunch of thieves takin' hard-earned money off the likes of gullible girls like Betsy and old women like Luty.'

Mrs Jeffries gave up. She might as well let them argue.

'A fat lot you know about it,' Betsy responded. 'You've never been to one.'

'And I've got too much sense to go to one too.'

Oh well, Mrs Jeffries thought as the debate raged around the table, there was nothing wrong with a free exchange of ideas and opinions. Her gaze fell on the newspaper. She scanned the page quickly, and a small article at the bottom of the front page caught her eye. She snatched the paper up and hurriedly read it.

'You've just got a closed mind,' she heard Betsy snap.

'And I intend to keep it closed to bloomin' rubbish like that,' Smythe shot back.

'Why does anyone think the dead wants anyone talkin' to 'em?' Wiggins asked.

'This is quite an interesting article,' Mrs Jeffries began. Everyone ignored her.

'You can get advice from 'em,' Betsy said heatedly. 'They're on the other side, they can keep you from makin' terrible mistakes, help you with your investments and such.'

'Investments!' Mrs Goodge was outraged. 'What do they know about investments? That's a bit risky, if you ask me. I don't see that just 'cause someone dies he gets any smarter. Just look at old Mr Trundle, he was the half-wit that lived over on Faverhill Road. Could you imagine the likes of him telling you what to do or where to invest your money?'

'I really think you ought to listen to this.' Mrs Jeffries tried again. 'It may be very important.'

They took no notice of her.

Exasperated, she shouted, 'There's been a murder.'

The word was magic. Silence descended as everyone stopped talking and turned to her.

'A murder?' Mrs Goodge took her elbows off the table and sat straight up. 'Where?'

Betsy's blue eyes widened. 'Who?'

Smythe leaned forward, his expression serious and intense. 'Is it in the inspector's district?'

Wiggins's mouth turned down in a dismal frown. 'Oh no,' he moaned. 'Not again.'

CHAPTER TWO

'GET ON WITH you, boy,' Mrs Goodge snapped. 'Stop your moanin'. What does it say, then?' She nodded at the newspaper in Mrs Jeffries's hand.

The housekeeper cleared her throat. 'Woman Found Murdered,' she began. 'This morning the body of Mrs Abigail Hodges of number eight Camden Street was discovered by her husband, Mr Leonard Hodges. The police were notified and the deceased was taken to a mortuary. The police would only confirm that the victim had died of gunshot wounds. Reliable sources, however, have said the deceased may have been murdered in the course of a robbery. An inquest will be held tomorrow.'

'Is Camden Street on our inspector's patch, then?' Betsy asked hopefully.

'Should be. I think it's one of them posh streets near the Royal Crescent,' Smythe replied. He grinned slowly. 'Looks like the inspector's got himself another one!'

'Not necessarily,' Mrs Jeffries said. She shook her head, dislodging a dark auburn tendril from her

24

well-kept bun. 'This case could very well be given to Inspector Nivens.'

'Inspector Nivens!' Smythe yelped. His grin disappeared. 'That ferret-faced little toff. Bloomin' Ada, that one couldn't find a horse at a racecourse, let alone a murderer.'

Mrs Jeffries smiled at the coachman's colourful description of Inspector Nivens's ability. She didn't think highly of the man herself.

'I couldn't agree more,' she said. 'The odious man is constantly interfering in Inspector Witherspoon's cases, or at least trying to, but disliking him won't change the facts. If this article is correct and the murder was committed during a robbery, I expect the case will go to him. Inspector Nivens is the Yard's resident expert on burglary. He's far more experienced with that sort of crime than our own Inspector Witherspoon.'

'Well isn' that just the worst luck,' Betsy complained. 'We finally comes across a decent murder and we're not goin' to get it. It's not fair.'

'What's so unfair about it?' Wiggins asked. He brushed a lock of light brown hair off his forehead. 'Seems to me our inspector gets more than his share of murders. Maybe this Inspector Nivens wants a turn too.'

Mrs Jeffries gazed down the length of the table. Except for Wiggins, everyone else looked as glum as an undertaker. She raised her eyes and stared blankly at the opposite end of the kitchen to the set of windows that faced onto the street. This floor of the house was built below ground level, so the melancholy music of the drizzling rain was louder, more intense. The miserable weather now matched their moods. Mrs Jeffries sighed. She wished she had kept quiet about that article. There was nothing worse than raising false hopes. And there was nothing she could say to cheer anyone up. It would be terribly wrong to wish for another murder merely because the household of Upper Edmonton Gardens was bored.

She turned her head slightly as she heard the clip-clop of horses' hooves stop on the pavement outside the house. A moment later there were pounding footsteps. 'There's the inspector now,' she said, getting to her feet. 'Not to worry, then. There's always the chance that this case has been given to him. And if so, I shall find out all the details I can.'

'Should we meet back here for cocoa after he's gone up?' the cook called. She gazed at the housekeeper hopefully. 'Just on the off chance he did get it?'

'That'll be fine, Mrs Goodge,' Mrs Jeffries said as she hurried up the stairs. 'Cocoa at ten o'clock.'

'Good evening, sir,' Mrs Jeffries called out cheerfully as the inspector stepped through the front door and into the hall. A gust of cold January rain came in with him, sprinkling water on the brand-new Oriental rug. The housekeeper hurried forward. 'Gracious, sir, what a dreadful evening.'

'Yes, it is rather,' Witherspoon replied morosely as he took off his hat and coat. A cascade of water dripped off the rim of his bowler. The inspector didn't seem to notice.

Mrs Jeffries watched him carefully as he hung up his wet things. His bony, angular face was set in lines of despair, there were deep creases around his clear grey-blue eyes, and when he'd taken his hat off, the thinning dark brown hair on the top of his head was standing on end, as though he'd spent hours running his fingers through it.

'It may be wet outside, sir,' she said, 'but we'll soon have you warm and dry.' She hid her delight behind a sympathetic smile as she turned and led the way to the dining room. From his expression, she'd bet six months' housekeeping money that he'd got the Camden Street murder. 'Mrs Goodge has a lovely dinner waiting for you. That'll soon fix you right up.'

'Er, I say.' The inspector hesitated at the door of the drawing room. 'I've no wish to inconvenience the cook, but do we have time for a spot of sherry? I dare-say, on a day like this that'll warm me up even faster than one of Mrs Goodge's superb meals.'

'Of course, sir,' Mrs Jeffries agreed, stepping back smoothly and entering the drawing room. She walked to the walnut table upon which the sherry decanter and a set of glasses rested and poured two glasses of amber liquid.

They frequently had a glass of sherry together before Witherspoon's evening meal. The inspector had started the custom soon after Mrs Jeffries had arrived in his household. He'd claimed that drinking alone wasn't a healthy habit. Mrs Jeffries agreed, but she also knew that he really liked these little chats together so he could unburden himself. People had been unburdening themselves to her for as long as she could remember. She was not only used to it, she encouraged it. For she knew that one of her greatest assets in life was her ability to listen.

27

With her plump motherly face and dark brown eyes, she inspired confidence in those who desperately needed someone to confide in. This ability had stood her in good stead over the years and she'd developed a sixth sense, an almost uncanny talent for getting information out of people. Even when they didn't want to say a word.

'Here you are, sir,' she said, placing his glass on the table next to the inspector's favourite chair and then sitting down on the settee. 'Now, why don't you tell me all about it, sir.'

'About what?' Witherspoon asked.

'About whatever it is that's making you so morose this evening, sir. You're not your normal, cheerful self. Come, come, I know you, sir. You're far too hardy a man to let a spot of bad weather take the spring out of your step.'

The inspector sighed and settled himself more comfortably in his chair. The fire crackled merrily in the hearth, the air was tinged with the agreeable scent of lemon polish and his wonderfully understanding housekeeper was inviting him to share his cares with her. Perhaps this wasn't going to be such a bad day after all, he thought. 'Naturally one doesn't like to complain, of course, but there is something troubling me.' He sighed deeply. 'It has been a terrible day.'

'You never complain, sir,' she assured him quickly.

Witherspoon smiled faintly. 'To put it bluntly, Mrs Jeffries, I'm feeling rather put-upon at the moment.'

'Oh dear.' She clucked sympathetically. 'How so, sir?'

'There's been a murder.'

'How very dreadful.' Mrs Jeffries waited patiently for him to continue.

'Well, you see, I've been given the case and I don't really think it's fair.'

'Not fair?' She took a dainty sip of sherry. 'In what way?'

'Because, by rights, this one really shouldn't have been given to me, it should have been given to Inspector Nivens.'

'Why would you say that, sir? Surely you don't believe that Inspector Nivens is anywhere near as good as you are at solving murders.' Mrs Jeffries knew precisely why Witherspoon was feeling put-upon. Obviously he'd been handed the Camden Street murder and he wasn't happy about it. She decided to use this opportunity to bolster his confidence. 'Why you're a positive genius when it comes to catching killers.'

The inspector smiled self-consciously and sat just a bit straighter in his chair. 'That's most kind of you to say, but be that as it may, this particular murder isn't really a murder at all. At least not in the sense I usually deal with. The victim was shot during a burglary. By rights, it should be Nivens who gets this one.' He gestured impatiently. 'Dash it all, Mrs Jeffries. This is a most awkward situation. Nivens is always going about saying I'm hogging all the murders, and now that there's finally one that should be his, he has the audacity to have measles.'

'Measles.' The housekeeper quickly lowered her chin to prevent the inspector from seeing the laughter on her face. 'Not a bad case of them, I hope.'

'I shouldn't think so. But nonetheless his being

covered in spots is causing me no end of trouble. I'm stuck with this wretched case,' Witherspoon complained. 'And I don't mind telling you, I don't think it's at all right. No, not at all right.'

Mrs Jeffries stared at him in some alarm. Complaining and shirking his duty were definitely not in his normal character. Obviously it was going to take more than a few words to bolster his self-confidence, for she had no doubt that he was feeling less than equal to the task ahead of him. Inspector Witherspoon was having a bad case of nerves.

'Perhaps it isn't right, sir, but you're the best man for the task.' She smiled gently. 'And I think you know it, sir.'

'If only I could believe that was true.' Witherspoon's own smile was wistful. 'The chief inspector said much the same thing when I brought the matter to his attention,' he admitted slowly. 'But honestly I'm not terribly sure I'm up to it. You know, sometimes when I look back on the cases I've solved, I can't quite recall how I actually did them. And today, when I was standing over that poor woman's body, I kept thinking that perhaps I'd only been lucky in the past, perhaps I'd fail this time and never catch the beast that had taken her life. It was a most depressing thought, Mrs Jeffries. Most depressing.'

Mrs Jeffries's heart went out to him. Of course he couldn't recall how he'd solved those cases, she thought. If he could, it would be obvious he'd had help and that would never do. 'Now, sir, don't be absurd. Why you know very well how you've tackled each and every case.'

'I do?' Witherspoon looked genuinely surprised.

'Now stop teasing me, sir.' She laughed. 'You know you always do a superb background check on the victim and you know good and well that unlike most police officers, you're willing to go beyond what's right under your nose and keep digging until you find the truth. Just look at how you solved that last case. You kept asking questions and picking up small bits and pieces of gossip, which, as we all know, turned out to be vital clues. Then your brilliant mind came to the only possible conclusion. The results were, as they nearly always are when you're on the case, justice for those poor unfortunate victims who without you would have gone unavenged by their own society.'

Witherspoon sat straight up in the chair. By golly, Mrs Jeffries was right. But of course, one couldn't come right out and say so; modesty prevented such disclosures. He felt ever so much better.

'Really, Mrs Jeffries. You mustn't keep saying I've a brilliant mind,' he murmured, his lips quirking in a smile he couldn't quite hide.

'I can see that I've embarrassed you,' she said briskly. 'So I'll speak no more about the subject. Why don't you tell me all about this latest murder?'

Betsy stuck her head into the drawing room. 'Should I serve dinner now?'

'Not just yet, Betsy,' the housekeeper replied. 'The inspector needs to dry off a little before he goes into the dining room. It's a bit drafty in there.'

The maid nodded. 'I'll ask Mrs Goodge to delay it for fifteen minutes, will that do you?'

'That'll be fine.' Mrs Jeffries turned back to the

inspector and gave him an encouraging smile. 'Do go on, sir.'

His confidence restored, Witherspoon cleared his throat. 'The victim was one Abigail Hodges, aged fifty-two. She was married and lived in one of those big houses in Camden Street, that's just off the Queens Road. Very wealthy neighbourhood, but not one that's had many housebreakings lately. Unfortunately it looks as if the poor woman came home after an evening out and walked in on a thief. He shot her once in the head and once in the chest.'

'How appalling.' Mrs Jeffries clucked her tongue appropriately. 'Who found the body?'

'Her husband, Leonard Hodges.'

Mrs Jeffries regarded him curiously. 'I take it Mr Hodges came home later than his wife? Or was he in the house when the shooting happened?'

'He wasn't there. The house was empty when Mrs Hodges came home. Poor Mr Hodges didn't find the body until the next morning when his wife didn't come down to breakfast on time.'

'Surely that's unusual,' Mrs Jeffries said. 'The house being empty, I mean. Where were the servants?'

'They'd been given the evening off.' Witherspoon shrugged. 'Mr Hodges hadn't a clue there was anything wrong until this morning. Poor fellow, blames himself, you know. Suspects that one of the servants let it be known the house was going to be empty and the robbers found out about it and came in.'

'Hmmm,' Mrs Jeffries said thoughtfully. 'I presume you've reasons for the assumption of murder committed during the course of a burglary.'

She knew this was a very important point.

'There's absolutely no doubt about that. Even Mr Hodges realized what must have happened. Mrs Hodges's jewellery box was upside down and emptied on the bed, all the drawers in the bedroom had been rifled and several expensive pieces of jewellery are now missing.' He took another sip of sherry. 'Mrs Hodges obviously surprised the thieves and she was shot to keep her from identifying them. We found a broken window in the kitchen where the thief or thieves had gained entry to the house.'

'I see,' Mrs Jeffries replied. She still needed to know exactly where Mr Hodges had been while his wife was being murdered, but she'd get back to that point later. She wanted to get the actual murder scene set in her mind first. 'Where was the body found?'

'At her house in Camden Street,' Witherspoon replied, giving her a doubtful look. 'Haven't I already mentioned that?'

'I mean where precisely in her house was the body found?'

'Why, her bedroom.' He cocked his head to one side. 'I thought I'd said that too.'

'Perhaps you did, sir,' Mrs Jeffries assured him. 'What I meant was, was the body in the doorway, or behind a dressing screen or lying on the bed?'

'Oh, the body was lying in front of her dressing table. The sleeves on her dress were undone, and from the position of her arms it looks as if she were starting to, er' – he broke off and coughed delicately, his pale cheeks turning a bright pink – 'undress herself.'

Mrs Jeffries's eyebrows drew together. 'Really, sir?

Now, that is peculiar. Let me make sure that I understand. Mrs Hodges was standing in front of her dressing
table getting ready for bed. Correct?'

'Er, yes.'

'Presumably the bedroom door was closed? Right?'

Witherspoon's face puckered into a puzzled frown.
'Yes, that's correct.'

'So the thieves opened a closed door in an empty
house and walked in and shot her? Is that how you
think it happened?'

'That's certainly how it appeared.' Witherspoon
peered at her closely. 'I mean, I don't think the woman
would have begun disrobing with the door open.
Do you? Come now, Mrs Jeffries, you obviously find
something amiss here, what is it?'

'It's really nothing, sir. It's just that my late husband always maintained that most housebreakers go
unarmed.' She smiled sweetly while that bit of information sank in. The late Mr Jeffries had been a constable
with the Yorkshire police for over twenty years.

'Well, yes, I quite understand that, but what's that
got to do with the bedroom door being closed?'

'Simple, sir. If Mrs Hodges were inside her bedroom,
why didn't the burglars leave? Why commit murder
when they could have slunk out the front door? Even
if Mrs Hodges had become aware of their presence,
surely any burglar worth his salt could move faster than
a fifty-two-year-old woman.'

'But if they'd done that, they wouldn't have got
the jewellery,' he explained. 'And that obviously was
why they were in the Hodges house in the first place.
Now, even I know it's unusual for burglars to carry

34

firearms, but these villains are obviously more ruthless than most. They came to steal and they were willing to murder anyone who got in their way.'

For the moment the inspector's mind was made up. Mrs Jeffries knew that at this stage of the investigation it would be useless to attempt to get him to consider another point of view. But she knew how to bide her time. He was only sticking like a burr to this burglary notion because he was still unsure of his own abilities.

'How are you going to approach this case, sir?' she asked.

'Naturally we're going to try to trace the jewellery.'

'What jewels were actually stolen?'

'A string of pearls, an opal ring and a garnet brooch.'

Mrs Jeffries stared at him in surprise. 'That's all? Pearls, an opal ring and a garnet pin? None of that sounds particularly valuable, not valuable enough to commit murder over, anyway.'

Witherspoon gave her a pitying look. 'Dear Mrs Jeffries, you're so very innocent. Why, there are places in this city where a thief would cut your throat for two shillings.'

'But surely a wealthy house off the Queens Road isn't one of them.' She smiled briefly. 'Did the thief empty the jewellery box?'

'Er, no.' Witherspoon had been puzzled over that himself. 'There were several pieces he didn't take. A gold necklace and a couple of rings, but Mr Hodges assured us those things were merely baubles. Most of Mrs Hodges's really good jewellery is kept in a bank vault.'

'Hmmm,' Mrs Jeffries replied. 'Where did you say the husband was last night?'

'He was at his club.' Witherspoon didn't like the doubts Mrs Jeffries had raised about the subject of burglars. But he comforted himself with the knowledge that there was a first time for everything, including a housebreaker arming himself.

'And where had Mr and Mrs Hodges gone before the murder?'

'To visit a medium, a Mrs Esme Popejoy.' Witherspoon gave her his man-of-the-world smile. 'It seems Mrs Hodges was a devotee of spiritualism and séances. I daresay it's quite shocking what nonsense otherwise respectable people get up to, isn't it?'

Mrs Jeffries didn't think that spending one's money on a séance was any more ridiculous than most entertainments, but for the moment she'd keep her opinion to herself. She didn't want the inspector's mind to wander. 'Quite. And after visiting this Mrs Popejoy, Mr Hodges went to his club, is that correct?'

'Not entirely. You see, Mrs Popejoy had put poor Mr Hodges in a bit of a spot.' The inspector dropped his voice to a conspiratorial whisper. 'She'd asked Mr Hodges to escort her to the train station. Mrs Hodges was not pleased. That's why Mr Hodges went off to his club afterwards instead of going home. He didn't want to have to face Mrs Hodges when her temper was up.'

'I see,' Mrs Jeffries replied. She saw that this 'burglary' had more holes than a sieve and that the husband seemed to have an alibi. Mrs Jeffries was very suspicious of people who had alibis. 'I take it you've checked Mr Hodges's whereabouts at the time of the murder?'

'Of course, we did that right after we spoke to the poor man. He was at Truscott's, all right. The club manager confirms that he arrived there by half past ten. Several other club members also saw Mr Hodges arrive. We've also spoken to the other guests who were at Mrs Popejoy's last night. Everyone agrees that the séance was over by nine-thirty. Taking into account the time it would have taken Mr Hodges to escort Mrs Popejoy to the station, he'd hardly have had time to nip home, shoot his wife and get to Truscott's by half past ten.'

'And you've confirmed with Mrs Popejoy that Mr Hodges actually escorted her to the station?' Mrs Jeffries asked innocently.

'Well, er, no. As a matter of fact we haven't. Mrs Popejoy is still at her friend's, in Southend. But the servants and one of the other guests told us they saw Mr Hodges get into a hansom with Mrs Popejoy.' He broke off and laughed. 'Really, Mrs Jeffries, you've a most suspicious mind. Why, anyone would think you didn't believe this was a simple, straightforward burglary.'

'Of course it's not a simple burglary,' Mrs Jeffries insisted. She gazed at the faces staring at her from around the table. Mrs Goodge's head was nodding up and down in vigorous agreement, Betsy's eyes were narrowed in concentration as she tried to take in every word Mrs Jeffries had said and Smythe's lips were curved in approval. Only Wiggins looked doubtful.

'But how can you be sure it weren't just a thief?' he asked plaintively. 'If the inspector says they was after jewels and the poor lady just 'appened to walk in on 'em, how can you know for certain that ain't what really 'appened?'

'Because she didn't just happen to walk in on the thieves,' Mrs Jeffries answered. 'From what the inspector told me, she was standing in front of her dressing table getting ready for bed. That means the door to the bedroom was closed. Now, if you walk innocently into your own home, you're not particularly quiet about it. Doors slam, dresses rustle, one doesn't tiptoe up a staircase because one is alone. Therefore we can assume that Mrs Hodges made a reasonable amount of noise when she entered the house.'

'All right, so the poor lady weren't bein' quiet,' Wiggins argued. 'I still don't see what you're gettin' at.'

'It's very simple. She went into her room without spotting the burglars. Therefore we can assume she didn't know they were there. But they probably knew she was home – she wasn't being quiet, so why wouldn't they have heard her come into the house? Now, why would a couple of housebreakers, who rarely go armed, hotfoot it into Mrs Hodges's room and murder the woman when they could just as easily have slunk out the front door with no one being the wiser? Burglars just don't take those kinds of risks.'

'Maybe they was in the bedroom when she walked in,' Mrs Goodge put in helpfully.

Mrs Jeffries shook her head. 'No. She'd already undone the buttons on the sleeves of her dress. She was getting ready for bed. That means the room was empty and the drawers and jewellery box were still untouched when she entered. She'd have hardly begun undressing if she'd found her room in disarray. Furthermore, there are several other odd aspects to this murder.' She paused for breath and then plunged into telling them the rest of the information she'd wormed out of the inspector over dinner. 'The servants weren't just given a few hours off last night, they were given the whole night off. The two housemaids, Ethel and Hilda Brown, went to visit their grandmother in the Whitechapel district and didn't arrive home until early this morning. The footman, Peter, spent the night in Brixton with his father, and the housekeeper, Thomasina Trotter, visited her old nanny who lives in Fulham. And Mrs Hodges's niece, Felicity Marsden, who lives there too, was out at the ballet with some friends. She wasn't home last night either.'

'Did the inspector check up on 'em?' Betsy asked.

Mrs Jeffries nodded. 'This afternoon. Mr Hodges was supposedly too grief-stricken to answer many questions, so Constable Barnes and the inspector questioned the servants and then confirmed their whereabouts when the murder took place. None of the Hodges servants appear to be lying.'

'And Miss Marsden,' Smythe asked, 'did he check on 'er?'

'Not yet.' Mrs Jeffries shook her head. 'The inspector's planning on interviewing her tomorrow morning. But you know, it's quite strange. It was Mr Hodges who gave the servants the night off, not Mrs Hodges.'

'What's so strange about that?' Mrs Goodge asked. 'The inspector gives us plenty of free time; maybe Mr Hodges is as good a master as our inspector.'

'I don't think so,' Mrs Jeffries replied slowly. 'Inspector Witherspoon mentioned he'd asked the housekeeper if it was usual for Mr Hodges to give them additional free time. She said this was the first time it had ever happened. Furthermore, it was generally Mrs Hodges who directed the servants and not her husband.'

Smythe leaned forward and planted his elbows on the table. 'So where do we start?'

'Where we always start,' Mrs Jeffries said with a smile. 'With the victim.' She turned to the cook. 'I think you know what to do, Mrs Goodge.'

'Do you just want me to find out about Mrs Hodges?' The cook pushed a lock of iron-grey hair off her plump face.

'Not just her. Find out anything you can about Mr Leonard Hodges and Felicity Marsden. Miss Marsden was supposedly with a family named Plimpton last night. She spent the night at their house after the ballet.' Mrs Jeffries started to turn to Betsy and then remembered something else. 'And see what you can learn about the medium, Mrs Esme Popejoy.'

'You know,' Betsy said thoughtfully, 'Edmund may be able to help there.'

'Oh, it's Edmund now, is it?' Smythe said sarcastically.

Betsy glared at the coachman and Mrs Jeffries quickly raised a hand, effectively silencing them before they could start to bicker.

'Mr Kessler probably could help,' she said to the maid, 'but please be careful about how you ask. As you all realize, it's imperative we keep any knowledge of our activities about the inspector's cases confined to a few trusted individuals.'

'What else do you want me to do, then?' Betsy asked eagerly.

'Start with the shopkeepers around Queens Road,' Mrs Jeffries said. 'Do the usual, find out everything you can about Mr and Mrs Hodges and Felicity Marsden. Keep on the alert for any interesting gossip concerning anyone in the Hodges household.'

'What about me?' Wiggins asked grudgingly, his tone less than enthusiastic. Another murder meant that his courting time would be seriously limited. And just when he was makin' some progress with Sarah too. Cor, he thought, it just in't fair.

Mrs Jeffries patted his arm. 'It's good of you to ask. Believe me, Wiggins, we all must make sacrifices in the interests of justice. I want you to try to make contact with the footman from the Hodges household. The inspector said young Peter has been in service there for several years. He'll probably know many useful things about the Hodgeses. Try to find him. See if you can loosen his tongue a bit.' She sat back in her chair. 'Also, keep in mind that the inspector said that Mr Hodges appeared to be a good deal younger than his wife.'

Mrs Goodge snorted. 'Hmmph, he's probably married her for her money, then.'

'That's rather a cynical attitude,' Mrs Jeffries said. 'But possibly true. Inspector Witherspoon didn't actually say so, but I got the impression that it's Mrs Hodges who had the money and not Mr Hodges. Additionally – and getting this tidbit out of the inspector took some doing, believe me – I also got the impression that Mrs Hodges wasn't a particularly attractive woman either in appearance or character.'

'Is there anythin' else?' Betsy stifled a yawn.

'Let me see.' Mrs Jeffries frowned thoughtfully. She'd given them all the information she'd got out of the inspector at dinner. It wasn't much in the way of facts, but it was a start.

She lifted her chin until she met Smythe's gaze. But before she could give him any instructions, he rose to his feet and gave them all a cheeky grin. 'No need to tell me, Mrs J, I'm on me way. Lots of good pubs round the Queens Road. I should be able to come up with somethin' for ya by tomorrow mornin'.'

'Tomorrow mornin',' Betsy yelped. 'That's not fair, I can't even get to them shopkeepers till half past nine.'

'What are you carpin' about?' Mrs Goodge snapped. 'We're not gettin' any deliveries tomorrow at all. I'll have to sit at the back window all day and snatch whoever walks by before I can start askin' my questions.'

Mrs Goodge was the only one of the household who managed to obtain her information without even leaving the kitchen.

The cook had a well-developed network of delivery people, rag-and-bone men, chimney sweeps, washerwomen and tramps whom she regularly paraded through the Witherspoon kitchen. With this ragtag band, whom she fed and plied with dozens of cups of hot tea, she obtained every single morsel of gossip about everyone of importance in London.

'Now, now, this isn't a competition,' Mrs Jeffries interjected. Really, a bit of healthy competitiveness was fine, but they were beginning to carry things a bit far. 'Remember why we're doing this. It's to help the inspector.' And also because they were all born snoops. Solving murders was far more exciting than counting bed linen and polishing silver.

'We're not forgettin' the inspector,' Betsy said, her expression sober. 'We all owe 'im too much.'

Immediately Mrs Jeffries's annoyance faded as she looked at the sombre expressions surrounding her. She knew that despite their natural love for detecting, the real reason they all worked so hard on the inspector's cases was because they all wanted to. It was a way of paying him back, without his knowledge, of course, for what he'd done for each and every one of them.

Betsy had been a half-starved waif on the inspector's doorstep when he hired her. Wiggins and Smythe had both worked for the inspector's late aunt Euphemia. But Wiggins was no more trained as a real footman than a dancing bear and the inspector needed a coachman and horses about as much as he needed a hole in his head. But rather than toss them both out onto the street to fend for themselves as best they could, he'd kept them on. And her. She sighed deeply.

Mrs Jeffries knew that she'd been in need of a brood to mother and an outlet for her own intellectual curiosity when he'd hired her as his housekeeper. When she'd realized that he could and did need someone to talk his cases over with, she'd been so delighted she'd almost convinced herself that fate had deliberately brought the two of them together. The only fly in the ointment, as far as she could tell, was that Inspector Witherspoon wasn't married. She knew the dear man was lonely. He was also notoriously shy – why, one could almost call him backward – with the fair sex. But Mrs Jeffries wasn't giving up. She knew that with a bit of help and a few gentle nudges, she could eventually find her inspector just the right woman.

Betsy's voice broke into her thoughts.

'But it in't fair that 'e' – the maid pointed at the grinning coachman – 'should get such a 'ead start.'

Mrs Jeffries noticed that Betsy was so annoyed she was dropping her hs again.

'Smythe is not getting a head start,' she repeated firmly. 'It's merely that it is easier for him to pursue his enquiries at night than it is during the day . . .' Her voice trailed off as she suddenly remembered something else the inspector had told her. She turned from Betsy to look at the coachman. 'Smythe, Mrs Hodges was sent home in a hansom, and from what the inspector said, Mr Hodges and Mrs Popejoy took a hansom to the train station as well. It might be a good idea to try to track the drivers down.'

Smythe's cocky grin faded. He'd much rather hang about in pubs than pound the streets looking for cabdrivers. 'Bloomin' Ada, Mrs J. That's a tall order. Remember the last time you 'ad me trackin' down cabdrivers? It might take days.'

'I remember the last time quite well,' she replied calmly. 'And if you'll recall, we learned a substantial amount of information about that case from all your hard work.' She smiled softly. 'I know it's asking a lot. But I really think it might be useful.'

'All right,' he said, his tone filled with grudging respect. 'Where does this Mrs Popejoy live? I might as well start checkin' the cabbies in that area first. And what station was she leavin' from?'

'Number seven, Edinger Place. It's less than half a mile from the Strand. The inspector hasn't been there yet. He was merely repeating what Constable

44

Barnes had found out. Mrs Popejoy's friend lives in Southend—'

'Southend!' Smythe yelped. 'Blimey, that's the T and S Line. Them stations is clear over to the East End. It'll take me 'alf the night to track down that cabbie.'

'Yes, I know it's inconvenient, but the sooner we get started, the sooner we'll have some real facts to sink our teeth into.'

'Is this Mrs Popejoy still in Southend?' Mrs Goodge asked.

'As far as I know,' Mrs Jeffries replied. 'Inspector Witherspoon is planning on speaking with the lady tomorrow afternoon.'

'Why not tomorrow morning?' Smythe asked, his dark eyes narrowed thoughtfully.

'Tomorrow morning is the inquest. The inspector says he wants to hear Mrs Popejoy's evidence at the inquest before he questions her.'

CHAPTER THREE

'WHAT DID YOU think of Mrs Popejoy, sir?' Constable Barnes asked as he and the inspector hurried down Camden Street to the Hodges house. 'Not one for hidin' her light under a bushel, is she?'

'No,' the inspector agreed, 'she isn't.' He was only half listening to the constable. His mind was preoccupied with other matters.

They'd just come from the inquest. Witherspoon knew he should be feeling far happier than he was. The ruling had been as expected. Mrs Abigail Hodges had been murdered. Dr Potter's evidence along with the evidence of the burglary left no doubt that the death had occurred during the commission of a crime.

Well, obviously, the woman was killed during a robbery, the inspector told himself sternly as they approached the victim's house. Everything pointed to that. He absolutely refused to allow himself to be sidetracked into thinking this crime was a complicated murder plot when everything, including the coroner's inquest, clearly showed it to be a simple robbery with very tragic results.

Yet despite his resolve, he couldn't quite shake the suspicion that there might be more to this case than he'd first anticipated.

He kept remembering his housekeeper's comments. 'Housebreakers rarely go armed,' she'd said. And then she'd pointed out the matter of the bedroom door being closed and why didn't the thieves simply slip out the front door. Witherspoon sighed. Something else was bothering him as well, something Constable Barnes had mentioned yesterday when they'd been examining the broken window in the Hodges kitchen. The window the thief or thieves had used to gain entry to the house.

The inspector came to a dead stop and turned to face Barnes. 'What did you say about all that glass yesterday?'

The constable's craggy face went blank for a moment and then cleared. 'You mean the broken window in the kitchen?'

The inspector nodded.

'All I said was the glass fragments looked a mite peculiar.'

'I remember that,' Witherspoon said earnestly, 'but we were interrupted and I never got a chance to ask you what you meant by that remark. How did it look peculiar?'

'The glass was on the wrong side,' Barnes explained. 'If the window had been broken from the outside, then most of the glass pieces should have been on the kitchen floor. The force of the blow, so to speak. But I happened to notice there were more glass on the out-side of the house than on the kitchen floor. The ground outside the window was covered with fragments.' He smiled self-consciously.

'Then you're suggesting that the window was broken from the inside of the house and not the outside, is that correct?' Witherspoon asked.

'Well, sir, I'm not exactly suggesting anything, I'm only saying that in my experience, finding the window glass the way it was, was downright odd.'

'Are you sure about this, Constable?' Witherspoon persisted. His spirits were sinking by the minute. If that ruddy window had been broken from inside the kitchen, then this crime wasn't a simple, straightforward robbery at all. Drat. 'I mean, surely, one can't tell from which direction a window was broken by the way the glass is arranged.'

'I didn't say I could, Inspector,' Barnes replied with a lift to his chin. 'But I've done a number of housebreakin's and it's been my experience that when someone's breakin' a window to get inside a house, there's usually more broken glass on the inside of the room than on the outside. That's all I'm saying.'

'Hmmm.' Witherspoon started walking again. 'I daresay, this case is getting more muddled by the minute.'

'Certainly looks that way, sir. Are we goin' to be speakin' with Mrs Popejoy today?' Barnes asked. They'd reached the steps of number eight. 'You know, I've met her kind before. I wouldn't put it past the woman to know a bit more than she let on at the inquest.'

'Why, Constable,' Witherspoon said in surprise, 'whatever do you mean? I know Mrs Popejoy's, er, activities are a tad unusual, but she seemed a nice enough woman to me.'

'She calls herself a spiritualist, sir,' Barnes exclaimed. 'Why, in my day we used to call 'em charlatans! And the way she was cosying up to them reporters, hmmph. Ought to be a law against such things. And the way she was muckin' about with our case, trying to tell everyone at the inquest that she'd warned Mrs Hodges on the night of the murder.' He snorted derisively. 'Whoever heard of such nonsense.'

'Mrs Popejoy claimed she'd had a message from beyond. She certainly never claimed to have told Mrs Hodges not to go home that night. I expect the lady was merely trying to gain a bit of notoriety.' The inspector smiled wryly. 'In her, er, occupation, I expect one needs to get one's name in the paper occasionally. She certainly appeared to enjoy all the attention she received at the inquest.'

'She were positively revelling in it, sir,' Barnes said in disgust. 'Hangin' all over the press, makin' sure they spelled her name right.' He clucked his tongue as he banged the brass door-knocker. 'Blimey, you'd think she were a bloomin' politician or somethin'.'

'I must admit, I didn't think speaking with the press was a good idea. But, of course, it would hardly be our place to try to stop her. She's a right to talk to them if she likes, though I can't imagine anyone wanting to actually speak to a journalist.' He shuddered delicately.

The door opened and a plump red-haired maid stuck her head out. 'Oh, it's you,' she said with a cheerful grin as she opened the door wide and ushered them inside. 'Mr Hodges said you'd be round again. He's in the study with Miss Marsden. If you'll wait here, sir, I'll announce you.'

Witherspoon nodded absently and stepped into the hall. He fixed his gaze at the floor, a frown creasing his face. He really didn't know how to approach this case any more. Much as he wanted to believe this had been a simple robbery with most tragic results, he wasn't sure he could any longer. Mrs Jeffries had been right when she'd mentioned that housebreakers didn't generally go armed. And now that Barnes had told him about the broken glass being on the wrong side of the window, well, he just wasn't certain how to proceed. Much as Witherspoon wanted to ignore this new evidence, his conscience wouldn't let him.

He heard the approaching footsteps of the maid as she returned, and lifted his chin and straightened his shoulders. He'd investigate this foul crime precisely as he'd investigated his other cases. With resolve, determination and perseverance.

They followed the girl down a long hallway and into the study. The room was dismal despite the fire blazing in the hearth. The heavy bronze curtains were drawn against the pale light from the overcast day, the ticking of a mantel clock seemed overly loud in the gloomy silence and the massive, dark furniture lent an air of depression to the whole room.

Leonard Hodges rose from the settee as they were ushered inside.

'Inspector Witherspoon,' he said politely. He gestured to the young woman sitting in a chair next to the fire. 'Please allow me to present my late wife's niece, Felicity Marsden.'

'Good day, Miss Marsden,' the inspector replied. He introduced Constable Barnes.

Felicity Marsden smiled nervously. 'Good day, gentlemen,' she murmured.

The inspector gazed at the young woman, seeing in her a distinct resemblance to her late aunt. She had the same dark hair, but in her case the curls were soft and drawn back with a ribbon at the nape of her neck. Her skin was a pale ivory and her nose strong without being large. Her face was more refined, more delicate than Abigail Hodges's, her cheekbones high and her brows perfectly arched black wings over the darkest, biggest brown eyes the inspector had ever seen. Beside him, he heard Barnes cough lightly.

Witherspoon realized he was staring. 'I'm dreadfully sorry to have to intrude upon you,' he began.

'That's quite all right,' she replied. 'I realize it's necessary.'

'We've a few questions that need to be asked' – the inspector deliberately tried to make his tone kind and gentle – 'and I assure you, we'll do our very best to make them as brief as possible.'

'Thank you.' She clasped her hands together in her lap. 'I expect you want to know where I was on the night my aunt was . . .' She faltered and then quickly recovered. 'On the night it happened.'

The maid who'd announced them suddenly appeared in the doorway. 'Would you like tea, ma'am?' the girl asked.

Though the maid had directed the question to Miss Marsden, it was Leonard Hodges who answered. 'That won't be necessary, Hilda,' he replied. 'This is hardly a social call. I don't expect these gentlemen will be here very long.' He smiled briefly at the inspector. 'That's correct, isn't it?'

Taken aback, Witherspoon blinked. 'Er, yes.'

'Inspector.' Miss Marsden's husky voice drew his attention. 'I was at the ballet. I was with my friends the Plimptons. We had supper together and then went to the theatre. Afterwards, I spent the night there.' She unclasped her hands and drew a deep breath. 'I'm afraid there's nothing else to tell you. The first I heard of the . . . tragedy was when a police constable fetched me from the Plimpton house.'

'Yes, I'm quite sure it was a dreadful shock for you, Miss Marsden,' Witherspoon said sympathetically. 'But even though you weren't here, you may be able to help us.'

'I don't see how.' She began to fidget with the buttons on the sleeve of her black mourning dress. 'My aunt was killed by burglars. How could I possibly know anything about that? I really don't understand why you're here. Surely you don't think any of us had anything to do with Abigail's death? Why aren't you trying to catch the thieves?' Her voice rose. 'I don't understand this, I don't understand why you're asking us all these questions.'

Witherspoon stared at her in alarm. He hoped she wouldn't become hysterical. Certainly she was still in somewhat of a state of shock and no doubt very upset, but really she was decidedly overreacting here. He didn't think he had asked all that many questions in the first place.

'Please, Felicity,' Leonard Hodges said firmly, 'the

inspector is only trying to do his job. Naturally this tragedy has deeply distressed you, it's deeply upset everyone in the household, but we must cooperate in any way we can.' He paused and gave her a slow, sad smile. 'Now please, get a hold of yourself. You do want your aunt's murderers brought to justice, don't you?'

She bit her lip and nodded. Hodges turned to the inspector. 'By all means, sir. Ask anything you like.'

'My apologies, Inspector Witherspoon,' Miss Marsden murmured. 'Please continue with your questions.'

From the corner of his eye, Witherspoon saw Barnes whip out his notebook. 'It would be most helpful if you could tell us exactly what time you left the house,' the inspector said.

'It was early,' Felicity answered slowly. 'I wanted to spend some time with Ada's mother before we had supper, so I expect it was about five.'

'You went alone?' Witherspoon wasn't sure that was useful information, but he felt compelled to ask anyway. He wasn't certain whether or not it was common for young women to travel out and about on their own at that time of the day. His housekeeper did, but then she wasn't a young woman.

She nodded. 'Peter went to the corner and got a hansom cab.'

'And you took the cab directly to the Plimptons' home?'

Again Felicity nodded. 'Yes. It had just gone half past five when I arrived.'

'Did you happen to mention to anyone at the Plimpton residence that this house was going to be empty that evening?' Witherspoon asked quickly.

'How could I?' Felicity said earnestly. 'I didn't know that Uncle Leonard had given the servants the night off until I arrived home the next day.' She tilted her chin and looked directly at Leonard Hodges. 'I must say, I was surprised by that.'

Leonard arched one eyebrow. 'Surprised; why? I felt that after what had happened last Sunday, the servants deserved some free time.'

'What happened last Sunday?' Witherspoon blurted.

Hodges stared at him coldly. 'It has nothing to do with this, Inspector. Nothing whatsoever.'

The inspector suddenly didn't know what to do. He didn't wish to interfere in anyone's domestic affairs, but on the other hand, he felt he really should be in possession of any facts relating to servants and their time away from the house. Servants were notorious gossips. One of them could easily have let it slip that the house was empty. He was saved from having to argue with Mr Hodges by the intervention of Constable Barnes.

'Begging your pardon, sir,' the constable said calmly. 'But you really should answer the question. The inspector needs to know if any of your servants might have had a reason to be angry with Mrs Hodges.'

His implication was obvious.

'Oh, all right,' Hodges replied grudgingly. 'Last Sunday my wife didn't let the servants have their usual afternoon off. She was annoyed with them. A few minor tasks had been left undone and Abigail got very angry. I felt badly for the staff and so I gave them all the evening off. That's all there is to it.'

Witherspoon stared at him incredulously. 'Why didn't you tell us this earlier?' he asked. 'Gracious, if the servants were angry with your wife, then any one of them could have deliberately passed the information that your home was going to be empty that night.'

'Surely that's a bit farfetched,' Hodges muttered. He looked embarrassed. 'And I didn't mention this before because I didn't want anyone thinking less of Abigail. She occasionally lost her temper, but she was a good woman. I won't have anyone saying any different.'

'We wouldn't think of it, sir,' Witherspoon assured him. He glanced at Felicity Marsden. She was watching her uncle with an unreadable expression on her exquisite face. He suddenly remembered he'd been in the process of questioning her when he'd become distracted.

'Now, Miss Marsden,' he began briskly. 'You went to the ballet with your friends, correct?'

'Yes.'

'And what theatre would that have been?' Barnes asked softly.

'Sadler's Wells Theatre,' she replied.

'And you were with the Plimpton family the whole time?' Witherspoon asked. He saw a blotchy red colour bloom in the woman's cheeks.

'Of course I was,' she replied. 'They've a box at the theatre. We were together the whole time.'

'Oh, come now, Felicity,' Leonard Hodges interjected, 'surely you're mistaken. Why, I saw Horace Plimpton at Truscott's. He'd been there the whole evening.'

'I meant, Mrs Georgianna Plimpton and Ada and I were together.'

'Mrs Georgianna Plimpton is Ada Plimpton's

grandmother,' Hodges explained to the policemen. 'So it was only the three of you ladies who went to the ballet? Ada didn't have a gentleman in tow to act as escort?'

'Mr Plimpton sent the footman with the carriage,' Felicity replied defensively. 'Don't be so old-fashioned, Uncle. The evening was quite respectable.'

Witherspoon was getting confused, but he struggled not to let it show. Clearing his throat, he said, 'May I have the Plimptons' address?'

'Number fourteen Tavistock Street,' Felicity replied. She suddenly got to her feet. She was small and slim and very delicate-looking in the heavy black mourning dress. The inspector felt such pity for the poor girl. Her aunt's death had been a terrible shock. Why, merely talking about the night it had happened had caused her to go completely pale. He noticed her hands were trembling as well.

She looked at him with a dazed, stricken expression of pain. 'Inspector, if you don't mind, I must retire. This has all been a dreadful experience. I must go and rest. If you've any more questions, you'll have to ask them later.' With that, she hurried to the door and disappeared.

'I say,' Hodges said, 'I'm most dreadfully sorry. Felicity isn't herself today.'

'No apologies are needed,' the inspector said quickly. 'I can see that your niece is terribly upset. Sometimes one forgets what delicate creatures women are.'

'Thank you for being so understanding,' Hodges said. 'Now, if you've no more questions for me, I really must be going. The vicar is waiting for me.'

'Ah yes, the funeral arrangements.' Witherspoon knew there were one or two more questions he should ask, but he couldn't think just what they were. Something that Mrs Jeffries had mentioned this morning at breakfast. Something to do with . . . He sighed, he simply couldn't remember what it was. Perhaps it would come to him later. Aware that the man was watching him expectantly, he said, 'Is it possible for us to have a word with the housekeeper now?'

Hodges looked surprised. 'Of course, but I thought you spoke with Mrs Trotter yesterday.'

'We've a few more questions, sir,' Barnes said firmly. 'Mrs Trotter wasn't in the best of states yesterday.'

Thomasina Trotter had completely recovered. Tall, grim-faced, grey-haired and ramrod-thin, she walked imperiously into the servants' hall and stared at the two policemen with the same suspicious expression she reserved for tradesmen and shopkeepers trying to cheat her. 'You wanted to see me?'

The inspector swallowed. This woman definitely didn't have the deferential manner one associated with a servant. As a matter of fact, with her regal bearing and distinct upper-class accent, he found her somewhat intimidating. 'Yes, Mrs Trotter, we did. We're hoping you can help us.'

'If you're referring to the robbery and murder of Mrs Hodges, then I'm afraid you're wasting both of our time. As I told your man yesterday, I wasn't even here. As you know, Mr Hodges gave us the night off. From six o'clock onwards, I was in Fulham.'

Witherspoon refused to be cowed. He was serving

the interests of justice here. 'Visiting your old nanny, I understand. A Miss Adelaide Bush. Is that correct?'

'As I told the police yesterday, that is correct.'

'Did you, by any chance, happen to mention to anyone that the house was going to be empty?' Witherspoon asked. 'Perhaps you may have mentioned it to someone on your way to Fulham, someone on the tram or the train?'

'I'm hardly in the habit of confiding in complete strangers,' Mrs Trotter said. 'Furthermore, though I may be forced by circumstances to use common public conveyances, I certainly don't speak to anyone.'

Witherspoon was suddenly curious. Thomasina Trotter had definitely known better days. 'How long have you worked for Mr and Mrs Hodges?'

Mrs Trotter's thin eyebrows rose. 'The terms and conditions of my employment in the Hodges household haven't anything to do with this crime. Therefore it is hardly the business of the police.'

The inspector tried to think of a reasonable reply. He was saved again by Constable Barnes.

'We're askin', ma'am.' Barnes said quietly, 'because if you've been here a while and you know the neighbourhood, you just might be able to tell us if you saw any strangers hangin' about afore you left?'

'I see.' She smiled slightly. 'Well, in that case, I shall answer the question. I've worked for Mrs Hodges for twenty years, and as it happens, I did see a stranger in the neighbourhood on the night she died.'

'Before you go into that,' Witherspoon interrupted. He'd suddenly remembered there were several basic questions concerning this household that he hadn't asked. 'Could you please tell us precisely what everyone in the household was doing prior to being given the evening off?' He was quite proud of himself for thinking of that line of enquiry.

Surprised, Mrs Trotter stared at him.. 'How on earth is knowing our movements going to help?' She shrugged. 'But I assume you should know your business.' She made it clear from her tone that she didn't believe this for one minute.

'Just tell us what everyone in the house was doing from,' he said slowly, ''er, five o'clock onwards.'

'Everyone with the exception of myself was eating their supper here in the servants' hall. We'd already been told Mr and Mrs Hodges were going out for the evening.'

'They weren't planning on dining at home?' Witherspoon asked.

'No. They were dining with Mrs Hodges's nephew, Jonathan Felcher. He'd offered to take them out to dinner and they'd accepted.' She laughed harshly. 'They were so stunned to actually receive an invitation from him! He's usually around here cadging meals off them. But that's neither here nor there. At half past five, the maids cleared up the dishes and cleaned the hall. Cook left to visit her half-sister in Notting Hill.'

'So you knew by this time that Mr Hodges was giving you the evening off?' the inspector said quickly.

'Oh no. Cook always went to her half-sister's on Wednesday evening,' Mrs Trotter replied. 'Mr Hodges didn't tell us we had the evening free until well after cook had left. It was probably close to six o'clock. The maids – they're sisters – immediately left to catch the late train. Peter, the footman, disappeared, probably to go to his father's, and I gathered my things and went to visit my old nanny in Fulham.'

The inspector's head was spinning. He took a deep breath and tried to think of the next reasonable question. 'May we have the lady's name and address?'

'Wouldn't you rather I tell you about the strange person I saw hanging about?'

'Er, uh, yes.' Witherspoon decided he could wait a few moments for the nanny's address. He hated being rude.

'It was a woman. She was standing just at the corner and I happened to notice her because she was completely veiled.'

'Perhaps she was in mourning,' Witherspoon suggested.

'In a red veil?' Mrs Trotter replied. 'No, this woman was standing at the end of the street. Just standing there. It didn't strike me as odd at the time; I thought perhaps she was waiting for someone. But given what happened, it seems to me she was watching the house.'

Beside him, Witherspoon heard Constable Barnes sigh softly and he knew what that meant. This evidence, if evidence it even was, was utterly useless. After a crime had been committed, people could always remember a suspicious character or two in the neighbourhood. However, none of these people were ever suspicious enough before a crime was committed to warrant anyone even mentioning them to a policeman! And finding a lone woman who'd happened to be standing on the same street as the Hodges home on the day of the murder would be an impossible task. And on top of that, the woman probably had absolutely nothing to do with the crime.

Mrs Jeffries paused at the corner and gazed at her surroundings, looking for a likely hiding place in the event that Inspector Witherspoon or one of his constables happened to come out of the Hodges house. She could hardly claim she'd come to return his glasses or his watch. The inspector had slipped out this morning before she'd had an opportunity to appropriate either item from his coat pockets. But she wasn't going to let that stop her. It was imperative she see the house and, if possible, the scene of the crime itself.

Camden Street came off the busy thoroughfare of the Queens Road. The Hodges house was a large red-brick Georgian at the end of the street. It was separated from its neighbour by a large stretch of garden on one side and enclosed by a six-foot stone wall on the other side.

She hurried to the corner and came alongside the ivy-covered stone wall. Her footsteps seemed inordinately loud as she walked along the pavement searching for a gate. When she found the gate, it was locked. She glanced up and saw the tradesmen's bell and, for one long moment, seriously considered giving it a good yank. But she immediately discarded that idea. It was far too likely that a policeman might answer that summons.

Thinking hard, she continued walking, her hand trailing idly against the wall, her fingers skimming over the leaves and brushing lightly against the stone. Suddenly her fingers stilled and she stopped. Leaning close, she saw that there was another, smaller, wooden gate set in the wall. Because of the heavy foliage, it wasn't noticeable. She pushed slightly against the wood and smiled as it silently swung open a few inches. Peeking inside, she saw that the latch was gone and the gate had been held shut merely by the connecting strands of ivy. She shoved again and managed to open up a space big enough to squeeze through.

Once inside, she stood stock-still and examined the area.

The ivy extended for a distance of about eight feet. Mrs Jeffries could see that only inches from where she stood, the plants had been trampled. A vague but direct line of trampled vines led from the gate to the grass. She suspected she knew now how the killer had made his escape. Turning, she looked at the gate again and shook her head. If her fingers hadn't been brushing that wall as she passed, she'd have missed it completely.

Mrs Jeffries didn't usually leap to conclusions. However, in this case she made an exception. If, indeed, the killer was the one who'd made those faint tracks through the ivy to get away, then that person was someone who knew this garden well. That gate was too well hidden to be discovered by a casual thief.

Mrs Jeffries wasted no time. Keeping her head down and dodging from one low-lying clump of bush to another, she was making her way to the Hodges house when the back door opened and a man and woman came outside.

The woman was dressed in an elegant, long-sleeved mourning dress and the man was wearing a well-cut suit. She didn't think they were servants.

Praying they were too preoccupied with one another to notice her, she trod softly across the grass to the only available hiding place, a giant oak tree. In front of the tree was a bench. Mrs Jeffries made it to the other side of the trunk only seconds before the two stepped off the path and onto the grass verge leading to the bench.

'Well, my dear cousin,' the man said as soon as the woman had seated herself. 'Don't you think wearing mourning is a mite hypocritical, or did you and dear Aunt Abigail manage to settle your differences?'

'We had no differences,' the woman replied. 'Furthermore, I'm of age. Aunt Abigail couldn't stop me from doing as I chose.'

He laughed. 'Come, come now. This is Cousin Jonathan you're talking to, remember. We both know you'd never risk your comfortable life here by offending our late, sainted aunt.'

'Don't be disgusting, Jon,' she snapped. 'Abigail's dead. Can't you let her rest in peace?'

'My, my, little cousin,' he said. 'Have we had a change of heart now that she's gone? Or could it be that now that you're set to inherit half of everything, you're inclined to be generous?'

Mrs Jeffries held her breath and flattened herself closer to the tree. She prayed that neither of them suddenly got the urge to get up.

'I'm not interested in Abigail's money,' the woman cried passionately.

'Aren't you?' he replied, his voice so low that Mrs Jeffries had to strain to hear. 'Aren't you in the least interested in money, my dear cousin? Now that she's gone, you can marry that poor clerk you're in love with. Isn't it fortunate how things work out?'

'I'm not in love with anyone,' she cried. 'And if you're implying I had anything to do with Abigail's death, you're wrong. You've more reason to want her dead than me. You hated her, remember?'

'I remember,' he replied grimly. 'And unlike you, I won't play the hypocrite. I'm glad she's dead. With her gone, I shall have control over my father's estate.'

'What makes you think so?' she said cattily. 'You've no reason to think that Leonard will instruct the solicitors any differently than she did for all those years.'

He sighed. 'Oh Felicity, you're so very naive. Dear Uncle Leonard doesn't give a toss about my piddly little trust. He's getting the other half of Abigail's estate. Other than money, Leonard's only interested in one thing, and it isn't business.'

'You're being revolting again.'

'I'm being truthful. Now that Abigail's out of the way, he'll have even less reason for being discreet. I'm sure with the proper persuasion I can convince Leonard to let me have control of my trust. Why not? I'm thirty years old.' He laughed again. 'You're the one with the problem, my dear. Last I heard, that clerk of yours had other fish to fry. Even with half of Abigail's money, it may be too late.'

She jumped to her feet. 'You really are revolting. Benjamin loves me, and if it hadn't been for Abigail's wretched interference, we'd have been married by now.'

'Calm down, calm down,' the man said soothingly. 'You're right, I'm being dreadfully rude. Forgive me, despite my cavalier attitude, hearing about Abigail's murder has upset me. After all, I was one of the last people to see her before she died.'

'Don't be so melodramatic,' the woman replied. 'Leonard told me that after they left you at the restaurant, they went on to the stupid séance. There were at least seven other guests. By the way, how did you come up with the money to take them out for a meal?'

'I had a spot of luck on a horse and decided to repay my dear aunt's many kindnesses to me,' he said, his voice dripping with sarcasm.

'You mean you wanted to trap her long enough so she'd have to listen to another one of your silly business schemes.'

'They aren't silly,' Jonathan snapped vehemently. 'If the old witch had given me my money when I wanted it last year, I'd be a rich man now. Do you have any idea how much silver that mine has produced?'

Mrs Jeffries straightened nervously as she heard the sound of footsteps pounding across the grass.

'Excuse me, sir,' an excited female voice exclaimed, 'but the inspector from Scotland Yard would like to have a word with you now.'

As soon as the twosome had followed the maid back into the house, Mrs Jeffries peered out from behind the tree to make sure the coast was clear.

Keeping her head low, she crept closer. A series of steps led from the edge of the garden onto a low-walled terrace that opened from what looked like the drawing room. Ducking down, Mrs Jeffries made her way to the other side of the terrace and the small back door that led off the flat, rough-stone service porch.

She studied the area carefully. The first thing she noticed was the service door didn't have a keyhole, which meant that it latched from the inside. Next to the door was a long, rectangular pane of glass, and beside that, the broken shell of a larger window that had had all its glass knocked out. Mrs Jeffries frowned. Why hadn't the burglar knocked out the small window and then reached inside and unlatched the door? Why take the risk of someone hearing the shattering of a large pane of glass when one could just as easily have knocked out the small one and gained entry through the door?

Suddenly she heard the inspector's voice from deep inside the house. She quickly crept back behind the wall surrounding the terrace and hurried back the way she'd come.

As she walked towards the Queens Road Mrs Jeffries realized she'd learned an enormous amount of information. Now she had to think of a way to ensure that Inspector Witherspoon learned it as well.

But there were two very important facts that were uppermost in her mind. First, Abigail Hodges had not been much loved, and second, whoever killed her was either the worst kind of bungling burglar or a very clever murderer.

CHAPTER FOUR

INSPECTOR WITHERSPOON WAITED patiently for Jonathan Felcher to sit down. He'd been waiting now for a good two minutes. The fellow couldn't seem to find a place to settle. He'd paced between the fireplace and the settee half a dozen times. Finally the young man stopped in front of a leather wing chair, smiled at the inspector and sat. He gazed at Witherspoon out of a pair of wary hazel eyes and casually flicked a lock of wavy brown hair off his forehead.

'All right, Inspector,' Felcher said as he began stroking his beard, 'go ahead and ask your questions. Though, I must say, I don't think you're going to learn anything useful. I certainly don't know a thing about who robbed and murdered Abigail.'

'I understand you took your aunt and uncle out to dinner on the night of the murder,' Witherspoon began. The moment the words were out of his mouth, he wanted to bite his tongue. He really must refer to this crime as a robbery. Blast it, this wasn't a murder plot. Was it? He wasn't sure any more, just as he wasn't sure what this fidgety young man could possibly tell him.

But dash it all, he had to keep trying. Nothing else about this case was going right. Despite a massive effort by the uniformed lads, they hadn't heard hide nor hair about the missing jewellery. It hadn't turned up in any pawnshops or any of the usual places stolen goods frequently appeared.

'That's true. They've had me round for meals so many times I felt I really ought to return their hospitality.' Felcher smiled slightly. 'It's difficult, though. I live in lodgings, so I had to take them to a restaurant. We went to Clutter's. It's a nice little place near Covent Garden. Do you know it?'

'Er, no. What time did you finish your meal?' the inspector asked. He knew this line of enquiry would probably lead nowhere, but he felt he must do a thorough job of interviewing everyone.

Felcher plucked a piece of lint off the lapel of his brown jacket. 'It was rather early, actually. Abigail and Leonard had another appointment. So it must have been half past seven or so when I saw them off in a hansom.'

'Did your aunt tell you where they were going?' Really, the inspector thought, the man acted as if he were bored. Wasn't he in the least concerned with helping to catch his aunt's killer?

Felcher gave a condescending smile. 'No, but Leonard did. Abigail had the good sense to be embarrassed by her foolishness. But her dear husband isn't anywhere near as discreet! He let the cat out of the bag.' He broke off and laughed. 'I don't know who she thought she was fooling. Everyone knew she was always trotting off to mediums and spiritualists or whatever it is those people call themselves.'

'So you knew she had an appointment with Mrs Popejoy?'

'But of course. Madame Esme Popejoy is the newest rage in some circles. Once Abigail heard of her, she didn't rest until she'd badgered Leonard into wangling an introduction.'

'Why did your aunt have such an interest in spiritualism?' Witherspoon asked curiously.

'My late aunt was obsessed with communicating with the spirit of her son.' He yawned exaggeratedly. 'A rather pointless exercise if you ask me. The boy died when he was five. The lad could hardly be expected to have much to say.'

Witherspoon stifled a sigh. This was getting him nowhere. What could Mrs Hodges's interest in spiritualism have to do with her murder?

'Yes, yes, I'm sure that's probably quite true,' the inspector muttered. He searched his mind for another pertinent question. 'Did Mr Hodges happen to mention to you that he'd given the servants the evening off?'

Felcher's eyebrows shot up. 'Certainly not. Why would he tell me? I'm hardly likely to care one way or another.'

'That is as it may be,' the inspector replied, refusing to give up, 'but there is always the possibility he did mention it to you and you inadvertently mentioned that fact to the wrong person.'

'The wrong person?' Felcher snapped, half rising from his chair. 'Now, see here, I'm not sure I like your implication, sir.'

'I'm implying nothing, Mr Felcher. I'm merely

trying to determine how the miscreants that robbed and murdered your aunt could have known the house was going to be unattended that evening.'

Felcher relaxed back into his seat, his bluster dying as quickly as it had come. 'Well, no one heard that information from me! I didn't even know about it. I'm hardly privy to my aunt's domestic arrangements.'

'After you and the Hodgeses had finished your meal,' Witherspoon asked, 'what did you do for the rest of the evening?'

'What did I do?' Felcher stared at Witherspoon incredulously. 'That's hardly any of the police's concern. Look here, I thought my aunt was murdered by a burglar. What's that got to do with me? What's that got to do with how I spent my evening?'

'Calm yourself, Mr Felcher,' Witherspoon said firmly. 'Our questions are merely routine. You mustn't read anything sinister into them. We're asking everyone who saw Mrs Hodges on the evening of her death the same thing.'

Felcher didn't look convinced. But he answered the question. 'As soon as I put Abigail and Leonard into the cab, I went back to my lodgings. I stayed there for the rest of the evening. My landlady can confirm that.'

It was mid-afternoon when Mrs Jeffries arrived back at Upper Edmonton Gardens. The house was very quiet. Wiggins, Smythe and Betsy were still out.

Mrs Jeffries paused at the top of the backstairs. She heard the low murmur of voices. Quietly she tiptoed downstairs and peeked into the kitchen. She saw the cook sipping tea and chatting with the butcher's boy and a man from the gasworks. Obviously Mrs Goodge had got busy.

She went back upstairs and pulled a feather duster out of the cupboard. As she dusted the drawing room Mrs Jeffries thought about what she'd learned so far. She no longer had any doubts about this crime. It certainly hadn't been a burglary gone bad.

From what she'd overheard about Abigail Hodges she'd wager a year's wages that the woman had been the victim of a well-planned murder. The robbery was merely a trick. A rather clumsy attempt to divert the police's attention from the real motive for the crime. Someone wanted Abigail Hodges dead. But who?

Mrs Jeffries hovered in the hallway near the back-stairs. She'd finished dusting a rather ugly portrait of one of the inspector's ancestors when she heard the back door slam.

Tossing the duster into the cupboard, she dashed for the kitchen.

'Good afternoon, Mrs Goodge,' she said cheerfully, taking the chair next to the cook, 'you certainly look like you've been busy today.'

Mrs Goodge smiled widely. 'Haven't done much cooking, but I've heard a thing or two.' She sat back and crossed her arms over her massive bosom. 'Let's hope the inspector's not too particular about what he eats tonight.'

'Don't fret about that. The inspector enjoys everything you cook. Now, what have you found out?'

'Well, I didn't learn all that much about Abigail Hodges, but I heard a bit about her husband. He was married before.'

'He was a widower when he married Mrs Hodges?'

'Right. He married Mrs Hodges almost a year to the day after his first wife died. Interestin', isn't it?' Mrs Goodge smiled smugly. 'And his first wife died in a funny way too.'

Mrs Jeffries leaned forward. 'A robbery?'

The cook shook her head. 'A drowning. Her name was Dorothy. She were a Throgmorton before she married Leonard Hodges.' She gazed at the house-keeper expectantly. Mrs Jeffries knew the name was supposed to ring a bell, but it didn't.

'Throgmorton?' Mrs Jeffries repeated.

'Of Throgmorton's Carriages. They're up Nottingham way, surely you've heard of them. One of the wealthiest families in the Midlands.'

'Oh yes, of course. Please go on.'

'A couple of years after they was married, Dorothy Hodges went off by herself to the Lake District. She drowned when the skiff she were in overturned.'

'Presumably, then, Mr Hodges had a substantial amount of his own money when he married his second wife. He probably inherited quite a bit from his first wife's death,' Mrs Jeffries mused.

'Not a penny,' Mrs Goodge said smugly. 'He probably thought he were going to, but them that's got money knows how to hang on to it. When she drowned, her people made sure that Hodges got nothing. All of her money was tied up in trusts and such.'

'Were you able to find out where Leonard Hodges was when his first wife died?'

'He was in Scotland – he worked for Dorothy's father. Old Mr Throgmorton had sent Hodges to Edinburgh.'

Mrs Goodge shrugged. 'But peculiar as it is – I mean, Mr Hodges losin' both wives in strange ways and him not even forty yet – there weren't no hints of foul play attached to Dorothy Hodges's death. And from what I've heard of the Throgmortons, if they'da thought that Hodges had anything to do with the drowning, they wouldn't have let it go.'

'Coincidences do happen,' Mrs Jeffries said thoughtfully.

'Yoo-hoo,' shouted a familiar voice from the top of the stairs. 'Anyone home?'

'What's Luty doin' here this time of day?' Mrs Goodge asked as they waited for the elderly American woman to make her way down the stairs. 'She and Betsy aren't going out until this evening.'

'Afternoon, Hepzibah, Mrs Goodge,' Luty Belle Crookshank said as she came into the kitchen.

They both gaped. Luty Belle, who favoured bright colours despite her advanced years, had outdone herself. Today she wore an emerald-green-and-white-striped day dress with a heavily draped apron over a kilted skirt. A velvet hat with a bottle-green feather was perched jauntily on her white hair.

'Are you two gonna gape at me all day or ask me to sit down?' Luty asked with a grin.

'Oh please, sit down, Luty,' Mrs Jeffries said hastily. 'You know you're always welcome here.'

'I come by to offer ya some help,' Luty said eagerly. 'Heard ya was workin' on another one of the inspector's murders.'

Mrs Jeffries was taken aback. 'Gracious, how on earth did you learn we're working on a case?'

Luty chuckled. 'Stop frettin', Hepzibah. It ain't common knowledge if that's what you're a-thinkin'. But I was shopping on Regent Street today and I happened to run into Wiggins.'

'What's Wiggins doin' on Regent Street?' Mrs Goodge muttered. 'I thought he was supposed to be gettin' that footman at the Hodgeses' to chat a bit.'

Mrs Jeffries brushed that aside. 'How much did Wiggins tell you?'

'About Abigail Hodges?' Luty pursed her lips. 'Not much, just what little he knowed. But once he mentioned the word "murder", I knew you'd be wantin' my help.'

'That's very kind of you, Luty,' Mrs Jeffries began cautiously. 'But so far—'

'I'da been here earlier only I was already promised to go over to Stockwell to the orphanage.' She frowned. 'They's a-havin' prizes' day and 'course I had to go. Without me all those pious old biddies that show up for that kinda folderol woulda had some of them young'uns thinkin' they ought to be grateful for the very air they breathe.' Luty shook her head in disgust. 'Land's sake, why can't people just give generously outta the kindness of their hearts instead of makin' them puir young'uns put on a show fer 'em. But that's enough about that. I'm here now and rarin' to get started.'

Mrs Jeffries stared at her helplessly. Though Luty Belle Crookshank was fully aware of their activities in helping the inspector, she wasn't sure if including her in every investigation was a wise idea. Despite her liveliness and energy, Luty was no longer young. And on their last case, it had been Luty herself who'd come to them for help. But as she gazed at the elderly American's sharp brown eyes and determined expression, she knew she didn't have the heart to turn her away.

Besides, Luty could be very useful.

'What time are you and Betsy meeting Edmund Kessler this evening?' Mrs Jeffries asked.

'Seven. Why?'

'Because the spiritualist Edmund is taking you to visit may know something about one of the other persons in this case.' At Luty's puzzled frown she broke off and smiled. 'Let's get you a cup of tea while I explain everything we've learned so far.'

Half an hour later Mrs Jeffries had finished telling Luty everything when the back door opened and Betsy stepped inside.

The maid took off her coat and hat. Her mouth was curved in a dejected frown and her shoulders slumped. 'I didn't learn nuthin',' she said disgustedly as she hung up her things on the coat rack.

'You mean none of the shopkeepers would talk about the Hodgeses' household?' Mrs Goodge asked in alarm. The very idea of such tight-lipped discretion filled her with horror.

'Oh, they talked all right,' Betsy muttered, 'but none of 'em had anything worth 'earin'.' She plopped down onto the nearest chair and accepted a cup of tea.

'Now, I'm sure that's not true, Betsy,' Mrs Jeffries said soothingly. 'Why don't you tell us what you've heard. As I've said before, at this stage of an investigation, it's very difficult to tell what will or will not be important.'

'All right.' She sighed dramatically. 'The grocer told

me the Hodgeses pays the bill regular like and don't haggle none over the prices. Though they was always ready to point out a mistake. I mean, they didn't complain about the prices, but if the bill was added wrong or they was charged for somethin' they didn't get, they'd let the grocer know about it quick enough. The fishmonger and the butcher said the same. Though the boy at the grocer's said that he didn't see how a household the size of the Hodgeses' could be fed properly on the amount of food they bought.'

'Now, you see, that's important. There's an indication that the household was stingy with food. They probably underfed the servants,' Mrs Jeffries said, though she wasn't sure she believed it. However, she didn't want Betsy to become discouraged. 'Who was in charge of the accounts?'

'The housekeeper, Mrs Trotter. But sometimes Mrs Hodges would come in and order things too,' Betsy explained. 'You'd think that rich people wouldn't be so careful with their money, wouldn't you, seein' as how they have plenty.'

'That's how they got rich in the first place,' Mrs Goodge commented. 'By watchin' their pennies.'

Mrs Jeffries didn't think watching one's pennies had all that much to do with getting rich, but she wasn't going to pursue the point just now.

'Betsy,' she said thoughtfully, 'what else makes you think that Mrs Hodges was overly careful with her money?'

'The girl at the dress shop did tell me that Mrs Hodges was always complainin' about the cost of her clothes. Not that the cost ever stopped her from buyin', mind you. She even used to complain about the cost of her husband's clothes.' Betsy shook her head. 'Honestly, Mrs Hodges were in there on the day she died to get an evening dress fitted and she spent the whole time bendin' the poor shop girl's ear about what a fool of a husband she had.'

Luty snorted. 'Women been complainin' about that fer a long time.'

'What precisely had annoyed Mrs Hodges?' Mrs Jeffries asked.

'Oh, you know. He spent too much time at his club and he didn't pay enough attention to her. He spent too much money and then he didn't spend enough.' She laughed. 'First she moaned about all the money he was spendin' at his club and then she whined about him buyin' a ready-made coat and bowler from one of them cheap shops down the East End. I tell ya, there's just no pleasin' some people.'

Mrs Jeffries hid her disappointment well. Betsy hadn't learned anything really useful. She'd picked up a few tidbits of marital gossip, but that was all. 'Were you able to learn anything about anyone else in the Hodges household?'

'Not really,' she replied dejectedly. She brightened suddenly. 'Exceptin' I did hear that Mrs Hodges's niece just broke off her engagement a while back. That's somethin', isn't it?'

'Of course it is.' Mrs Jeffries forced an enthusiastic smile to her lips. She'd have to find a way to break it gently to the girl that she'd already picked up that particular item from the conversation she'd overheard at the Hodges house.

'Addie,' Betsy continued excitedly, 'that's the girl at the dress shop, said that a couple of months ago Felicity Marsden came in an' cancelled an order for some clothes she'd ordered for her trousseau. Addie was right annoyed about it too.'

'Addie didn't, by any chance, know the name of Felicity's fiancé did she?' Mrs Jeffries asked eagerly. Thwarted love was sometimes a motive for murder. And the only name she'd overheard this morning had been Benjamin. A surname would be most useful.

'She didn't know his name,' Betsy admitted reluctantly. 'But she did say that ever since then she 'adn't seen hide nor hair of Felicity. But that don't do us any good. An engagement that ended two months ago isn't goin' to 'elp us find Abigail Hodges's killer.' She slumped in her chair. 'Sorry. I didn't learn much today, did I?'

'You did well, Betsy,' Mrs Jeffries assured her.

'I don't know. Smythe has probably already tracked down both them cabbies . . .'

Mrs Jeffries pursed her lips. 'No, he hasn't. He popped in early this morning. So far he's found nothing.'

'Well, one of us better come up with somethin',' Betsy exclaimed. 'I've got a feelin' this case is goin' to be real difficult.'

Luty Belle reached across the table and patted Betsy's hand. 'It ain't gonna be any more difficult than any of the other cases. Now stop frettin', girl. It's early days yet.'

'It's a rather sordid story, inspector, and not one that I'd care to repeat.' Esme Popejoy smiled sadly as she handed Witherspoon his cup of tea. 'But I do understand that you're investigating a terrible crime, and therefore you need to know.'

'Er, actually, all I wanted to know was whether or not Mr or Mrs Hodges had mentioned their house being unattended,' Witherspoon sputtered. Really, this interview wasn't going at all well. He knew he should have taken Barnes's advice and gone on home, leaving the interviewing of Mrs Esme Popejoy until tomorrow. But dash it all, he'd wanted to get it over and done with.

'That's all you wanted to ask me? But surely you don't believe Mrs Hodges was killed in a robbery?' Mrs Popejoy exclaimed. 'Surely you can see that she was murdered. You're not having much success tracing the jewellery, are you?'

Inspector Witherspoon was so startled his hand jerked, slopping tea into his saucer and rattling the cup. 'Oh dear,' he groaned. 'How on earth do you know that!' He caught himself abruptly, realizing he really shouldn't be admitting such a thing to one of the principals in this case. 'Really, Mrs Popejoy, I've no idea what you're talking about.'

This, his last interview of the day, was turning out to be his worst.

Women like Esme Popejoy made him fidgety. With her delicate features, slim womanly figure, dark auburn hair and lovely blue eyes, she made him nervous. Very nervous indeed. He was never precisely sure how to talk to such creatures. They were so very different from men. When they smiled and laughed and raised their perfectly shaped eyebrows, well, a fellow practically became tongue-tied.

Embarrassed by his thoughts, the inspector quickly

looked away and focused his attention on his surroundings. He stared fixedly at the voluminous folds of the elegant blue silk drapes before dropping his eyes to the royal-blue carpet. The settee and other furniture in Mrs Popejoy's drawing room were white damask and he was terrified he was going to spill his tea all over the cloth and leave a horrid stain if that woman didn't stop staring at him. Drat it all, he really should have let Barnes handle this interview.

'Come now, Inspector,' Esme Popejoy replied. 'You needn't pretend with me.' She leaned forward and looked Witherspoon directly in the eye. 'You see, I know. I know it wasn't a simple robbery gone wrong. It was cold-blooded murder.'

'But how could you possibly know such a thing!'

She gave him a slow, wise smile. 'You wouldn't understand,' she said softly. 'Men so rarely do. But then again, perhaps you're not like other men. I've heard you're exceptionally intelligent.'

'Oh, well,' Witherspoon murmured modestly. Perhaps it was just as well that he hadn't let Barnes interview this lady. Why, talking to her was getting easier by the minute. Gracious, she was such a perceptive woman. He was surprised to find that his nervousness had almost completely gone. 'I have had some modest success . . .'

'But of course you have,' she agreed, reaching over and patting him gently on the arm. 'And it's because you're so brilliant, so much more broad-minded than the average person, that I'm willing to speak so openly with you. You see, I know it was murder because Lady Lucia warned Mrs Hodges.'

'Lady Lucia?' Witherspoon repeated. 'Who's she?' He felt a flutter of apprehension.

'My spirit guide.' Esme gave him another dazzling smile. 'She almost didn't come that evening, you see. I'd told Mrs Hodges that Lady Lucia really only likes to come at dusk, when one lights the gas lamps, but Abigail was late, so Lady Lucia was, well, annoyed. That's why the warning was so muddled. She's generally much clearer than that.'

The inspector felt as if he was losing control of the conversation. He decided to try to tactfully ignore this rather peculiar digression and backtrack. 'Er, yes, I'm sure she was annoyed. Now, if you'll recall, I did ask if Mr or Mrs Hodges had mentioned that their home would be empty. Not only were the servants not home, but their niece was out as well.'

Mrs Popejoy stared at him for a long moment before answering. Her voice, when she finally replied, was rather cool. 'Yes, Inspector, you did. To answer you, Abigail had told me Felicity was out for the evening, but she hadn't mentioned the servants being gone.'

'I see.'

'Do you?' Mrs Popejoy raised one perfect eyebrow. 'I don't think so. You see, Abigail was rather concerned about Felicity. She didn't trust the girl. That's what I was trying to tell you earlier, but you insisted upon digressing.'

Witherspoon would have liked to have told Mrs Popejoy that he wasn't the one who'd digressed, she was. But naturally one didn't like to contradict a lady. 'I'm dreadfully sorry,' he murmured. 'Please do go on.'

He might as well listen. Not that he thought for a

moment that Mrs Popejoy had anything but gossip to tell him. And as for her assertion that Mrs Hodges was murdered and that the robbery wasn't real, well, that was sheer dramatics on the woman's part.

'As I said before,' she began, 'it's rather sordid. Felicity Marsden got herself engaged. But her fiancé was most unsuitable. He was a fortune-hunter by the name of Benjamin Vogel. A nobody. Abigail loathed the man. But as Felicity was of age and threatened to elope, she knew there was nothing she could do about it. Abigail finally decided to pay Vogel off, and the dreadful creature took the money and broke his engagement to Felicity.' Mrs Popejoy laughed harshly. 'But do you think the girl was grateful? No, she blamed her poor aunt for Vogel's disgusting character. Abigail was beside herself. She confided in me. Told me how worried she was, how desperate she was to have her niece love her again. That's one of the reasons she wanted to come to me on the night she was killed. She was going to ask Lady Lucia for advice. But as I told you, she got a warning instead. And the warning, though it was muddled and unclear at the time, has become very clear to me now. Lady Lucia was warning her to be careful of her niece.'

'Did Lady Lucia actually say that?' Witherspoon asked before he realized how ridiculous the question sounded.

'Not in so many words,' Mrs Popejoy stated. 'But Abigail had just asked her a question about Felicity's future and Lady Lucia's only answer was to tell Abigail she was surrounded by darkness, death and despair.'

'But that could mean anything.'

'Only to those who don't understand,' Mrs Popejoy

cried passionately. 'Don't you see? Sometimes the veil between the flesh and the spirit is so strong we only receive part of their message. But I know Lady Lucia. She was warning Abigail Hodges to be careful of her niece.'

'Really, Mrs Popejoy,' the inspector warned, 'you mustn't say such things. We've accounted for Miss Marsden's whereabouts on the night of the . . . er, robbery and she couldn't possibly have done it. Furthermore, where would a young woman like that get hold of a firearm?'

'From her former fiancé, Benjamin Vogel. He had a gun. Why don't you ask him what he was doing that night!'

Mrs Jeffries glanced at the clock and then back at the impatient faces sitting around the kitchen table. They were waiting for Betsy and Luty Belle. Smythe was glaring at the floor, Mrs Goodge was nursing a last cup of cocoa and Wiggins was yawning.

The inspector had finally gone to bed. He'd come home in an awful state and Mrs Jeffries had spent the evening listening to him recount every detail of his day. She'd learned quite a bit. Now they seemed to have several suspects. Why, even the inspector was almost convinced that the robbery hadn't been genuine, though he'd been loath to admit it at first.

'Cor, what's takin' 'em so bloomin' long?' Smythe snarled as he scowled at the clock for the twentieth time. 'Don't that silly girl realize we've all got a lot to do tomorrow? We can't hang about all night waitin' for her to get herself home.'

'It's not that late,' Wiggins soothed.

Just then they heard the rumble of carriage wheels and the clip-clops of horses' hooves as Luty Belle's coach pulled up at the front door. As Betsy had her own key, it took only a few moments before the two excited women came hurrying into the kitchen.

'It's about time,' Smythe said.

'Land's sake,' Luty exclaimed as she sank into the chair next to Mrs Jeffries, 'what a folderol. I tell ya, tonight was better than a Barbary Coast saloon on payday. Yes indeedy . . . that woman puts on quite a show.'

'I take it you're referring to your evening with Madame Natalia.' Mrs Jeffries smiled, delighted to see that her friends had enjoyed themselves.

'It were ever so excitin'.' Betsy giggled. ' 'Course no one would believe it for a moment. There were six of us, countin' Luty Belle and Edmund and me. We all sat around this tiny little table and held hands. Madame Natalia went into a trance, sort of like bein' asleep only you're really awake, and then she called up her guide. His name was Soaring Eagle.'

Luty snorted. 'Soaring Eagle, stupid name. Knew a few Indians, none of 'em had names that silly.'

'Well, go on,' Wiggins said eagerly. 'What happened then?'

Betsy giggled again. 'Everyone started askin' questions – some of them were really funny too. That Mrs Parnell, she were there with her husband, she wanted to know what cemetery she ought to be buried in.'

'Yes, well, I'm delighted to see it was so entertaining for you,' Mrs Jeffries began.

'That's about all it was,' Luty interjected. 'If that woman was really talking to a dead Indian named Soaring Eagle, then I'm the Queen of Sheba. But what was really important was that we got an earful about Esme Popejoy.'

'Why, that's wonderful,' Mrs Jeffries said, glad that neither Betsy nor Luty Belle was taking this spiritualism business too seriously. 'The rest of us have had a fairly good day with our enquiries too. Before any of you begin, why don't I tell everyone what I've learned and, more importantly, what the inspector's learned.'

For the next half-hour they sipped cocoa and listened as the housekeeper recounted her experiences at the Hodges home. Then she told them about Inspector Witherspoon's interviews with Thomasina Trotter, Jonathan Felcher and Esme Popejoy.

'Sounds like Mrs Popejoy's puttin' a flea in the inspector's ear about Miss Marsden,' Smythe said when she'd concluded. 'From what I found out at the pubs, no one believes Mrs Hodges was killed by a robber. For one thing, there ain't been no burglaries in that neighbourhood in months, and for another, one of the footmen from the house next door to the Hodgeses' told me he were out on the street fer half the evenin'. Lookin' for the family cat, he was, and he didn't see no one comin' and goin' to the Hodges house. All he saw was Mrs Hodges's hansom drive up and her havin' a go at the driver before she flounced into the house.'

'What were she goin' on at the poor driver about?' Mrs Goodge asked.

Smythe shrugged. 'I don't know, the footman was too far away to make out what she was sayin', alls he could tell was that she were madder than a crazy cat. 'Course, he says she were always yellin' at somebody. I didn't have much luck findin' the driver that drove her cab.'

'Did you have any luck finding the driver that took Mr Hodges and Mrs Popejoy to the station?' Mrs Jeffries asked hopefully.

'Yeah, I found 'im,' Smythe admitted, 'but he weren't much 'elp. He just said he picked the two of 'em up and took 'em to the station.'

'What about the gun?' Wiggins said. 'Is the inspector going to ask this Mr Vogel about his gun?'

' 'Course he is,' Smythe snapped. ''E's duty bound to at least have a chat with the bloke, even if he did get his information from that Mrs Popejoy.'

'I don't think the niece had anything to do with it,' Luty declared. 'Seems to me if she was goin' to shoot someone, it would be her ex-fiancé. He's the one that took the money not to marry her. Besides, from what we found out about Esme Popejoy, I wouldn't credit much of what she says.'

'Here, wait a minute before you start in about this Mrs Popejoy,' Mrs Goodge said tartly. 'I've got my bit to say about Mr Hodges.' She then spent the next ten minutes telling everyone at the table exactly what she'd already told Mrs Jeffries. By the time she'd finished, they were all shaking their heads.

'This is gettin' really confusin',' Wiggins muttered.

'Kin I tell what we learned about Mrs Popejoy now?' Luty Belle asked.

'Yes, please,' Mrs Jeffries soothed. She didn't know what to make of anything she'd heard this evening, but

86

as was her habit, she tucked all the information safely in the back of her mind. She wouldn't think about it until she had the peace and quiet of her bedroom.

Luty cleared her throat. 'Well, fer starters, Madame Natalia says that Mrs Popejoy ain't no medium. Claims the woman used to work in the music halls, did some singin' and dancin' and some kind of mind-readin' act.'

'And she charges an arm and a leg too,' Betsy chimed in.

'But the best part is that we heard she don't just charge people fer a readin', that's what they call goin' and watchin' a medium try all that mumbo jumbo. She keeps on chargin' them.'

Mrs Jeffries stared at Luty quizzically. 'Whatever do you mean?'

'I mean, according to Madame Natalia, Esme Popejoy don't charge people fer puttin' 'em in touch with the dead, she charges them from then on.' Luty shook her head in disgust. 'After she gets her spirit guide to find someone's dear departed relative, she starts givin' 'em warnings. Pretendin' the warnin's is from the great beyond, from a relative they loved and trusted. Then she tells 'em if they don't come back the next week to find out what's goin' to happen next, that she can't be responsible for what befalls them.'

CHAPTER FIVE

'WHAT A PERFECTLY appalling way to behave,'
Mrs Jeffries exclaimed. 'You don't mean to say
that every time some poor unfortunate soul gets one of
Mrs Popejoy's warnings, she then keeps them coming
back in order to avoid disaster?'

'And she charges them a pretty penny for the advice
too,' Betsy said.

'Doesn't this Madame Natalia charge too?' Smythe
asked.

'Sure,' Luty agreed. 'But Madame Natalia gives
ya yer money's worth. There ain't a bunch of spirits
moanin' gloom and doom at her séances. Soaring Eagle,
fer whatever he's worth, jawed out more advice than a
preacher on a rainy Sunday. You wouldn't have to go
back to git yer answers. And accordin' to what Madame
Natalia said, that's jus' what you'd have to do if Esme
Popejoy got her hooks into ya. Not only that, but this
Popejoy woman won't sit fer jus' anyone, no sirree. Ya
gotta be well-off before she'll even let ya through the
door. Ya gotta be recommended by someone.'

'Sounds to me like Mrs Popejoy isn't much more

than a refined sharper,' said Smythe, referring to the class of professional tricksters that induced unwary innocents into card games or skittles for money and then cheated them ruthlessly before disappearing.

'Or maybe the madame,' Smythe continued thoughtfully, 'may be just tryin' to cut out the competition. 'Ow do we know she's not makin' up tales. I don't expect this Natalia woman likes losin' customers to Mrs Popejoy, especially if Mrs Popejoy's gettin' all the people with fat purses.'

'You may have a point there, Smythe,' Mrs Jeffries said earnestly. 'And there's something else we need to consider. Mrs Popejoy was on her way to the station or on a train to Southend when the murder was committed. She may well be an unprincipled person or a trickster, but if what Madame Natalia told us is true, she'd be the last person to want Abigail Hodges dead. One can't extort money from a corpse.'

No one had an answer to that. They sat silently, all of them trying to understand the separate pieces of the puzzle they'd each brought to the table.

'Hmmph,' Luty finally said. 'I was lookin' forward to havin' Edmund fix us up a séance with Mrs Popejoy. Be fun to let her try her tricks on me. But you're right, Hepzibah. She wouldn't have no reason fer wantin' Abigail Hodges dead, so I expect we'd better concentrate on someone who would.' Birdlike, she cocked her head to one side. 'Who's gonna git her money?'

'Well, from the conversation I overheard this morning between Jonathan Felcher and Felicity Marsden, I think we can assume Mrs Hodges's estate is going to be divided between her husband and her niece.'

'I know what you overheard, but jus' because some-one thinks they're gonna inherit somethin' don't make it a fact. I remember ol' Cyrus Plummer back home, he was always tellin' everyone he was gonna get his great-aunt Polly's farm, but when Polly died, she'd up and left the farm to Norman Heckler. Made ol' Cyrus madder than hell, but weren't nothin' he could do about it. No one knows who's gonna get what until the will is read.'

'Hmmm,' Mrs Jeffries murmured. 'You may be right. But we won't know who stands to benefit financially from Mrs Hodges's death unless the inspector speaks to her solicitor. And until the inspector determines that this case is murder and not robbery, I don't suppose he'll pursue that line of enquiry.'

'You mean he's still thinkin' this was just a robbery?' Smythe asked incredulously.

Mrs Jeffries sighed. 'I'm afraid so, even though they haven't had any success in tracing the stolen jewellery.' She paused and drummed her fingers on the tabletop. 'You know,' she finally said, addressing the group at large, 'the more I think about it, the more I realize Luty's right. It's imperative we find out who benefits from Abigail Hodges's will.'

''Ow can we do that?' Wiggins said as he stifled another yawn. 'Mrs Hodges's solicitor in't likely to tell us.'

'But that shouldn't stop us from tryin',' Smythe argued. 'Seems to me if we start askin' around, we can at least find out who was likely to inherit. Maybe it really is Mr Hodges and Miss Marsden.'

'That's precisely what I had in mind,' Mrs Jeffries

said. 'From what I've heard of Mrs Hodges's character, it wouldn't surprise me if she wasn't one of those persons who is quite vocal about the intended disbursement of her worldly goods.'

Wiggins frowned. 'Huh?'

'She means the old woman might be one of them that's always threatenin' their nearest and dearest with bein' disinherited,' Luty explained.

'Exactly,' Mrs Jeffries said. 'But that isn't all we must do. We've also got to ascertain if Jonathan Felcher, Felicity Marsden and Thomasina Trotter were where they said they were when Mrs Hodges was murdered.'

'Why the housekeeper?' Betsy asked. 'Why not the rest of the servants too?'

'Because none of them had gone to school with Mrs Hodges. According to the inspector, Thomasina Trotter was once of the same social class as her employer. Then she ended up working for her. Something about that doesn't seem right. So it's very important we confirm her whereabouts,' Mrs Jeffries explained. She wasn't sure what she was after here, but she knew they still didn't have nearly enough information. 'Now, Wiggins, did you have any luck with Peter the footman today?'

Wiggins shook his head. 'No, I hung about the 'ouse for the better part of the day, but 'e didn't come out.'

'You didn't happen to notice anything else interesting, did you?' Mrs Jeffries asked kindly. She didn't want him to feel as though he'd failed.

'I didn't see anything,' Wiggins said eagerly, 'but I 'eard somethin' that might be useful. One of the housemaids from across the road from the Hodges place told me the lights was lit at the Hodges house.' He leaned forward eagerly, putting his elbows on the table. 'But the funny part is – and Nellie saw this with her own eyes; she's got a room on the top floor and she could see right across the road to the house – that around ten o'clock, all the lamps started goin' out. One by one. She watched it go from room to room, candles and lamps and even the gaslights were put out.'

'All right,' Mrs Goodge put in, 'so the killer turned off the lights. That doesn't tell us anything.'

Wiggins looked crestfallen. Mrs Jeffries hastily intervened. 'Thank you, Wiggins. That particular fact may be very important eventually.' She rather agreed with Mrs Goodge, but she didn't want to say so. 'Are you up to more footwork tomorrow, lad?'

' 'Course I am. What do you want me to do?'

'I want you to keep an eye on Felicity Marsden tomorrow. Keep watch on the house, and if she leaves, be sure and follow her.' Mrs Jeffries thought that was a safe enough task for the boy. She'd send Betsy to have another go at talking with the Hodgeses' footman.

'Is she pretty?' Wiggins asked hopefully.

'What difference does it make what she looks like?' Smythe snapped. 'She might be a murderess, so make sure she don't spot you.'

The coachman looked at Mrs Jeffries. 'Do you still want me to try and find the driver that brought Mrs Hodges 'ome that night?'

'Yes, I'd like to know why she was so angry with him.' Mrs Jeffries cocked her head to one side. 'But I'd also like you to see if you can find out any information about Jonathan Felcher. Double-check his whereabouts the night of the murder and find out as much as you can about his character.' Mrs Jeffries turned her attention to Betsy and Luty Belle. 'Betsy, I think you need to try to make contact with someone from the Hodges household. A maid or a footman, perhaps you can find that young boy Peter. Find out anything you can about Felicity Marsden's broken engagement and also whether or not it's true that Mrs Hodges paid Benjamin Vogel not to marry her niece.'

'What about me?' Luty asked.

Mrs Jeffries gazed at her helplessly. The others were young and strong and could easily take care of themselves. But she didn't want Luty Belle Crookshank lurking in passageways or trying to pry a few words out of servants. She was too old for that. Yet she couldn't come right out and say so. Luty would be mortally offended.

'Come now, Hepzibah,' Luty said tartly. 'I ain't askin' to follow anyone or some such foolishness as that, I knows what I'm capable of doin'. But surely I can do somethin'?'

'Of course you can,' Mrs Jeffries assured her. 'You're a valuable asset to our enquiries.' She broke off, still trying to think of something for Luty to do, when inspiration struck. 'I've just the thing. Gracious, why didn't I think of it before? Felicity Marsden was allegedly with the Plimptons on the night of the murder. Try to find out if she actually was at Sadler's Wells watching the ballet. And more importantly, can you find someone who will confirm that Felicity Marsden was with them all evening?'

Luty nodded eagerly, her dark eyes flashing with

enthusiasm. 'That oughta be easier than shootin' fish in a barrel. I know plenty of folks who's always goin' off to the ballet. I can find someone who was there that night.'

Mrs Jeffries heaved a silent sigh of relief. Luty's chore wasn't really needed. The inspector had already confirmed that the Plimptons had taken Felicity out that evening. But it was important that she be made to feel wanted and useful.

'Now, I believe we'd all better get some rest.' Mrs Jeffries stood up. 'Tomorrow is going to be a very busy day.'

Benjamin Vogel lived in a ground-floor room in a run-down lodging house in Paddington. Inspector Witherspoon and Constable Barnes arrived before nine in the morning, hoping to catch the young man before he left for his employment.

Barnes rapped lightly on the door and it was opened a moment later by a tall, blond-haired young man dressed in a white shirt, tie and brown trousers.

'Yes,' he asked cautiously, eyeing Barnes's police uniform warily. 'What do you want?'

Despite the man's careful diction, the inspector could faintly hear the flat, nasal accent of east London working class. The young man might be respectably dressed and well educated, but he wasn't all that many years out of Whitechapel.

'Are you Mr Benjamin Vogel?' the inspector asked.

'I am, and who might you be?'

'Inspector Witherspoon of Scotland Yard. This is Constable Barnes. We'd like to have a word with you, sir.'

Vogel opened the door wider and motioned for them to step inside. The room was small, ugly and crowded with mismatched furniture. There was a bed covered with a mustard-coloured bedspread, a wardrobe with two of the knobs missing from the bottom drawers, a threadbare green-and-brown carpet and a pair of limp-looking dull-brown curtains at the one dirty window. Opposite the bed was a cracked leather divan and next to that a scarred table and a single cane-back chair. On the floor beside the table were several stacks of books.

'Now, what's all this about, inspector?' Vogel asked. He didn't invite either man to sit down. 'I'm a bit short on time. I don't want to be late for work.'

Witherspoon could understand that. 'We won't keep you long, Mr Vogel. Could you please tell us where you were on the night of January the fourth?'

Vogel's light eyebrows drew together in a puzzled frown. 'January the fourth? Well, let me see. I'm not all that sure I can remember.'

'It was only three days ago, sir,' Constable Barnes stated.

Vogel drew a deep breath. 'Oh? Well, I was probably right here. Where else would I be? Yes, that's right. I came straight home from work and spent the evening reading.'

'Are you acquainted with Mrs Abigail Hodges and Miss Felicity Marsden?' Witherspoon asked. He could see Vogel stiffen.

'Yes.'

The inspector watched him carefully. 'Were you aware that Mrs Hodges was murdered on January the fourth?'

Vogel's eyes widened. 'Good Lord. Really, no, I must say I hadn't heard.'

Witherspoon didn't believe the man. There was something very theatrical about Vogel's reaction, he thought. The inspector was quite pleased with himself. 'Theatrical' was a word he'd heard his chief use more than once when he was describing a suspect's expression.

'You didn't read about it in the papers, sir?' Barnes said softly.

'Newspapers are useless,' Vogel declared firmly. 'I never waste my time on them. How was Mrs Hodges killed?'

The inspector glanced at the constable. Barnes shook his head ever so slightly, indicating that he didn't believe one word Benjamin Vogel was saying.

Witherspoon sighed silently. Really, Vogel was a terrible actor. The man's tone, his manner, his expression. Goodness, his act was so patently false a two-year-old could see through it.

'She was shot,' the inspector replied slowly. 'Twice. Once in the head and once in the heart. It happened during the course of a robbery.'

'That's dreadful.' The Adam's apple in Vogel's throat bobbed up and down as he swallowed. 'Appalling.'

'Were you engaged to Miss Felicity Marsden?' Witherspoon cocked his head to one side.

'I was,' Vogel admitted. A dull red crept up his cheeks. 'But Miss Marsden and I ended our engagement over two months ago. I haven't heard from or seen her or anyone else in her family since then.'

The inspector hoped the next question would take

the man by surprise. Really, he so hated it when people tried to lie to the police. 'Didn't Mrs Hodges help to end that engagement? Didn't she pay you a great deal of money not to marry her niece?'

'That's a lie,' Vogel snapped. He clenched both his hands into fists. 'A filthy disgusting lie. I love Fliss, I wouldn't have taken all the money in the world to break our engagement.'

Startled, Witherspoon blinked. Benjamin Vogel sounded like he was telling the truth.

'But we have it on good authority that Mrs Hodges did pay you to break your engagement to her niece.' The inspector phrased his question carefully. 'Are you denying it's true?'

Vogel laughed harshly. 'Of course I'm denying it. No doubt you've heard all sorts of nasty gossip about me. Mrs Hodges made sure that everyone including Fliss would believe the worst about my character. The old harridan even tried to get me sacked. Oh, I don't deny that she came around here offering me money, but I refused to take it. I threw her out. Somehow, though, she convinced Fliss that I had taken money not to see her any more. She sent the ring back.'

'So you've had nothing to do with the Hodges household since Miss Marsden returned your engagement ring?' Witherspoon asked.

'That's right,' Vogel answered.

'Where's the engagement ring that Miss Hodges returned?' Witherspoon asked. He was quite proud of that question. Surely if Mr Vogel were telling the truth about his association with Felicity Marsden, he'd be able to produce the evidence of his broken engagement.

'I didn't keep it,' Vogel replied harshly. 'I'm not a rich man. When Fliss sent the ring back, I sold it. What did you expect, that I'd keep it for sentimental reasons?' He laughed bitterly. 'Between Abigail Hodges and Felicity they managed to kill any tender feelings I might have once had. If you want to see that ring, Inspector, you can take yourself down to Webster's on Kensington High Street and buy it yourself.'

The inspector was suddenly embarrassed. The anger and pain in Vogel's voice were real. 'I, er, don't think that will be necessary.' He would, however, send a constable to check Vogel's story.

'So you've had nothing to do with anyone in the Hodges household in two months?' Barnes persisted.

'As I've already told you, no.' Vogel sighed deeply. 'Now, if you don't mind, I'd like to finish dressing for work.'

'Just one more thing, sir.' The inspector had suddenly remembered Mrs Popejoy's wild assertion. Naturally he didn't believe much of what she'd told him. Certainly he didn't for one moment believe in gaslight spirits warning victims of their intended deaths, but he couldn't in good conscience ignore the one fact that might be of importance.

'Please, Inspector,' Vogel replied, heading for the wardrobe. 'Do make it quick. I mustn't be late.'

'Do you have a gun?'

Vogel stopped in his tracks and whirled around. 'A gun? Why on earth do you think I've a gun?'

'Never mind why, sir,' Constable Barnes interjected. 'Just answer the question.'

Vogel cleared his throat and cast one quick, nervous

glance towards the wardrobe. He looked like he was trying to decide whether or not to tell the truth. 'Yes. I do. It's a—'

Witherspoon cut him off. 'May we see it, sir?'

Constable Barnes had put his notebook away and now watched Benjamin Vogel carefully as the man hesitated.

'Yes, of course.' Vogel went to the wardrobe, pulled open the door and yanked a small, square case off the top shelf.

Taking the case to the table, he slammed it down and turned to stare belligerently at the two policemen who were right behind him.

'You've not got a warrant, have you?' Vogel said. His voice cracked ever so slightly.

'No, Mr Vogel,' the inspector replied. 'We haven't. You'd be well within your rights to refuse to show us the gun.' Actually Witherspoon wasn't terribly sure about that; he'd dozed off during the lecture on legal search procedures.

Vogel took a deep breath and shook his head. 'I do want it noted that I'm cooperating with the police of my own free will.'

'That'll be noted, sir,' Barnes assured him dryly.

He unlatched the clasp and lifted the lid. 'My God,' he exclaimed. 'What on earth . . .'

Witherspoon and Barnes looked into the case.

The gun was gone.

'But of course I was at the ballet,' Miss Myrtle Buxton exclaimed. 'Why, everyone was there that night.'

Luty hid her satisfied smile by taking a sip of the fine

Indian tea Miss Buxton had so thoughtfully provided. Myrtle Buxton, wealthy, single and well past sixty, lived across the road from Luty's own Knightsbridge home. Myrtle wore a pale rose day dress that blended perfectly with the pink overstuffed settee and dark burgundy carpet. Her silver-grey hair was arranged in tight curls, her eyes were a vivid blue and Luty was sure the woman had on a bit of rouge. No one Myrtle's age had cheeks that bright. Not that Luty cared. If she wanted to paint her face, it was her business.

The important thing was, Myrtle devoted practically every waking moment to her social life. A notorious gossip, Myrtle Buxton had developed an eagle eye for noting who was where and with whom. Luty knew she'd come to the right woman.

'Too bad I missed goin',' Luty replied. 'But I've been kinda busy lately. Some friends of mine was there that night, though – the Plimptons. Did ya happen to see 'em?'

Myrtle waggled her ring-bedecked fingers coquettishly. 'I saw everybody,' she declared proudly. 'Of course I saw the Plimptons. But I didn't know they were friends of yours. Gracious, I wouldn't have thought you'd know that family. They are a very stuffy bunch.'

'Er, uh, I met 'em at a party last month,' Luty lied.

'Rather conventional people,' Myrtle mused. 'Not your sort at all, Luty. They've a box at the theatre, you know.'

'Was the whole family there?'

'Goodness no! Horace Plimpton wouldn't go near the ballet if his life depended on it and Henrietta

Plimpton's one of those women who continually fancy themselves as ill. No doubt she'd taken to her bed for the evening. It's old Mrs Plimpton, Georgianna, who's the social one in that family. She, her granddaughter and another young woman were in the box that night.' She paused and shook her head. 'Not that I understand why Georgianna bothers. She fell asleep the minute she sat down. Dreadful habit, falling asleep in public. Her mouth actually gaped open. It stayed that way through the whole performance. I must say, she makes a spectacle of herself. Still, if it wasn't for Georgianna, I don't suppose poor Ada Plimpton would have any social life at all.' Myrtle broke off and gazed at her friend curiously. 'Why are you asking?'

'No particular reason,' Luty replied with a casual shrug. 'I just happened to hear they was all there that night and I wondered how that could be? Ya see, I had an argument with a friend of mine who claimed that I was gettin' so old I couldn't see straight. I thought fer sure I saw Miss Plimpton and another young woman leavin' the theatre before the ballet even started. Well, Hepzibah – that's my friend – she claimed I was seein' things and that a decent young girl wouldn't be out on the streets at that time of night gettin' into hansom cabs.' She paused and smiled apologetically. 'I reckon she must be right, I couldn't of seen her if they was sittin' in the Plimpton box. Guess I'll have to tell Hepzibah she was right. I tell ya, Myrtle, it's hard gettin' old.' She lowered her head and sniffled pathetically.

'Nonsense.' Myrtle was instantly sympathetic. She reached across and patted Luty on the hand. 'You're not old at all and you most certainly could have seen Miss Plimpton and another young lady outside the theatre. Though I must agree with your friend, it isn't the sort of behavior decent young women should indulge in. But that's becoming the way of the world these days. Women wanting the vote, wanting equality and even going out to work . . . shocking. Not at all like in my day.'

Luty bit her tongue to keep from telling Myrtle that she thought women should vote, work and do anything else they danged well pleased. 'But I thought you just said you saw the girls sittin' with Mrs Plimpton?'

'Only at the beginning,' Myrtle explained. 'You see, I happened to notice that as soon as Georgianna Plimpton fell asleep, both young ladies slipped out of the box. Ada Plimpton came back a few minutes later. But the other girl didn't come back until the last curtain call.'

Luty tried to appear unconcerned. 'Reckon the girl must have gone and sat with someone else,' she replied casually.

'She most certainly did not,' Myrtle said archly. 'I looked. I tell you that young woman left the theatre. She was gone for at least two hours.'

Remembering she was supposed to be playing a pitiful elderly lady, Luty pretended to be shocked. 'Goodness gracious, where on earth do you think a young girl would be at that time of the evening?'

'Hmmph.' Myrtle snorted indelicately. 'Where do you think she'd be? She was probably off meeting some man.'

★　★　★

'Get off with ya,' Wiggins whispered. He stared in exasperation at the shaggy, skinny, long-haired brown-and-black dog who gazed back at him with adoration. 'You've served yer purpose, you silly hound, and I've given you a bit of bun, so scarper off.'

The dog sat down and rested his head on Wiggins's foot.

'Blimey, it seemed a good idea at the time,' he muttered.

Upon arriving at Camden Street, Wiggins had been dismayed to find the quiet residential road devoid of traffic. And he couldn't get to his usual hiding place because the butler from the house next to the Hodgeses' was standing outside his ruddy door.

Wiggins hadn't known what to do. Then, out of nowhere, this silly mutt showed up. The animal was very friendly, and took to the footman like a duck to water. He decided to pretend the dog was his. He'd spent the next ten minutes walking up and down the road with the dog trotting obediently at his heels. He hadn't had the Hodges house out of his sight in all that time, either.

Wiggins stamped his feet and pulled his coat tighter against the chill. The dog shivered. Wiggins sighed. Poor thing, you could see its ribs. When the butler finally disappeared, Wiggins had been able to dart into his usual hiding place, a narrow passageway between the two homes opposite the Hodges house. The dog had come with him.

'Look, boy,' he tried again, squatting down and patting the animal's head. 'Run along home now, I've got to keep watch and I don't have any more currant buns.'

The dog whined and nudged his nose against Wiggins's coat pocket.

'Oh, you're still hungry, aren't ya?' he said sympathetically. He wished now he'd given the poor animal all the currant buns and not just half of them.

Sighing, Wiggins glanced up just as the door of the Hodges house opened and Felicity Marsden stepped outside. She paused at the top of the stairs and turned her head quickly one way and then another before darting down the stairs. Under one arm she had a dark fur muff and she carried a small brown-paper parcel.

Wiggins straightened up and dashed into the road behind the girl. The dog followed.

Felicity hurried up the quiet street, her high heels tapping rapidly against the paving stones. At the corner, she turned towards the Queens Road.

'Go on home,' Wiggins hissed at the dog again as he quickened his steps to avoid losing sight of his quarry. The dog woofed softly and bounced around his ankles, almost tripping him.

'This in'a game.' He tried to push the furry bundle to one side without hurting the animal. 'And if I lose 'er, you'll never get another crumb out of me, you silly cur.'

The dog wasn't in the least intimidated. He continued to trail Wiggins as they moved rapidly up one street and down another. Several times Wiggins and the dog had to hide behind a tree or a postbox to avoid being spotted, for Felicity Marsden frequently stopped and looked behind her.

Breathing hard, Wiggins tried to keep the young woman's slim back in sight. As they turned onto the

Uxbridge Road he almost lost her in the now crowded street, then he spotted her crossing to the opposite corner in front of the Uxbridge Road station.

Darting in front of an omnibus, Wiggins spared a worried glance at the dog and was relieved to see it keeping pace with him.

Felicity Marsden had turned onto Holland Road. Wiggins and friend followed. He wasn't worried about getting lost. He knew this area well.

She stopped suddenly, turned to glance behind her and then slipped through a gate. Wiggins waited for a moment and hurried after her.

He frowned as he reached the spot where she'd disappeared. Felicity Marsden had gone into St John's Church. For a moment he wondered what to do, whether or not he should go in after her. The dog woofed softly. Wiggins made up his mind. He pushed open the gate and went into the churchyard.

'I 'eard that Mrs Hodges broke up her poor niece's engagement,' Betsy said to the young man. He was the footman from the Hodges household.

Peter Applegate smiled shyly and deftly plucked off his rather soiled porkpie hat. He dusted the park bench carefully and then motioned Betsy to sit down.

'Aye, that she did,' he said as he sat down beside her. 'She didn't think Mr Vogel were good enough for Miss Fliss. But she were wrong. He's a nice man, he is.'

Betsy gazed around the small park where the two of them were resting and stifled a twinge of conscience. She was investigating a murder here, she told herself sternly. All's fair. But she felt bad about shamelessly flirting with the lad in order to loosen his tongue. He'd practically fallen over his feet when she'd suggested a stroll in the park. And he was only a child. He couldn't be more than fourteen.

'But being nice weren't all that important, at least not to one like Mrs Hodges,' Peter declared. 'Look how she's treated poor old Mrs Trotter all these years and them two went to school together!'

'Really?' Betsy said, though she already knew that information. 'You mean she weren't very good to her servants?'

'Good!' He laughed harshly. 'Mrs Hodges didn't know the meaning of the word. Worked us like dogs, she did.'

'Even Mrs Trotter?' Betsy decided to pursue that line of enquiry.

'Especially Mrs Trotter,' he declared. 'Had her fetchin' and carryin' and doing all sorts of things no housekeeper I ever saw did.'

'Why did Mrs Trotter put up with her? Surely she could have got a position somewhere else?' Betsy shrugged nonchalantly. 'I once worked in a miserable place, but I didn't put up with it. I took myself right off and got another position.'

Peter eyed Betsy slyly. 'You're askin' an awful lot of questions. Why? What's it to do with you?'

She racked her brain to come up with a reasonable excuse. Then she gave him a brilliant smile. 'Well, if you must know, I work close by here' – she giggled – 'and the truth is, my mistress is as nosy as anything. She sent me over here to learn what I could about the murder. I didn't want to do it, mind you. But, well . . .'

She broke off and dropped her gaze, fluttering her eye-lashes in the process. 'I'd seen you about and I figured comin' round would be a good excuse to talk to you.'

Peter stared at her incredulously for a moment and then he smiled. 'Oh, well, that's all right, then.'

She silently drew a long breath of relief. Mrs Goodge was right, she thought, a few honeyed words and a bit of battin' the eyelashes and a man will believe any load of old rubbish you tell 'im.

'Anyways,' she said shyly, 'we was talkin' about Mrs Trotter. It's real interestin', I mean 'earin' about others and 'ow they live.' She deliberately began dropping her hs. 'You never said why the woman was putting up with Mrs Hodges.'

'Oh, that. Mrs Trotter was hangin' on because she wanted something from Mrs Hodges.'

'What?'

'Don't know. But I 'eard 'em talkin' about it a few times. Once when I was takin' coal to one of the upstairs fireplaces, I 'eard Mrs Trotter beggin' the old witch to tell her where someone was.'

'Who was she talkin' about?' Betsy said, leaning closer.

'Never 'eard no name. Just Mrs Trotter saying over and over, "Tell me where she is, tell me where she is." ' He shook his head. 'It were right pitiful, old straitlaced Trotter begging like that.'

'Poor Mrs Trotter.' Betsy shook her head sympathetically. 'I reckon she's right upset, what with Mrs Hodges gettin' 'erself done in that way.'

'Upset!' Peter laughed. 'Not bloomin' likely. I don't know who Trotter was on about that day, but I do know that since the old witch's death, Mrs Trotter's been happier than I've ever seen her. Walks about the house hummin' and smilin' and talkin' to herself. Barmy, if you ask me.'

Betsy wondered what to ask next. Then she wondered how on earth she was going to get rid of Peter. 'Is Mr Hodges a nice master, then?'

'He's all right,' Peter replied. 'Nicer than she was. Bit of a dandy, but other than always brushin' lint off his sleeve or havin' me put more polish on his boots, he's not too bad.'

'I suppose Mr Hodges wasn't too happy about Mrs Hodges wanting to go to séances?'

'Where'd you hear that?' Peter's brows drew together.

'You mean it isn't true?'

' 'Course it's not true. Goin' and tryin' to talk to the spirit of Mrs Hodges's dead son were Mr Hodges's idea. He started talkin' about it right after he and Mrs Hodges got married. Mind you, that caused a bit of a stir.'

'Are you sayin' it were Mr Hodges that believes in spiritualism, then?' Betsy asked, just to be sure she understood him correctly.

' 'Course it were him. Mrs Hodges didn't believe in all that silly stuff.'

'How did Mrs Hodges meet up with Mrs Popejoy then?' Betsy asked.

Peter stared at her suspiciously and she quickly added, 'I read about her in the papers. Caught me eye, it did. I'm interested in spiritualism myself. You never know, do you? Could be there's lots the dead could tell us. And that Mrs Popejoy did claim some spirit tried to warn poor Mrs Hodges to be careful.'

'Yeah,' he muttered. 'She did say that, din't she. But I don't believe a word of it.'

'Well, Mrs Hodges must of, she kept goin' to see the woman.'

'Only because Mr Hodges wanted 'er to,' Peter declared. 'Mr Hodges claimed it would give Mrs Hodges a bit o' peace.'

'You never answered me question. 'Ow did Mrs Hodges meet up with Mrs Popejoy?' Betsy asked quickly, now that she'd finally loosened Peter's tongue again.

The boy gave her a slow, sly grin. 'It were Mr Hodges that introduced them. Fact of the matter is, I reckons Mr Hodges knows Mrs Popejoy from way back. They was old friends. Good friends too. If you get my meanin'.'

CHAPTER SIX

Mrs Jeffries spent the afternoon sorting linens. The task freed her mind to concentrate on the case. She was convinced that the death of Abigail Hodges wasn't a simple robbery gone wrong. It was murder. Premeditated murder. She could feel it in her bones. But there were still far too many unanswered questions for her to make any assumptions as to the identity of the killer.

Picking up an armload of tablecloths and napkins, she made her way downstairs to the kitchen.

'Hello, Mrs Goodge,' she said brightly as she opened the door to the cupboard and slipped the linens inside.

'Good afternoon. Miserable day out, isn't it?' The cook was standing at the table next to a large earthenware bowl filled with ground meat. Beside the bowl was a silver cast-iron sausage maker and a tin of sausage casings.

'Yes, it is. I do hope all this rain isn't hampering the others in the investigation. Are we having sausages for dinner?'

'No, I thought I'd do these for a late-night nibble

– it's chicken tonight for all of us. But sausages can come in handy when we're all round the table givin' our news.'

'What a good idea,' Mrs Jeffries said. 'And you do make such lovely sausages, so much better than the ones available at the butcher's.'

'I should hope so,' Mrs Goodge exclaimed. 'Lord knows what goes into those others. Wouldn't have them in the house.' She finished grinding the last of the meat and wiped her hands on a towel. Mrs Jeffries noticed her stretching her fingers and flexing them before she reached for the tin of sausage casings.

'Your rheumatism is bothering you today, isn't it?' Mrs Jeffries said, watching as the cook fumbled with the lid on the tin.

'Always does when it rains. But at least in this house a body can sit a spell when the pain gets too bad.' Mrs Goodge put the tin down and plopped into a chair. 'Not like some houses I've worked in. Now, that reminds me, I found out a bit about Mrs Hodges and how she runs her house.' She gave an inelegant snort. 'Real strict, she was. Made the servants pay for their tea and sugar every month, prayer gong every morning before breakfast, with the housekeeper leadin' the prayers because Mr and Mrs Hodges couldn't bother to stir themselves out of bed that early. And cold meat from the day before for the servants' dinner at one o'clock. Sounds a right miserable place, doesn't it?'

Surprised, Mrs Jeffries gazed at the cook curiously. When she'd first taken up her post here, her own unorthodox way of running the household had caused Mrs Goodge much alarm. She'd put an end to any silly

111

divisions between the upper and lower servants, insisting that Smythe, Wiggins and Betsy be treated in the same manner as herself and the cook. She'd eliminated morning prayers with the comment that anyone who wanted could worship the Almighty in the privacy of their own room, and she'd informed them that as long as their duties were carried out, she had no need to supervise them directly. Meals were taken together with everyone waiting on themselves instead of expecting the lowest kitchen maid to do it all (not that they had a kitchen maid, but that onerous burden would normally have fallen to Betsy) and what was done on one's own free time was one's own business. Mrs Jeffries was well aware that her way of managing a household was unusual, but as long as the inspector was satisfied, she wasn't concerned.

'Mrs Hodges certainly seems to have run her household very strictly,' Mrs Jeffries finally agreed, 'but that's not so unusual. Most households function in much the same manner.'

'More's the pity,' Mrs Goodge muttered. She stared off into the distance for a moment and then shook herself out of her reverie. 'Well, we've not got all day, have we? I did just like you asked and found out a bit about that Mrs Trotter.'

Mrs Jeffries gazed at her in admiration. 'Goodness, Mrs Goodge, that's very quick.'

'You might say I had a bit of luck. The grocer's boy come by this mornin'. He delivers to the Hodges house too and he gave me a right earful about Thomasina Trotter.' Mrs Goodge leaned forward on her elbow. 'She's a real strange one, she is.'

'Strange? How do you mean?'

Mrs Goodge tapped her finger gently against her temple. 'Up here,' she said, her voice hushed. 'She's touched. Not right in the head. The woman spends her free time out walking the streets.'

Mrs Jeffries stared at the cook in bewilderment. 'Are you implying that Thomasina Trotter is a . . . a . . . prostitute?'

'No, no,' Mrs Goodge said impatiently. 'She's not lookin' for men, she's lookin' for women. She stares at young girls. Accosts them in the street. Goes right up and looks into their faces, studyin' 'em like. Why, she's gone as far as Whitechapel – and even worse, she's done it at night. Can you imagine that? Being on the streets in the East End after dark. I tell you, the woman's daft. Completely daft.'

'Goodness, that is most odd,' Mrs Jeffries replied. 'Were you able to find out why she does it?'

'No. I wasn't. But I'll keep at it. Just give us a few more days. I've got me sources askin' around.'

'You know,' Mrs Jeffries said thoughtfully, 'from what you've just told me about Mrs Hodges having been so very strict with her servants, I'm amazed she allowed her housekeeper to do such a thing. Surely she must have known Mrs Trotter was behaving rather oddly?'

'But she didn't know about it.' Mrs Goodge laughed. 'For goodness' sake, who'd tell Mrs Hodges anything? The servants didn't like her much and I'm sure she weren't the kind to sit and natter with the tradespeople who delivered to the house. And for all her daft ways, Thomasina Trotter's a bit of a sharp one. She obviously used to tell Mrs Hodges she were goin' to visit her old nanny.' She broke off and frowned. 'Now, what was the woman's name? Oh yes, Miss Bush. Anyways, after the grocer's boy left this mornin', I sent young Willie Spencer, the lad that works over the garden for Colonel Norcross, over to Fulham to have a gander at Mrs Trotter's nanny.'

'Why how very intelligent, Mrs Goodge,' Mrs Jeffries said. 'How did Willie do?'

'The boy did well enough, I reckon.' Mrs Goodge smiled smugly. 'He spoke to Miss Bush herself. Mind you, nothin' she said made any sense. Willie says the poor thing's half out of her mind. She's old, you know. Sometimes they get that way. So the way I figure is that Mrs Trotter used to tell her mistress she was visiting with Miss Bush, who wouldn't even know what day it was, let alone whether or not anyone had come calling, and then instead of actually goin' to see her, Mrs Trotter would wander the streets starin' at young girls.' She shuddered. 'Horrible, isn't it?'

'If you're right,' Mrs Jeffries mused, 'and there's no reason to believe you aren't, then that means Thomasina Trotter doesn't have an alibi for the time of the murder.'

'That's what I'm thinkin' too.'

'Gracious, this sheds a whole new light on the situation.'

'But why would Mrs Trotter want to kill her mistress?' Mrs Goodge shook her head. 'That's the part I can't understand. The woman might be a bit daft, but a murderess?'

'We don't know that she did kill Mrs Hodges, but

then again, we don't know that she didn't,' Mrs Jeffries murmured thoughtfully. After a moment she smiled at the cook. 'Keep digging, Mrs Goodge. I think we might be onto something here. Tell the others we'll meet back here after the inspector's gone to bed this evening. Perhaps we'll have even more pieces to add to this puzzle.'

As Mrs Jeffries went back up the stairs to finish her linens, she made a mental note to urge the inspector to double-check Thomasina Trotter's alibi. And just to make sure, she thought, I'll send Betsy or Smythe around to talk to Miss Bush and her neighbours.

'Now, Constable Barnes,' Inspector Witherspoon said patiently, 'we didn't really have any grounds to arrest Mr Vogel. A missing gun isn't reason enough to take him down to the station to help us with our enquiries.'

Barnes pulled the door of the hansom shut. 'Ladbroke Road Police Station,' he called to the driver before turning to the inspector. 'Yes, sir, I know that. But what about his landlady? She claimed she never saw him come in that night.'

'Yes, but she also told us she doesn't see him come in most evenings. Her rooms are at the back of the house,' the inspector replied tiredly. 'Furthermore, we've no idea if his gun has anything at all to do with Mrs Hodges.'

'She was shot with a revolver,' Barnes insisted. 'And his revolver's missin'. We know he needs money and we know he hated Abigail Hodges for interferin' in his relationship with Miss Marsden. He knew the layout of the house, he could have found out that the Hodgeses was goin' to be out that evening and he could have broke in just plannin' on robbin' them when Mrs Hodges surprised him. That would explain why she was shot. Vogel knew she could identify him.'

'Then where is the jewellery?' Witherspoon asked. 'As far as we know, it hasn't turned up at any of the usual places and we know it wasn't in his room. Mr Vogel was quite within his rights to refuse to let us search, but he didn't and the jewellery wasn't there.'

'He could have hidden it somewhere,' Barnes suggested, but he didn't sound very sure of himself. 'I expect you're right, sir. We didn't have all that much evidence against the man.'

'Vogel's not the only man in London who owns a revolver,' the inspector said.

'True, but most of them that owns guns can probably produce them,' Barnes muttered. 'Still, I'm sure you know what you're doin', sir.'

Witherspoon hoped the constable was right. At this point he wasn't all that sure he did know what he was doing. Perhaps he should have brought Mr Vogel in – but then again, he hated making an arrest unless he was absolutely certain.

'But it's still hard for me to believe it was professionals that broke into the Hodges house and killed that poor woman,' Barnes continued thoughtfully. 'It just didn't have the right feel, if you know what I mean, sir.'

'I do indeed, Constable. As a matter of fact, I've recently come to the same conclusion myself,' Witherspoon admitted. 'There are simply too many peculiar circumstances in this case. I think we'll just have to keep at it. Did the lads come up with anything useful from the neighbours?'

'Not really, sir.' Barnes reached for the door latch as the hansom pulled up in front of the station. As soon as the horses stopped, he opened the door and leaped out. The rain, which had started out as a drizzle when they'd left Vogel's rooms in Paddington, was now a downpour. 'Better make a run for it, Inspector,' Barnes called as he took care of the driver.

The Ladbroke Road Police Station was a large brick building with a paved yard in front. The larger and more conspicuous of the two doors led into the front office with its constables behind the counter and the charge room, while the other, smaller door led to a main staircase, which in turn led to offices and the canteen.

It was this smaller door that Witherspoon made a dash for. Inside, he stopped and shook the water off his bowler. He was reaching for his spectacles when a uniformed constable appeared at the top of the staircase.

'Good afternoon, sir,' the young policeman called down. 'The station officer would like to see you. He says it's urgent. He's in the charge room, if you'd care to go in.'

Witherspoon, who'd hoped to get a cup of tea, stifled a sigh. He went through the connecting door into the front office. After nodding politely at the constable on duty behind the counter, he entered the charge room.

Witherspoon grimaced as he stepped inside. He hated this bleak place. There were no windows and the walls were painted a dull, ugly green. The hardwood floor was scarred and stained from years of heavy, weary feet. There was a plain wooden bench alongside one wall for the prisoners to sit on, a wooden table for them to turn out their usually meagre personal effects and a tall desk for the station officer to sit at as he listed the charges against the prisoners in the crime book. At the end of the room was another door, which led to the detention room. All in all, Witherspoon found the whole place dreadfully depressing. Not at all like the records room at CID headquarters at Scotland Yard. He sighed wistfully at the thought of his former position and then straightened his shoulders, remembering his duty.

The door from the detention room opened and the station officer stepped inside. 'Oh, good day, sir. I see you got my message. Sorry I wasn't here,' he said politely, 'but we've had a busy day. Two in lockup in the last hour.'

'That's quite all right, Constable, er . . .'

'Kent, sir. Constable Kent. I was on my way in today when I was stopped by Constable Griffith. He's got a message for you about the Hodges case. They've found the stolen jewellery.'

'Really?' Witherspoon was genuinely surprised. He'd never expected those jewels to turn up.

'Yes, sir. Constable Griffith wanted me to make sure you stayed here until he arrived. He should be here anytime now.' Kent hurried over and stuck his head out of the door. 'Can't imagine what's keeping him.'

'Goodness, did he say where the jewels were found?' Witherspoon fervently hoped the stolen items had been found at one of the shops in Shoreditch or St Giles that the police knew solicited stolen merchandise.

'No, sir, he didn't,' Kent said. 'But here he is now, sir. Griffith,' he called across the front office. 'Inspector Witherspoon's in here.'

The inspector would have liked to have left this miserable room for the front office or, better yet, for the canteen, but he didn't get the opportunity. Constable Griffith, all six feet two inches of him, was already inside the charge room. Barnes was right behind him.

'Sir,' Griffith exclaimed. 'We've found the jewels.' He handed the inspector a black cloth bag.

Witherspoon opened the bag and spilled its contents onto the table. 'Where did you find them, Constable?'

'At the Hodges house,' Griffith replied. 'In Felicity Marsden's bedroom. The bag was pinned to one of the folds in the curtains, up along the upper rails.'

'Looks like you were right, sir,' Barnes said. 'This wasn't a bloomin' robbery. No thief in his right mind leaves the goods behind.'

Witherspoon's spirits sank. Drat. The murderer was far too clever for his liking.

'Took us a while to find them,' Griffith continued proudly. 'I almost missed them too, but then I noticed one of the curtain rings was angled crooked and there was a funny bulge in the fabric right below it.'

Witherspoon dragged his gaze from the jewels and stared at Constable Griffith. 'Why on earth did you search Miss Marsden's bedroom?' he asked.

Constable Griffith's bright smile faded. 'But, sir, you told me to. At least you sent me a note.'

'I most certainly did not,' the inspector protested. He thought back on everything he'd done that day and he was absolutely sure he hadn't sent Constable Griffith a message to search the Hodges home. Witherspoon knew perfectly well that he occasionally got a bit muddled, but even he'd remember writing a note.

'But, sir,' Griffiths pleaded. He stared at his superior in panic. 'I've got the note right here.' He reached into the pocket of his jacket and pulled out a piece of paper, which he immediately thrust into Witherspoon's outstretched hand.

Opening the folded paper, Witherspoon frowned as he scanned the contents. 'My apologies, Constable,' he said, looking up. 'This is indeed instructions from me authorizing you to search the house.'

Griffith sighed in relief.

'But I didn't write it. How was it delivered?'

'A young lad brought it to me as I was leaving the house across from the Hodges home,' Griffith explained slowly. He looked terribly confused by this turn of events. 'We were finishin' up the house-to-house, trying to talk to all the neighbours. The boy, he was just one of them street arabs, sir, couldn't have been more than eight or nine, he told me it had been given to him by Inspector Witherspoon.'

'I do believe, sir, that I really should get you a headache powder,' Mrs Jeffries said to the inspector. The poor man looked positively dreadful. He'd come home with his shoulders slumped and rain pouring off the rim of his hat. She'd immediately ushered him into the drawing room, put him in his favourite chair and poured a nice glass of sherry. She'd then sat down and listened to his tale of woe.

'That won't be necessary, Mrs Jeffries. As soon as

I've had a bite to eat, I'm sure I'll feel much better.' He took another sip of his drink. 'It's just, well, one gets embarrassed when one's been made to look a fool.'

'Now, sir. Don't be ridiculous. How could you possibly have been made to look foolish?' She clucked her tongue. 'It's hardly your fault that someone forged your signature onto a note.'

'It's good of you to say so, but that's not the only reason I feel badly,' he confessed. He stared morosely at his sherry. 'I think perhaps I should have listened to Constable Barnes. He wanted to bring Mr Vogel into the station for questioning and I didn't think we had sufficient evidence.'

Mrs Jeffries clucked her tongue again. 'Now, now, sir. I'm sure you made the right decision. Why don't you tell me everything that happened today. It'll do you good to get it off your chest.'

She straightened as she heard a harsh, muffled rumble that sounded like it was coming from belowstairs. The inspector heard it too.

'I say, did you hear that?' he asked.

'Yes. It was probably something falling off the back of a cart.' She didn't care what the sound was. Unless the house was on fire, she wanted nothing to distract the inspector from telling her what had transpired that day.

'Thought it sounded like a dog,' he murmured. Then he took a deep breath and told his dear housekeeper all about his utterly dreadful day.

Mrs Jeffries listened very carefully.

The inspector retired early that night. Mrs Jeffries waited until he'd disappeared up the stairs and she heard his bedroom door close before she hurried down to the kitchen.

For once, everyone was there. Even Luty Belle had managed to come.

'Hatchet said he'll be back fer me in an hour,' Luty said, referring to her butler. 'His nose is out of joint on account of havin' to go out in the wet, but he'll git over it. I couldn't wait till tomorrow. I've found out some information that's gonna set your hair on fire.'

There was another muffled rumble sound and everyone started in surprise.

'What was that?' Betsy asked.

'Sounded like a dog,' Mrs Goodge replied.

'I heard the same sound a while ago,' Mrs Jeffries said.

'It's thunder,' Wiggins put in.

'Thunder?' Smythe exclaimed. 'It weren't a bit like thunder. You'd better get the muck out of yer ears, boy.'

'And I'd better get them sausages,' Mrs Goodge said as she stood up and bustled down the hallway towards the cooling pantry. 'Don't anyone start until I get back.'

They all waited patiently, sipping at the cocoa the cook had put in a pot on the table. Mrs Jeffries could tell from their faces that each of them had something to report.

'Arrg!' Mrs Goodge screamed. Despite her rheumatism, she fairly flew down the hall, clutching an empty platter in her hands.

Alarmed, Mrs Jeffries and Smythe both jumped to their feet. Betsy scooted back from the table to get a better view, Wiggins sank into his chair and Luty pulled a pistol out of her fur muff.

'For goodness' sake, Luty,' Mrs Jeffries cried when she saw the gun, 'put that thing away before you shoot someone.'

'I'll put this away when I know why Mrs Goodge is howling her head off,' Luty retorted.

'Me sausages,' the cook yelped. She slammed the empty platter onto the table. 'They're gone.'

'Is that what all the shoutin's about?' Smythe said in disgust. 'For pity's sake, Mrs Goodge, someone probably ate them.'

'But they was there less than ten minutes ago,' Mrs Goodge insisted. 'And I've been hearin' strange noises all evenin'. I tell you somethin's in the house.'

Another rumble exploded from the back of the hall.

'Now I know that weren't thunder,' Luty said. She aimed the pistol at the dimly lit passage and got to her feet.

Wiggins leaped up. 'Don't shoot,' he shouted. ''E's only a puppy.' He threw himself in front of Luty. 'Please, put that gun away. 'E was hungry. 'E followed me home and I didn't have the heart to turn 'im out. He's a good dog, Fred is.'

Wiggins turned and rushed down the hallway towards the small, rarely used storage room. A few moments later he returned with the dog in tow.

'Fred's sorry 'e ate the sausages,' Wiggins said apologetically to Mrs Goodge. The animal looked at Mrs Goodge and licked his chops. 'But it were an accident. The door to the cooling pantry was open when I was bringin' 'im down the hall and the poor mite was so hungry that when 'e smelled that meat, 'e couldn't 'elp hisself.'

Surprised by this turn of events, they all stared at the footman and the dog. Fred wagged his tail.

Mrs Jeffries cleared her throat, Smythe chuckled, Mrs Goodge snorted, Betsy grinned and Luty put her gun away.

'Can 'e stay?' Wiggins asked as he knelt by the animal and started stroking his rather mangy coat. ''E's got nowheres to go and we can't just turn 'im out. 'E'll starve.'

'But, Wiggins,' Mrs Jeffries said gently, 'what will the inspector say?'

Still wagging his tail, Fred stepped closer to the table. Smythe tentatively put his hand out and the dog licked it. Then he went to Betsy and nuzzled his head against her chair.

'We can talk 'im into it,' Wiggins insisted. 'Our inspector's a kind'earted gentleman, 'e wouldn't want to see the poor little pup turned out in the cold.'

'Let's have a go at it,' the coachman put in. 'I don't mind sharing me room with a dog. As long as Wiggins agrees to keep 'im clean.'

'I don't know,' Mrs Jeffries said hesitantly.

'Oh please.' Betsy added her voice to the chorus. 'I like dogs and this one looks like he's right friendly.' Fred bumped his nose against her knee.

Mrs Jeffries didn't believe in dithering. She made a decision. 'All right, we'll ask the inspector if we can keep the dog. But, Wiggins, the animal will be your responsibility. You must treat him kindly, keep him clean and ensure that he's walked properly.'

'You won't regret it, Mrs Jeffries,' the footman promised. ''E's a good dog, is Fred. 'E'll even come in

'andy on our investigations. Why, with proper trainin'
and such 'e can probably learn to pick up the scent and
follow the trail.'

Fred chose that moment to flop down flat on the
floor and go to sleep. Everyone laughed.

'Mind you keep his nose off the trail of my sausages
in the future,' Mrs Goodge muttered. But she smiled at
the animal as she said it.

'Now that that's settled,' Mrs Jeffries said with a
worried glance at Fred, 'let's find out what each of us
has learned today. Luty, why don't you go first. We
don't want to annoy Hatchet any more than necessary.'

Luty told them all about her visit to Myrtle Buxton.
She was a good storyteller, and when she got to the part
about Felicity Marsden leaving the ballet, everyone was
leaning towards her, their faces alight with interest.

'Cor,' Smythe said when she'd finished. 'That means
that Miss Marsden don't have an alibi.'

'True,' Mrs Jeffries said, 'but it doesn't mean she
murdered her aunt. It could just as easily mean she
wanted a chance to see her young man.'

'Thomasina Trotter don't really have an alibi either,'
Mrs Goodge interjected. She told them what she'd
heard from her sources that day as well.

'Well, I've learned something important too,' Betsy
said when the cook had finished. She told them about
her conversation with Peter Applegate.

'Are you tellin' us that it were Mr Hodges that introduced Mrs Popejoy to his wife?' Luty asked.

Betsy nodded. 'And that's not the half of it, accordin'
to Peter. He thinks that Mr Hodges and Mrs Popejoy
knew each other from a long time ago.'

'Was he just guessing or does he know that for a fact?' Mrs Jeffries asked.

'He weren't really sure,' Betsy said cautiously. 'But a couple of months back, right after Mrs Popejoy had been round the Hodges house the first time, Peter claims he saw Mrs Popejoy and Mr Hodges together driving in a carriage down Oxford Street. But when Peter happened to mention it to Mr Hodges, Mr Hodges acted like he didn't know what he was on about.'

'I'm gettin' confused,' Wiggins said. 'Was the man Mr Hodges, then?'

'Hold yer horses, boy,' Luty interjected. 'She's gettin' to it. Go on, Betsy, what happened then?'

'Peter says he didn't think much about it, he just thought he'd made a mistake. But the very next day Mr Hodges left the house and forgot his walkin' stick. Well, Mrs Hodges gives Peter the stick and tells him he can probably catch up with her husband at Holland Park.' Betsy paused dramatically. 'But when Peter reached the park, he didn't just find Mr Hodges. He saw Mr Hodges and Mrs Popejoy together and they was huddlin' under a tree. They didn't hear Peter comin', so they weren't careful with what they were sayin' to one another.'

'What did Peter hear?' Mrs Jeffries asked quickly.

'He heard Mr Hodges sayin' that Mrs Popejoy had better be careful, that they wouldn't like it to be like the last time. Then he laughed like and said, "Remember what happened three years ago." '

Wiggins shook his head. 'I still don't get it.'

'Neither do I,' mumbled Mrs Goodge.

'Don't you see, if he's referrin' to something that

126

happened three years ago, something they both knew about, that proves he knew Mrs Popejoy three years ago.'

'Hmmm,' Mrs Jeffries said. 'Perhaps, or perhaps not. Mr Hodges could have been referring to a social or political event that everyone knew about. Something that was in the papers and was common knowledge, or he could have been chatting about something like last winter's weather. We've all commented that 1886 was the coldest winter anyone could remember. Mr Hodges could just as easily have been having a polite conversation with Mrs Popejoy.' She shook her head. 'Mr Hodges just isn't a reasonable suspect in this case. When Inspector Witherspoon was interviewing Mrs Popejoy yesterday, she mentioned a friend of hers, Harriet Trainer, was sitting in the ladies' waiting room when she arrived at the station with Mr Hodges. The inspector told me today that they'd confirmed Mrs Popejoy's story. Harriet Trainer positively identified Leonard Hodges as the man who accompanied Mrs Popejoy to the station. And several witnesses saw him at his club not long after.'

'So it doesn't matter if they knew each other or not before Mr Hodges married Mrs Hodges,' Betsy said glumly. 'And Peter were ever so sure they did. Said it wasn't just that incident in the park, it were other things too. Like the way they look at each other.'

'Huh?' Wiggins scratched his head.

'Like the way you look at Sarah Trippett, lad,' Smythe said, and Wiggins blushed.

Mrs Jeffries tapped her fingers against the table. They'd learned much so far. Felicity Marsden didn't have an alibi, Mrs Popejoy may have known Mr Hodges longer than anyone had thought and he'd been the one to encourage his wife to go to a spiritualist. But she still didn't have enough information. She smiled at Smythe. 'I believe it's your turn now.'

The coachman shrugged. 'My news isn't all that interestin',' he confessed. 'But I did track down the hansom driver that brought Mrs Hodges home. He claims she were angry because he'd driven her home by way of the Strand instead of the quieter streets. Said the woman was shoutin' so loud he never got a word in edgewise, otherwise 'e'd of told 'er it were 'er own husband who'd instructed him to take the long route.'

'You mean Mr Hodges told the driver to go down the Strand?' Luty asked.

'Indeed, Mr Hodges told the bloke exactly how to go. Told the driver he and the missus had words and 'e wanted to give 'er time to get over her temper.'

'That's very interesting,' Mrs Jeffries said. 'And quite possibly true.' She then told them what the inspector had confided to her. She told them about Benjamin Vogel's now vanished gun, the jewels being found in Felicity Marsden's room, the note to Constable Griffith that the inspector hadn't written and the fact that Vogel's landlady couldn't confirm his alibi.

'That's it then,' Mrs Goodge muttered darkly. 'They did it together. Felicity Marsden and Benjamin Vogel. Mark my words, they're the killers.'

'Now, we mustn't jump to conclusions,' Mrs Jeffries warned. 'We don't know that Mr Vogel and Miss Marsden were even together that night, and even if they were, I hardly think that proves them guilty of murder.'

'But they both got a motive! 'Is gun's missing, and the jewels was found in 'er room,' Smythe protested. 'Sounds to me like that's pretty good evidence.'

'On the surface it may well be,' Mrs Jeffries replied. 'However, the inspector mentioned that he didn't think Mr Vogel was stupid. Hiding jewels you've conspired to steal in one of the other conspirators' rooms strikes me as the mark of a very stupid man.'

'Maybe he's going to blame it on her,' Luty suggested. 'Wouldn't be the first time a man's taken advantage of a woman's love. I once knowed a woman, good woman too, right smart. She up and helped her feller rob a bank. When the law caught up with 'em, he left her holding the money and hightailed it down to Mexico.'

'That's terrible,' Wiggins mumbled.

'But why would he do that? The jewels weren't worth much,' Betsy said. 'Seems to me the object was to get rid of Mrs Hodges so he could marry her niece. With Mrs Hodges dead, Miss Marsden probably stands to inherit a tidy sum. Lots more money than those piddly pearls were worth.'

'Maybe all he wanted was vengeance,' Luty insisted. 'Lots of men have done that. Spent a lifetime trackin' someone down who'd done 'em wrong. Why, I knew a feller once who spent twenty years—' She broke off as Wiggins moaned. 'Land's sake, boy. What's ailing you? My stories ain't that bad.'

Wiggins moaned again and buried his face in his hands. Everybody stared at him, their expressions concerned.

'Wiggins?' Mrs Jeffries prompted gently. 'What's wrong? What is it?'

The boy looked up, his face a mask of misery. 'You 'aven't 'eard what I've got to say, and when you do, you'll all be wantin' to put the noose around poor Miss Marsden's neck for sure. And I know she couldn't have done it, I just know it.'

'You're only sayin' that 'cause you think she's pretty,' Smythe mumbled.

'Don't be ridiculous, Wiggins. We're hardly likely to want to put the noose around anyone's neck at this point in our investigation.' Mrs Jeffries didn't add that she personally didn't see the point of hanging criminals in any case. The criminal justice system in England had been doing that for years and she didn't see that it had done all that much good. There were still plenty of criminals about. But this was hardly the time to enter into a debate over one of her more radical views. That could wait.

'You will when I tell ya,' he moaned.

'Oh, go on and tell us, lad,' Smythe snapped. 'We're 'ardly like to grab a rope and go get the woman to string her up tonight.'

'Please,' Mrs Jeffries said quietly. 'Tell us what you know.'

Wiggins nodded and told them about following Felicity Marsden to St John's Church. 'When I was standin' in the churchyard, I saw the vicar come out the front door, so I nipped round the corner to the back and what do you think I saw?'

Luty rolled her eyes. 'Hurry up, boy. Hatchet'll be here any minute and I want to hear this.'

'Miss Marsden. They's a graveyard behind the church and she were dartin' from one 'eadstone to

130

another,' Wiggins continued. 'Well, as I 'ad Fred with me, it were kind of 'ard to keep 'er from spottin' me, so we finally 'unkered down in some bushes. Then I saw 'er stop beside a newly dug grave. She kneeled down like she were goin' to pray, only instead of prayin' she started diggin'. When she stood up again, the little brown parcel she were carryin' weren't in 'er 'ands.' He paused again. 'She'd buried it.'

'Did you go dig it up?' Smythe asked.

Wiggins blushed. 'Er, I were goin' to.'

'What do ya mean, you was goin' to?' Luty slapped her hand against the tabletop. 'What stopped you, boy?'

'It were gettin' dark,' Wiggins said defensively. 'And I didn't want to be late gettin' 'ome. I tell you, the place was right 'orrible. Startin' to rain, and Fred here was hungry and then it got black as night, and what with all this talk of spirits and communicatin' with the dead, well, I weren't goin' to 'ang about there diggin' in some grave on me own.'

'Oh, Wiggins,' Betsy teased, 'are you tellin' us you was scared?'

'I didn't say I was scared!'

Luty was shaking her head in disgust. 'What a greenhorn,' she muttered.

'Blast, boy,' Smythe snapped. 'The dead is dead. They'll do you no 'arm. You should have seen what Miss Marsden was buryin'. It might be too late now.'

''Ow do you know the dead is dead?' Wiggins argued.

'Silly goose,' Mrs Goodge muttered.

'Now, now,' Mrs Jeffries said firmly. 'Stop picking

on Wiggins. I hardly think Felicity Marsden would bury something in St John's churchyard this afternoon just to go back and dig it up this evening.'

'True,' Smythe agreed, 'but someone else might.'

CHAPTER SEVEN

Naturally, after smythe's pronouncement, everyone had an opinion concerning the best course of action. Wiggins wanted to go to bed and worry about someone digging up Felicity Marsden's cache in the morning. Smythe, Betsy and Luty Belle wanted to dash off to St John's instantly, and Mrs Goodge, who wouldn't have gone in any case, tended to side with Wiggins.

Undecided, Mrs Jeffries gazed at the footman thoughtfully. 'You weren't followed today, were you?'

' 'Course not. Even if someone did spot me, unless they was faster than Snyder's hounds, they couldna kept up with me and Fred. We barely kept Miss Marsden in sight ourselves.'

Satisfied, the housekeeper nodded. 'I believe then that as you're the only one who knows about Miss Marsden's trip to the churchyard, no one else could possibly get to it before we do.'

'Reckon you're probably right,' Smythe said. 'Wiggins and I can go do a bit of diggin' ourselves tomorrow morning. If we get to the church right after dawn, we can get in and out without anyone seein' us.'

'Go on with you, man,' Betsy snapped. 'Why should you and Wiggins get to do all the nice things? I want to go too.'

'Nice!' Smythe stared at the girl incredulously. 'I was only tryin' to be considerate. Diggin' about in a damp, cold churchyard at this time o' the year isn't exactly what I'd call nice.'

Luty yawned widely. 'Quit yer squabblin', if it's all the same to everyone, Hatchet and I'll be round tomorrow mornin' before yer inspector's stirrin'. We'll bring the carriage, that way we can all go.'

'That sounds like a fine idea,' Mrs Jeffries said quickly.

True to her word, Luty, with a grumpy butler in tow, called for them in her carriage at half past six the next morning. As there was little traffic at such an early hour, they made excellent time to St John's.

Dawn was breaking as they piled out of the carriage. Luty had directed Hatchet to bring them to the back of the church.

The churchyard was enclosed by a low stone wall capped by a thick iron railing. A small, locked gate was the only entry.

'Nells bells,' Luty exclaimed as she glared at the heavy black lock. 'How come you people lock up yer dead tighter than a bank vault? I ain't seen a cemetery yet in this country that wasn't surrounded by bars. What're ya expectin' them bodies to do? Come back and haunt ya?'

'Actually,' Mrs Jeffries explained cheerfully, 'the railings were erected around most cemeteries and churchyards early this century. It was an attempt to keep the bodies from being stolen.'

'Pardon the interruption,' Smythe hissed softly, 'but Wiggins and I'll have a hunt round the other side to see if we can't find a way in. If we can't, we'll climb the fence.'

'Good idea.' Mrs Jeffries said.

Luty tugged on her sleeve. 'Who the dickens would want to steal corpses?'

'Hmmm, oh, professional bodysnatchers,' Mrs Jeffries replied absently as she anxiously watched Smythe and Wiggins disappear around the corner. Then she turned to gaze at the back entrance of the church; she wanted to be able to call out a warning in case a vicar or someone else came out into the yard.

'Bodysnatchers,' Luty muttered. 'Why the dickens would anyone want a bunch of dead bodies?'

'To sell to medical schools,' Mrs Jeffries said, still keeping her gaze on the church. 'The students need them for dissection.'

Betsy winced. 'That's disgustin'.'

'There weren't enough bodies, you see,' Mrs Jeffries continued. She thought she might as well satisfy Luty's curiosity while they waited for Smythe and Wiggins. 'The problem was most prevalent in Edinburgh – they simply didn't have enough bodies for the students to dissect. Medical schools, which, from what I've heard, didn't ask too many questions about how the bodies were procured, would pay between seven and ten pounds per corpse. Surely you've heard of that dreadful Burke and Hare – they actually used to murder their victims in order to keep the supply available. Well,

135

with that kind of money in the offing, bodysnatchers began to prey upon recent burials. Naturally this upset the relatives, and so they started standing guard for a number of days after the loved one was buried.'

'Givin' the body time to rot, huh?' Luty asked with relish.

Betsy moaned softly. 'If you two are goin' to be so gruesome at this time of the mornin', I'm going to sit with Hatchet.'

Luty looked offended. 'We're not bein' gruesome. Hepzibah is just tellin' me some of the more interestin' bits about you English.' She grinned at the housekeeper. 'How come they put up the gates then, if relatives was standin' guard?'

'They wanted to be doubly sure.' She pointed to the spiked points on the top of the railings. 'The railings were designed to make it difficult to get a body over the gate. But the newest churchyards don't have them.'

Luty, who obviously found the subject fascinating, said, 'How come?'

'After the passage of the Anatomy Act of 1832 it became much easier for medical schools to acquire bodies legally. That, of course, took the profit out of stealing from graves and that particular crime has virtually died out. It was rather distasteful, I'll admit, but if you keep in mind the dreadful poverty so many people are forced to endure, you can understand why it happened.'

Smythe, with a panting Wiggins trailing him, appeared from around the corner. He waved them over.

'There's another gate on the side,' he whispered. 'We've got it open. But we'd better be quick, there's a few lamps coming on across the road.' Leaving Hatchet to keep watch for patrolling constables, they went into the yard. Wiggins led them to the spot where Miss Marsden had buried the parcel. It was just beneath the headstone of one Percival Pratt, who departed this world only a week ago.

Sinking to his knees, Smythe took a trowel from beneath his coat and began to dig. 'I've hit somethin',' he muttered as he tossed the trowel to one side and brushed some dirt off the package with his fingers. He brought out the parcel and handed it to Mrs Jeffries.

Everyone gathered closer as she carefully eased off the string and unwrapped the paper. 'Oh dear,' she murmured softly. 'It's a gun. Probably the one that killed Mrs Hodges.'

Wiggins made a sound of distress. 'Poor Miss Marsden. This'll put a noose round 'er neck for sure.'

'Not necessarily,' Mrs Jeffries replied. 'Just because she buried the gun isn't evidence that she did the shooting.'

'But who else could of done it?' Betsy asked. 'And if it weren't Felicity Marsden, then why did she come all the way over here to get rid of the gun?'

'That's a very interesting question,' Mrs Jeffries answered quickly, 'and one we'd better discuss thoroughly before we take any action.' She hastily rewrapped the weapon. 'Here, Smythe, hold this while I retie the string.'

'What'dya doin' that fer?' Luty asked. 'Ain't we gonna take the gun to the inspector?'

'No, we're going to put it back right where we found it and go back to Upper Edmonton Gardens,' Mrs

Jeffries declared. 'We've much to discuss before we tell the inspector anything.'

'Cor, Mrs J,' Smythe said with a shake of his head. 'Are you sure? I mean, this is hidin' evidence.'

'It most certainly is not.' Mrs Jeffries cast a quick glance to the back of the church. 'We're not hiding anything, we're replacing it. And we must hurry. It's getting late. I don't want to have to explain our presence here to the vicar. Now stop worrying, all of you,' she said earnestly as she looked from one concerned face to another. 'Believe me, I know what I'm doing.'

'We're going to have another little chat with that Mr Vogel today,' Inspector Witherspoon declared. He reached for another slice of toast from the rack and liberally smeared it with butter and marmalade. 'Then we're going to ask Miss Felicity Marsden to explain how that jewellery got into her room.'

'Perhaps Miss Marsden doesn't know,' Mrs Jeffries suggested. 'You know, it is possible the jewels were put there to throw suspicion on the young lady. After all, Miss Marsden was at the ballet that night.'

'Hmmm, I'm not so sure of that. I'm going to send Barnes around to the Plimpton house today to double-check Miss Marsden's statement.'

'Really? Why?'

'Actually,' the inspector replied, 'it was something you said that got me to thinking we'd better have another look at Miss Marsden's alleged movements on the night in question.'

'Something I said,' Mrs Jeffries repeated innocently, though she was much relieved. She'd been dropping hints that everyone's statements as to their whereabouts on the night of the murder should be double-checked.

'Certainly. You stated that once one was seated in a crowded dark theatre, it was jolly easy to slip out without anyone being any the wiser. Especially if one was seated next to an elderly woman who probably fell asleep as soon as the curtain came up.'

'Oh that,' she replied airily. 'Well, I only said it because I remembered how my great-aunt Matilda used to doze off when we took her to the theatre in Yorkshire.' She laughed gaily. 'But I must say, I'm very flattered that you took my little observations seriously.'

Witherspoon smiled. 'You mustn't be so modest, Mrs Jeffries,' he said as soon as he'd swallowed his toast. 'Why, you said it yourself, one of my characteristics as a detective is to take everything I hear seriously. Why, hearing your little bits about human nature seems to spark something in my own thoughts. Jolly good too; otherwise I'd never have been able to solve some of the difficult cases I've been given.'

'Are you going to examine Jonathan Felcher's and Mr Hodges's movements as well?'

Witherspoon shrugged. 'We've already double-checked Mr Hodges. As I told you last night, Barnes got a statement from Miss Trainer that she'd seen Mr Hodges escort Mrs Popejoy to the door of the ladies' waiting room.'

'So you did,' Mrs Jeffries murmured. 'How silly of me to forget.'

'You're not in the least silly,' the inspector declared. 'But I do believe we'll double-check Mr Felcher's whereabouts and perhaps even that housekeeper, Mrs

Trotter. She's an odd sort of person. Constable Barnes repeated the most peculiar rumour about her yesterday.' He then proceeded to tell her what she'd already learned about Thomasina Trotter's excursions into the streets of London.

'How very unusual,' she commented, when the inspector finished.

'Yes, isn't it.' Witherspoon sighed. 'But then lots of people have eccentric habits. It doesn't necessarily make them murderers.'

Mrs Jeffries waited until the inspector left before pouring herself another cup of tea. The house was very quiet. After they'd come back from St John's this morning, she had hastily given everyone another assignment and they were all out gathering information.

Betsy had gone to make contact with someone in Mrs Popejoy's establishment, though Mrs Jeffries didn't see that course of action as being particularly fruitful. Mrs Popejoy and Leonard Hodges were the only two people involved in the case who had unshakable alibis. Smythe had gone to have another word with the driver who'd taken Mrs Popejoy and Mr Hodges to the train station, though again, that was probably a waste of time. Luty had decided to try to ferret out any gossip she could find about Mrs Trotter, and Wiggins had announced he was off to find evidence that Miss Marsden was innocent.

Mrs Jeffries sighed. This whole case was so muddled. No one was where they were supposed to be that night. Everyone seemed to loathe the victim, so there was no shortage of suspects, and now it looked like the evidence was pointing directly to the one suspect who had the most to gain by Abigail Hodges's death. Felicity Marsden.

Or did she? The housekeeper tapped the side of her teacup. They still didn't know for sure that Miss Marsden was going to inherit a large portion of the estate, and until the inspector got around to questioning the woman's solicitor, they wouldn't know. And Mrs Jeffries didn't like the manner in which this new evidence against the girl was being discovered. It was too tidy. Too neat. Almost as though someone were directing the action from behind the scenes.

Someone who had sent Constable Griffith that note about searching the house. Someone who had wanted those jewels found. Someone who, if Benjamin Vogel were to be believed, had taken the gun out of his room without his knowledge. Someone who wanted to implicate Felicity Marsden and her former fiancé. Or maybe, she thought, they had done the murder and staged the robbery. But surely, she argued silently, no one is stupid enough to have made all those mistakes.

Or were they? Mrs Jeffries put her cup down.

She shook her head and decided to go over the reasons someone would want Abigail Hodges dead.

Felicity Marsden hated her aunt because she'd thwarted her relationship with Benjamin Vogel. But if that engagement was truly over, the two of them would hardly have conspired to fake a robbery and stage the murder. Mr Vogel deeply resented Mrs Hodges's lies; that could be his motive. But if it were, it was pretty weak. And what about the nephew, Jonathan Felcher? He hated the woman because he wanted control of his own money and she wouldn't give it to him. Then there was the housekeeper. Mrs Jeffries shrugged. Who knew what on earth possessed Mrs Trotter.

Mrs Jeffries knew she needed to do something. But what? Suddenly she leaped to her feet.

Jonathan Felcher. No one had really taken a good look at him. She hurried to the backstairs and called to Mrs Goodge that she was going out. It was time to take a closer look at Abigail Hodges's nephew. And after that, it was time to have a chat with Felicity Marsden.

'We'd like to speak to Miss Marsden, if you don't mind,' Inspector Witherspoon said to Leonard Hodges.

'Felicity? But she's resting now,' Hodges replied. 'Look, Inspector, I hardly think you need disturb the girl. She's told you everything she knows.'

Witherspoon stared at him curiously. 'But I'm afraid she hasn't. You realize, of course, that finding the jewellery here in this house – more specifically, in Miss Marsden's room – changes the entire nature of this investigation. We really must speak to her.'

Hodges nodded slightly in acknowledgment. 'I can understand your reasoning, Inspector, but I'm not certain I entirely agree with it. Couldn't the thieves have panicked when they murdered my wife and hidden the jewellery themselves?'

'If that were the case, I hardly think the miscreants would have bothered to hide the jewels! Why not simply take them along with them as they left?' Witherspoon suggested. 'And even if you're correct, pray remember where they were found, pinned inside the upper folds of the curtains. Hardly the actions of a person in an agitated state of mind, sir.'

Hodges sighed. 'Yes, I see your point.' He stepped over to the bellpull and yanked the cord. When the maid appeared, he instructed her to fetch Miss Marsden.

Without being asked, Witherspoon sat down. 'Mr Hodges, I presume your late wife made a will?'

Hodges slowly turned his head and stared at the inspector. 'Yes, she did.'

'Do you, by any chance, happen to have any idea as to how her estate was divided?'

'As a matter of fact, I do,' Hodges stated calmly. 'Abigail wasn't reticent about her plans. Everything she owned is divided equally between myself and Felicity.'

'What about Mr Felcher?'

'He has his own property. Now that Abigail is gone, he'll obtain control of his holdings.' Hodges brushed a piece of lint off the collar of his elegant black mourning coat. 'Unlike most women, Abigail controlled her own property.'

'That's most unusual, isn't it?' the inspector asked. He wasn't sure, but he'd always thought that once a woman married, her husband legally became the possessor of everything she owned. Of course he could be mistaken, there was something going on in Parliament about a Married Woman's Property Act, but he wasn't sure it had passed. Or had it? Yes, by golly, he thought, he did remember reading about that in the newspapers. Something about a woman owning two hundred pounds of her own money . . . no, that didn't sound right. Wasn't there another act in the offing? One that entitled them to keep all their own money? Oh dear, he thought, politics were such a muddle, one couldn't be expected to keep every little thing straight.

'Abigail was an unusual woman.' Hodges smiled sadly. 'And as to the laws and customs of our great nation, they had no influence on her. Her money and holdings were in the United States and the laws and customs of that land are far different than here. Interesting place, actually. Women are accorded a great deal more freedom, I believe.'

The inspector immediately thought of Luty Belle Crookshank. 'Er, yes,' he said with a smile. 'You're quite correct.'

'Abigail inherited substantial real-estate holdings in both New York and Baltimore from her first husband,' Hodges explained. 'The property is administered by an American law firm and quarterly funds are drawn on bank drafts through the Bank of New York.'

The inspector wondered what was keeping Miss Marsden. He was most impressed by Mr Hodges's openness. Quite grateful, as a matter of fact. Now he wouldn't have to have one of those tiresome conversations with Mrs Hodges's solicitor. He suddenly realized there was something very important he must ask. 'Mr Hodges,' he said cautiously, 'did Miss Marsden know she was going to inherit half of her aunt's fortune?'

'He drinks like a bloody fish, he does, and gambles too,' Elspeth Blodgett exclaimed. 'I say, it's right nice of you to bring me here. I've never been in one of these places. Tea shops, that's what they call 'em. I know 'cause one of me lodgers is always meetin' her young feller at the one in Piccadilly Circus. She's one of them typewriter girls, has her own Remington, she does, claims she makes twenty-five shillings a week.'

Mrs Jeffries waited patiently for Jonathan Felcher's landlady to pause for a breath. It had taken only the barest hint that she was enquiring into Mr Felcher's character on behalf of the family of a young lady to loosen Elspeth Blodgett's tongue. The woman certainly liked to talk.

Immediately Mrs Jeffries had known that if she could get a cup of tea in front of the landlady, she'd have a veritable gold mine of information. As Mrs Blodgett was on her way to do the shopping, it was quite easy to convince her to make a quick detour into a very convenient ABC Tea Shop.

A waiter pushing a trolley topped with seedcake, currant buns, digestive biscuits and meringues stopped beside their table.

Mrs Blodgett broke off in mid-sentence. Her eyes narrowed and she licked her lips as she stared at the tray of sweets.

'Oh please, order anything you like,' Mrs Jeffries said quickly. 'On a chilly day like today, a cup of tea just isn't enough. And it's so very good of you to help me in my enquiries.'

'Thank you, I don't mind if I do.' She pointed a chubby, rather dirty finger at the plate of meringues. 'I'll take a couple of those and two of them digestive biscuits as well.'

Though she wasn't hungry, Mrs Jeffries was determined to be sociable and keep the woman talking. She ordered a currant bun and more tea.

'Now,' she continued, when the waiter had left, 'about Mr Felcher? You were saying?'

'He's a rotter and a rogue, he is,' Mrs Blodgett said

as she dipped a biscuit into her tea. 'But that don't keep the ladies away, if you get me meaning. Not much of a worker, always takin' time off in the afternoons and holds on to his job by the skin of his teeth. He ain't above nickin' a few bits and pieces 'ere and there, neither.'

'Gracious.' Mrs Jeffries deliberately pretended to be shocked. 'Why on earth do you allow such a monster to stay on in your lodging house?'

'I'm no starry-eyed girl. He don't steal from me, I makes sure of that.' Mrs Blodgett cackled. 'He may be a rotter, but he pays his rent, and on time too. Besides, it's all the same to me. If that silly aunt of his wants to let him steal her blind, that's her business.'

'You mean he steals from his own relatives!'

' 'Course he does. I seen it with me own eyes.' Mrs Blodgett pushed a strand of dirty grey hair out of her eyes and tried to tuck it back beneath an equally dirty grey cap. 'I've seen him open her purse and help himself when she ain't lookin'.'

'How appalling,' Mrs Jeffries exclaimed. Obviously Mrs Blodgett didn't think it unethical to spy on her lodgers. 'How did you see Mr Felcher steal? It's rather important. I mean it's my duty to warn Elizabeth's family that the young man who has been paying court to their only daughter isn't to be trusted.'

'We've all got to do our duty,' Mrs Blodgett seconded. 'Well, like I was sayin', this here aunt of his used to come by occasionally and give Felcher a dressin'-down. Whenever she'd finish, she'd nip into the back room to put on her hat and coat. Felcher used to open her purse and help himself. Got right quick at it too. Her name was Abigail Hodges.'

'The woman who was murdered a few days ago?'

'That's the one, all right. Had lots of money, she did. Felcher was always lickin' her boots and tryin' to get on her good side, but I reckon she had him sussed out well enough.' Elspeth smiled slyly. 'She never paid no mind to his grovellin' and wheedlin'. But she sure kept him at her beck and call all the time, she did.'

'Perhaps Mr Felcher hoped to eventually inherit something from her estate,' Mrs Jeffries suggested.

Mrs Blodgett shook her head. 'Maybe, or maybe he was always dancin' to her tune 'cause if he didn't she'd tell his employer about Mr Felcher playin' about with Mr Macklin's wife.'

This time Mrs Jeffries didn't have to pretend to be shocked. 'I'm afraid I don't understand what you're saying?'

'I'm sayin' that Mr Felcher was playin' about with Mrs Macklin, his boss's wife. Mrs Hodges caught 'em together one afternoon. She's had Felcher under her thumb ever since. He's told me more than once 'e wished Mrs Hodges was dead. Looks like he finally got his wish.'

'Jonathan Felcher took them to dinner on the night that the murder occurred,' Mrs Jeffries said thoughtfully.

She spoke too soon, because Elspeth Blodgett suddenly sat back and gazed at her suspiciously. 'How do ya know that?'

'It was in the papers,' Mrs Jeffries said quickly, hoping that Mrs Blodgett hadn't followed the case in the dailies.

'Oh. For once Felcher were tellin' the truth. He did

take 'em to dinner that night. Claimed he had a big win at the races.' She snorted. 'More like one of his women had greased his palm with a bit of cash, if you ask me. Mrs Macklin wasn't the only rich woman he was spendin' his time with.'

'According to the papers, Mr and Mrs Hodges then went on to another engagement and Mr Felcher returned home. I wonder if that's true.'

' 'Course it in't true. Felcher never come home that night at all.'

Mrs Jeffries weighed her next words carefully. 'Have you told the police that he didn't come home?'

Mrs Blodgett shrugged. 'They haven't asked me. But if they did, I've got no reason to lie to save the likes of him. Why should I? Now that Mrs Hodges has up and died, he's give his notice. He'll be leavin' at the end of the week. Goin' to America.'

'I think, madam, I really ought to come inside with you.' Hatchet helped Luty Belle Crookshank out of the carriage and then turned to survey the area. He arched one silver brow disdainfully at the row of dingy grey houses, the unpaved road, the hordes of ill-kempt children playing in the mud and the unremitting stench from the poultry yard directly across from the home of Miss Bush.

'Don't be silly, Hatchet,' Luty replied as she brushed off his arm and headed up the broken walkway. 'You'll be of a lot more use out here.' She jerked her head towards the children, several of whom were eyeing her carriage. 'I can handle one old lady. All I want to do is talk to the woman. But if it eases yer mind, stay close to the door and I'll give a shout if I need any help.'

Leaving Hatchet muttering under his breath, Luty banged on the door. Several blotches of paint fell off onto the ground. From inside, she heard a shuffling noise, and several moments later the door slowly opened and a quavery voice said, 'Who's there? What do you want?'

'My name is Luty Belle Crookshank,' she replied. 'I'm a friend of Thomasina Trotter's. I'd like to speak to Miss Bush.' Luty sincerely hoped that Miss Bush wouldn't remember this little visit and mention it to Mrs Trotter.

The opening widened and a shrivelled-up woman leaning heavily on a cane appeared. Her white hair had thinned so much there were bald spots on the crown. Her face was a mass of wrinkles and her eyes were dull and glazed. 'Tommy?' she said in a singsong voice. 'Are you my angel? My Tommy?'

Luty wanted to stamp her foot in frustration. Miss Bush wasn't just elderly and a mite forgetful, she was completely loco. Then she was ashamed of herself as she saw the dazed eyes clear.

'Have you come to visit me?' The old woman smiled hopefully.

'Yes, ma'am, I surely have,' Luty replied. 'May I come in?' she asked, feeling a wave of pity wash over her.

'But of course you can.' Miss Bush turned and shuffled down a darkened hallway, leaving Luty to follow after her. 'I don't get so many visitors these days. Gets lonely, you know. I'd offer you tea, but . . . but' – she broke off as they came into the parlour.

Luty, who wasn't fussy about cleanliness, resisted the

urge to hold her nose. The room smelled as though something had died in it. There were huge patches of damp on the walls and ceiling, the wallpaper was gone in spots and the furniture was moth-eaten and covered in dust.

Miss Bush lowered herself into a chair and motioned to Luty to take the one opposite her. 'Where's Tommy?'

'Well, she's busy right now,' Luty explained gently, 'but she sent me to visit you for a spell.'

'Is she coming soon?' Miss Bush asked hopefully. For a moment her gaze sharpened again and she looked at Luty carefully, then her eyes dulled and she sighed. 'Did you say you'd stay for tea?'

'That'd be right nice,' Luty began, but Miss Bush didn't seem to hear her.

'Poor Tommy,' she moaned. 'She never gets to come and see me any more.'

'I expect she's busy what with her workin' fer Mrs Hodges and all.'

Miss Bush paid no attention to her; she rambled on and Luty quickly shut up. She was afraid she'd miss something important.

'She never gets to rest.' Miss Bush shook her head from side to side. 'Day in, day out, she spends every waking moment looking for the girl. Does all the errands for that wicked woman, all of them. Always on the streets, always looking. Never gets to rest. Oh, my poor angel.'

'That's right, she never gets to rest,' Luty repeated as she decided to change tactics. She reached over and patted Miss Bush's hand. 'But why don't you tell me a bit about your Tommy?'

A slow, dreamy smile spread across the old woman's face. 'She was such a pretty child, such a sweet thing. And she was all mine, practically from the day she was born. Her mother was ill, you know. I raised her.' Miss Bush suddenly giggled. 'But then again, if she hadn't been so pretty, she wouldn't have had all that trouble. I always used to tell her, pretty is as pretty does, but she'd never listen. Wilful, that's what she was.'

'What kind of trouble did she have?' Luty asked softly.

Miss Bush moaned. 'Trouble, always trouble. First the money gone and then him!'

'What kind of trouble?' Luty repeated. 'What "him" are you talking about?'

Suddenly Miss Bush banged her cane against the floor. Luty jumped.

'There was no Mr Trotter, you know.' Miss Bush leaned over and wrapped a clawlike hand around Luty's arm. 'He left. But Tommy always pretended there was, always pretended he was coming back to her, and then she'd find the child and the three of them would be together.'

'What child?'

Miss Bush ignored her. 'Tommy could have been happy, you know. But that wicked woman wouldn't let her. They could have come here, but Tommy wouldn't have it, wouldn't have the baby marked like that. She went to her instead. Stole the baby, she did, pretended she was doing it for Tommy, but she wasn't. Wicked she was, so wicked.'

'What woman?'

'Told Tommy she was a fool, that kind of wickedness

never repents.' Miss Bush sighed. 'But she was always so wilful. She insisted, insisted she did, that Abigail would tell her the truth. Now she can't. Gone she is, gone to the dead.' Miss Bush's eyes flashed fire. 'Gone to hell.'

'I say, Mr Hodges,' Witherspoon said as he glanced at his watch. 'Do you think perhaps you could send one of the servants to see what's taking Miss Marsden so long?'

Hodges looked surprised by the suggestion. 'I don't think it's been all that long, Inspector,' he said, reaching for the bellpull to summon the parlour maid, 'but if you insist, I'll send Hilda up again.'

The girl appeared in the doorway.

'Did you tell Miss Marsden we're waiting for her?' Hodges asked.

'I did, sir,' the maid replied. 'She were in the bathroom when I went up, so I rapped on the door and told her you and the gentleman from Scotland Yard wanted to see her.'

'Well, go and see what's taking her so long,' Hodges said impatiently. 'Perhaps she needs help getting dressed.' He turned to the inspector. 'You'll be gentle with Felicity, won't you? This whole situation has upset her dreadfully.'

'We are not bullies, sir,' Witherspoon answered. Really, the way some of these people went on; why, one would think the police were barbaric monsters! 'Miss Marsden will be treated with all due courtesy and respect. However, you must be aware that Miss Marsden is in a very precarious position.' He broke off as Mrs Trotter ushered Constable Barnes into the room.

Barnes didn't waste any time. He motioned for the inspector to step closer and then whispered, 'You were right, sir. Miss Marsden did leave the theatre. The lady who accompanied Miss Marsden and Miss Plimpton was old and she fell asleep. Miss Plimpton's confessed that her original statement was a lie and she was covering for Miss Marsden.'

'Oh dear,' the inspector said quietly, 'that doesn't look good, does it?'

'Has something happened, Inspector?' Hodges asked. 'What's all this whispering about? I demand to know what's happened. I am an interested party; it was my wife that was murdered.'

'I'm afraid, sir, I must insist that you bring Miss Marsden down immediately,' Witherspoon replied gravely.

'I'll get the girl myself,' Hodges said. 'Then perhaps we can get this situation straightened out. Whatever information you think you've learned, Inspector, I assure you, my niece is innocent.' He turned on his heel and stalked out of the room.

Barnes waited until he heard Mr Hodges's footsteps going up the stairs. Then he turned to the inspector. 'I'm still wonderin' who sent that note. Any ideas, sir?'

The inspector had actually given the matter a great deal of thought. He was rather glad the constable had asked. 'Actually I've already deduced who it must have been.'

Barnes looked appropriately impressed.

'Obviously' – Witherspoon lowered his voice – 'it was one of the Hodgeses' servants.'

'Really, sir?'

'But of course, who else could it have been? It was someone in the household who didn't want to risk losing their position by coming forward and telling the police what they'd learned, but on the other hand, they didn't want justice to be thwarted either.'

They heard the sound of pounding footsteps on the staircase. Alarmed, both men hurried into the hall.

Leonard Hodges, breathing hard and looking very agitated, stopped on the bottom step. 'I'm not really sure what to make of this,' he began. 'Honestly I'm certain there's a reasonable explanation, but I don't know what it could possibly be.'

'Please calm yourself, Mr Hodges,' the inspector said. 'Just tell us what's wrong.'

'It's Felicity.'

'Yes, what about her?' Barnes asked as he began edging towards the staircase. 'Is she refusing to speak to us?'

'She's gone.'

CHAPTER EIGHT

MRS JEFFRIES PAUSED across the road from the Hodges home. She pursed her lips, wondering what approach to take with Felicity Marsden. Perhaps she should slip around to the back of the house and wait and see if the girl came out into the garden, that would ensure them privacy. But then she glanced at the grey, darkening sky and realized that with the weather so bleak and cold, her quarry was hardly likely to come into the garden at all. Yet Mrs Jeffries didn't want to run into the police! For all she knew, Inspector Witherspoon might be inside the Hodges house at this very minute.

Suddenly the front door opened and the object of her thoughts appeared on the front steps. The inspector stood there, waving his hands and talking earnestly to Constable Barnes. His bowler was askew, as though he'd tossed it on his head without proper care, and his coat was undone. Mrs Jeffries could see he was extremely agitated. Something must have happened. But what? She had to know.

She saw the inspector point to his left, in the direction of the Queens Road, and then Constable Barnes nodded and hurried away. Mrs Jeffries decided to take the bull by the horns. She waited until Barnes was out of earshot and quickly crossed the road.

'Oh, Inspector,' she called gaily as she came up behind him, 'how very nice to see you, sir.'

Witherspoon jumped in surprise and whirled around. 'Why, Mrs Jeffries, what are you doing here?'

'I'm just on my way to Fitzchurch's,' she explained. 'They've such lovely linens and we've quite a few sheets that need replacing. Well, as I had to pass here to get to there, I thought I'd just have a peek at the' – she broke off and pretended to be embarrassed – 'scene of the crime. Oh dear, sir, I'm afraid you'll think me such a busybody, but I was so terribly curious.'

'That's quite all right, Mrs Jeffries,' the inspector said quickly, seeing his housekeeper's obvious discomfort. 'I understand completely. Naturally you would be curious.'

'How very understanding you are, sir,' she replied. 'But then, that's why you are such a brilliant detective. You understand people.'

Witherspoon's chest swelled with pride for a brief moment before he remembered the latest development in this baffling case. 'It's jolly good of you to say so,' he said. 'But I'm afraid this case has even me a bit flummoxed.'

'Nonsense, sir,' Mrs Jeffries said briskly. 'I've absolute confidence in your abilities. Whatever has happened is, I'm sure, only a temporary delay.'

'Do you really think so?' he asked hopefully.

'Of course. Now, tell me, sir. What has you so agitated?'

'I fear my prime suspect has flown,' he confessed on a sigh.

'Oh dear, how very tiresome for you.'

'It most certainly is. Really, young people these days! No respect for the law. I tell you, Mrs Jeffries, as difficult as it is to imagine such a thing, that young woman has something to hide.'

'I take it you're referring to Miss Marsden?' Mrs Jeffries asked. She was rather surprised by this new development. 'Did she know you were waiting to see her?'

'Yes. The maid told her we were downstairs waiting to speak with her,' the inspector replied, 'but when Mr Hodges went up to fetch the young lady, he found her gone. She'd also taken her carpetbag and some clothes.'

'Oh dear, sir.' Mrs Jeffries clucked sympathetically. 'That's most annoying, I'm sure. But not to worry, you'll soon catch up with her.'

'I've sent Barnes to get us a hansom,' Witherspoon continued, glad of the chance to unburden himself. 'We're going to see Benjamin Vogel. If he's gone as well, we'll know the two of them are our murderers.'

Mrs Jeffries almost bit her tongue to keep from telling the inspector he shouldn't jump to conclusions. Instead she said, 'But I thought Miss Marsden had broken her engagement to Mr Vogel?'

'That's just what they wanted everyone to think. But one of the housemaids has admitted that Miss Marsden and Mr Vogel have been secretly meeting with one another.' Witherspoon's eyes narrowed. 'Hilda Brown has been acting as their go-between. The supposed breakup of the engagement was just a ruse. No doubt they didn't want Mrs Hodges cutting Miss Marsden out of her will.'

'So you think that Miss Marsden and Mr Vogel conspired together?' Mrs Jeffries's mind was racing furiously. 'But why?'

'Because Miss Marsden stands to inherit a great deal of money upon her aunt's death, that's why.'

'She's the sole beneficiary to Abigail Hodges's estate?' Mrs Jeffries wanted to be absolutely clear on this point.

'Not the sole beneficiary,' Witherspoon said cautiously as he peered up the road for Barnes. 'Mr Hodges gets the other half. The estate's worth over a million pounds.'

'Gracious, sir, that is a lot of money.'

'Many would kill for such an amount,' Witherspoon replied, 'and I'm almost certain that Miss Marsden and Mr Vogel did.'

A cold blast of wind slammed into them, rattling the branches of the trees. Mrs Jeffries drew her cloak tighter as she saw a hansom cab turn into the road and come towards them. She was running out of time, but there was one last important point she needed to impress upon the inspector.

'But, sir,' she said softly, 'who sent the note to Constable Griffith?'

'Note?' Witherspoon stared at her blankly.

'The one purportedly from you, sir,' she explained. 'Constable Griffith searched the house and found the jewels because he thought you'd instructed him to do so, but you hadn't.'

'Oh that. Well, obviously, it was one of the Hodgeses' servants. Possibly even young Hilda Brown herself.' Witherspoon brightened perceptibly. 'Yes, I'm sure that's who sent the note. No doubt the girl realized what Miss Marsden had done. She probably felt very guilty for being a party, even an innocent party, to such wickedness.'

Mrs Jeffries thought that a possibly illiterate maid having the gumption to forge an inspector's name on a note was about as likely as pigs flying. She had to do something. She was sure that note hadn't been written by Hilda Brown, just as she was becoming more and more certain that Felicity Marsden and Benjamin Vogel weren't the killers.

The hansom drew up next to them. Mrs Jeffries smiled and patted the inspector on the arm. 'I'm sure you're right, sir. It probably was the maid. Mind you, the girl must be better educated than most servants.' She broke off and laughed gaily. 'Why, so many of them can barely read or write. The girl's obviously clever too, if she had the foresight to forge your name. Apparently Miss Brown knew exactly what to do to get the uniformed lads to make such a quick and thorough search. My thinking that perhaps someone was deliberately trying to lay the blame for this heinous crime at an innocent woman's feet is simply silly. Why, you're far too just a man to arrest someone for a crime merely because it's the easiest course of action.'

Her words had the effect she'd hoped. The inspector's face fell and she could tell he was truly unsettled. For the truth of the matter was that the inspector was a just man. Now that she'd hinted that Felicity Marsden might be an innocent victim instead of a heartless killer, she knew Witherspoon wouldn't rest until he got at the truth.

'Yes, well, I'll just be off,' the inspector said as he reached for the latch and opened the door. Constable Barnes caught sight of Mrs Jeffries and smiled. 'Hello, Mrs Jeffries,' he called. 'What are you doin' over this way?'

'I'm just on my way to Fitzchurch's,' she replied.

'Perhaps I'll give this whole situation a bit more thought,' Witherspoon muttered as his housekeeper and constable exchanged pleasantries. He was still muttering to himself when Barnes closed the hansom door and the horses clip-clopped briskly away.

Mrs Jeffries started walking. She thought about the various pieces of information she'd learned. It could well be that someone was indeed trying to make the police think that Felicity Marsden and possibly Benjamin Vogel were the killers. But then again, there was the chance that Inspector Witherspoon was correct and the note had been written by a servant or someone else who didn't wish to come forward. But that was rather farfetched. Again, she had the feeling that some unknown hand was moving the pieces of the puzzle to and fro. The note, the jewels, the ease with which Miss Marsden's and Mr Vogel's alibis had been shattered, it was all too neat and tidy.

She turned the corner onto Princes Road. Felicity Marsden and Leonard Hodges were the two who stood to benefit the most from Abigail Hodges's death and Felicity was the one without an alibi. But what about Jonathan Felcher, she thought. Didn't he benefit as well? He might not inherit anything directly from his aunt, but now that she was dead, he'd have control over his own money.

And, she reminded herself, Felcher was planning on leaving the country in a few days. That certainly bore thinking about.

She stopped at the corner of the Uxbridge Road and waited for several moments before there was a break in the traffic. But if Felicity Marsden was innocent, she thought as she darted behind an omnibus, why had she buried a gun in St John's churchyard? Mrs Jeffries had a twinge of conscience at this thought.

So far she'd done nothing to lead Inspector Wither-spoon to that gun and she knew she really should. Yet she couldn't help but feel that even with the inspector's passion for justice, with the kind of evidence that gun suggested, he'd have no choice but to arrest Miss Mars-den and Mr Vogel for the crime.

And Mrs Jeffries didn't want that. Something was seriously wrong with this case. The evidence against Felicity Marsden and Benjamin Vogel had seemed to happen in the twinkling of an eye. It had all come about too quickly.

Mrs Jeffries stopped and stood still. Of course. Why hadn't she realized it before? Shaking her head at her own stupidity, she quickened her pace. Someone was indeed trying to make it appear that Miss Marsden and Mr Vogel were the perpetrators of this terrible murder and now she understood why. The real killer had only started planting the evidence against the young lovers when it had become obvious the police weren't convinced Mrs Hodges had been killed by a burglar. When the burglary plan fell apart, she thought, whoever was behind this had switched to another plan. That was the way it must have happened. Nothing else made any sense.

With an increasing sense of urgency, Mrs Jeffries decided on a course of action. But first, she had to find Felicity Marsden and Benjamin Vogel before the police did.

'Can't say that I'm surprised, sir,' Constable Barnes said as they came down the steps of Benjamin Vogel's lodging house. 'Once we knew she'd run, it were only reasonable that he'd run too.'

'Now, now, Constable,' Witherspoon replied cautiously. 'We mustn't jump to conclusions.'

'But, sir, the landlady said that Vogel left with a young woman not more than half an hour ago. It were obviously Miss Marsden he left with and they've obviously decided to make a run for it. Do you want me to have some lads watch the railways and the liveries?'

Witherspoon thought carefully before answering. He couldn't stop thinking about what his housekeeper had said. Despite her assertion that she was just being 'silly', he knew that Mrs Jeffries had a valid point. That wretched note had to have been written by someone. And now that he'd had time to think about it, he didn't think it was Hilda Brown. Drat. But who had written it? And despite the fact that now two of their prime suspects in the case seemed to have disappeared, he didn't think either of them was the author. Why would they have written it?

The note had certainly tightened the noose around Felicity Marsden's throat and that fact, on top of Mr Vogel's gun being missing, could certainly lead the police into making a good case against the two of them. Especially now that they had evidence that Mr

Vogel had not broken off his relationship with Miss Marsden.

Witherspoon's head began to throb. Drat. Why couldn't it have been a simple burglary? Why did every case he was assigned end up being so complicated?

'Sir?' Barnes said impatiently. 'Did you hear me?'

'Er, yes, Constable.' Witherspoon made a decision. He wasn't going to chase Miss Marsden and Mr Vogel. Not yet at any rate. Much as he hated to consider the possibility, it did, indeed, appear as though someone wanted the police to think the two fleeing young people were guilty. But he refused to be manipulated.

'It won't be necessary to send our lads to the liveries or train stations. I'm sure neither Miss Marsden nor Mr Vogel has left the city.' He infused his voice with as much authority as he could. He hadn't the faintest idea whether they'd left the city or not, but if he himself was trying to avoid the police, the last thing he'd do is leave a big, crowded city like London and go somewhere where one stuck out like a sore thumb.

By later that afternoon, Mrs Jeffries had refined her plan of action. Everyone, except for Wiggins, had gathered back in the kitchen of Upper Edmonton Gardens.

'Have another cup of tea, Hatchet,' Luty commanded her butler. 'Yer still lookin' a mite blue around the gills.'

'Thank you, madam,' Hatchet replied. He helped himself to a second cup. 'It was rather cold in the carriage and you were gone quite a long time.'

'Yup, reckon I was,' Luty agreed, 'but ya can't rush

163

these things. Specially when yer tryin' to make sense outta the ramblin's of an old woman like Miss Bush. Lord A'mighty, I sure hope I don't end up like that poor thing. Unwanted, alone, half-mad and barely able to git around.' She shuddered slightly. 'I'd rather someone jes' put a gun to my head and put me out of my misery before endin' up like her.'

'I take it that means you weren't able to find out anything useful from Miss Bush,' Mrs Jeffries said.

'Oh, I found out lots, but I ain't sure if I found out anything that was true,' Luty stated. 'Miss Bush spins a right good yarn, but now whether or not what she told me really happened, or whether or not she's jes' tellin' tales, that's the part I can't figure.'

'Why don't you tell us what she said,' Mrs Goodge suggested, 'and we'll see if it fits with the other bits and pieces we've picked up.'

Luty put down her teacup and leaned forward on her elbows. 'From what I could make of what she was sayin', Miss Bush claims that Thomasina Trotter had an illegitimate child.'

'How long ago?' Mrs Jeffries asked. The more facts they had, the better.

'Twenty years ago.'

There was a gasp of surprise from Betsy, Mrs Goodge's jaw dropped, Smythe raised his eyebrows and even Mrs Jeffries looked stunned.

'Yup, that's right, twenty years,' Luty continued with a wide grin. 'That means Mrs Trotter weren't no young girl when she got into trouble. She's close to the same age as Mrs Hodges was, so that would put her about fifty-two now.'

'But that means she had the baby when she was thirty-two,' Betsy said with a shake of her head.

'That's right,' Luty said. 'Her family disowned her when they discovered she was with child and the man responsible did like a lot of men – he run like a scared rabbit rather than own up to what he'd done. Mrs Trotter had no one to turn to 'ceptin' her old friend Abigail. Anyhow, Abigail took her in, took care of her doctor bills and arranged for the baby to be adopted out.'

'So Mrs Trotter has been working for Mrs Hodges ever since?' Smythe asked.

Luty shook her head. 'No, after she had the baby, her daddy died and she went back and lived with her mother. A few years later the mother died. But Thomasina didn't inherit one dime, wasn't nothing left. So then she went to work for Abigail.'

Betsy sighed. 'It's a good story, but I don't see how it has anything to do with Mrs Hodges's murder.'

'Now hold yer horses, girl, I ain't finished,' Luty said impatiently. 'There's a few things I ain't told ya yet. Seems like Mrs Trotter began to think she made a mistake in givin' her baby up just a few months after she'd had the child. She got some idea in her head that if she could find the baby, she could get her back and take her away somewhere's like Canada or the United States. Only Mrs Hodges wouldn't hear of it, told Mrs Trotter she was a fool and a dreamer and she wouldn't tell her where the girl was.' Luty paused and took a deep breath. 'Then, after Mrs Trotter's mother died, Mrs Hodges changed her tune a bit, started saying that maybe it wouldn't be so bad if Mrs Trotter did find her daughter. Strung the poor woman on fer years, promising to tell her and promising to leave her some money in her will so she and the girl could go off and start a new life. But she never did. Never told her.' Luty broke off and sighed. 'Then, a few years ago, Mrs Trotter started walkin' the streets – lookin' for the girl, she was. It was a mad thing to do, but I think that by then, the poor woman was mad.' She smiled sadly.

'But how can she be so . . . so . . . lunatic and still keep workin' for the Hodgeses?' Betsy interjected. 'Didn't they notice there was somethin' not right with the woman?'

'There's all kinds of madness,' Luty said softly. 'It ain't all rantin' and ravin'.'

'So with Mrs Hodges dead, Mrs Trotter will never have any hopes of finding the girl,' Mrs Goodge interrupted.

'Poor thing,' Betsy murmured.

'I wish you'd all give me a chance to finish,' Luty complained.

'Perhaps they would, madam,' Hatchet said quickly, 'if you didn't stop speaking at the more melodramatic points in the story.'

'That's the best way to tell a tale.' Luty exclaimed indignantly. She glared at her butler.

'True, madam,' he replied smoothly, 'but as I understand it, you ought not to be telling tales here, you ought to be stating facts.'

'Oh, don't be such a stuffed shirt, Hatchet,' Luty snorted. 'What's the good of a bunch of dry old facts when you can string 'em out into a right good story.'

'That's true, Luty,' Mrs Jeffries said hastily. 'But

perhaps you'd better conclude, we've an awful lot of information to pass along here this afternoon.'

'Oh, all right. The point is, Mrs Trotter is going to find out who adopted her child.' Luty surveyed their stunned expressions with satisfaction. 'Abigail left a letter with the solicitor. Upon her death the letter is to be given to Thomasina Trotter and it contains the name of the couple who adopted her child.'

'Cor,' Smythe said thoughtfully, 'that's a pretty good motive.'

'Yes, but why now?' Mrs Jeffries mused. 'Why wait twenty years to kill someone?'

Again Luty smirked in satisfaction. 'Because Mrs Hodges only recently told Mrs Trotter about the letter. That's right, it was after she started goin' to them séances that her conscience seemed to start workin'. Miss Bush told me that it wasn't more than a month ago that Mrs Trotter come in all excited like and said that Mrs Hodges had written this letter and given it to her lawyer.'

Mrs Jeffries cocked her head to one side. 'Do you think Miss Bush was telling the truth?'

'She's got no reason to lie,' Luty replied thoughtfully. 'I don't think she really knew who I was or what I was doin' there, but once she started on about Mrs Hodges and Mrs Trotter, she sounded right sure of herself.' She made a sweeping gesture with her hands. 'But I reckon it could jes' be a story. The poor old thing's not right in the head.'

'Well, we'll just have to see how your information fits in with other facts as we go along, won't we?' Mrs Jeffries gave Luty a wide smile. 'You've done a remarkably good job.'

'Better than I have,' Betsy chimed in. 'I didn't learn nothing today.'

Mrs Jeffries patted the girl on the arm. 'That's all right, dear. You've certainly done more than your fair share in the past. By the way, does anyone know what's keeping Wiggins?'

Mrs Goodge frowned darkly. 'He's probably out chasin' after that Sarah Trippett and forgettin' he was supposed to be back here.'

'If not Miss Trippett,' Betsy said, 'then some other girl. Honestly, sometimes that lad gets his head turned by nothing more than a hint of a smile.'

Smythe snorted. ''E's not the only one.'

'What do you mean by that?' Betsy demanded, crossing her arms over her chest and glaring at the coachman.

'I expect my meanin's clear enough,' he replied. 'You've got no call to always be on about Wiggins when you're no better than 'e is. All that Edmund has to do is crook 'is little finger and you go runnin'.'

'That's a bloomin' lie.' Betsy leaped to her feet, her blue eyes blazing fire.

'Now, now, you two,' Mrs Jeffries interrupted. 'Stop it this instant. We've enough problems on our plate just now without the two of you quarrelling.' She turned her head and gazed sternly at Smythe. 'I do believe you owe Betsy an apology for that last remark,' she said firmly.

Smythe's lips flattened to a thin, mutinous line.

'And,' Mrs Jeffries continued, turning her gaze to the maid, 'I believe Smythe does have a point. None of us has the right to constantly assume Wiggins shirks his duty because of a pretty face.'

Betsy dropped her gaze and slipped back into her chair. 'All right, I'm sorry for what I said about the lad.'

'Sorry, Betsy,' Smythe mumbled.

Everyone turned and looked at Mrs Goodge. She sighed. 'Oh, all right, I shouldn't have said what I did either. Now, is everyone happy? Can we get on with this?'

'Indeed we can,' Mrs Jeffries stated firmly. She told them all about her visit with Elspeth Blodgett, stressing the fact that Mrs Blodgett claimed the police had never bothered to ask her whether or not Jonathan Felcher had been home on the night of the murder.

'That don't sound right,' Mrs Goodge said. She sliced off another slab of seedcake and put it onto her plate.

'I know,' Mrs Jeffries agreed. 'It certainly is peculiar. The police are generally very thorough in their investigations.'

'Do you think this Mrs Blodgett could be lyin'?' Smythe asked.

Mrs Jeffries thought about it for a moment. 'I don't think she's necessarily lying, but I do think it's possible she's made a mistake.'

'Mistake?' Luty asked. 'Hepzibah, no offence meant, but the way the law dresses in this country, it's purty danged hard to mistake them for anything other than what they are.'

'I quite understand your point, Luty,' Mrs Jeffries explained, 'but what I'm saying is that I don't think that the police neglected to go round to Mr Felcher's lodging house and ask about his whereabouts, but I do think it's likely that they didn't speak to Mrs Blodgett. They probably spoke to her hired girl. Mrs Blodgett seems to spend a good deal of her day out of the house.'

'But why would the hired girl lie for Mr Felcher?' Betsy asked.

'I don't think she did. But she's Russian. Mrs Blodgett told me herself that the girl can barely speak English.' Mrs Jeffries stared thoughtfully at Luty. 'With all your connections, Luty, do you happen to know anyone who speaks Russian?'

'Russian, huh?' Luty's eyes narrowed and she shook her head. 'Don't think I can help you much there. Now, if you were lookin' for some Germans, I could find you a couple of them faster than hot beer down a hog's gullet.'

'I know some Russians,' Hatchet announced.

They all stared at him in surprise.

'I've several acquaintances from Russia,' he continued, ignoring their incredulous expressions. 'And if it would be helpful, I'll be happy to take one to Mrs Blodgett's lodging house and see if the girl did indeed speak to the police.'

'Why, thank you, Hatchet,' Mrs Jeffries said. 'That would be very helpful indeed.'

'Why?' Luty asked. 'What difference does it make? We already know that Mrs Blodgett said Felcher wasn't there that night.'

'True, but I'd like to know why the police have given up their investigation into Mr Felcher's movements,' Mrs Jeffries explained. 'And furthermore, Mrs Blodgett has a bit of a grudge against Mr Felcher. She seems most put out that he's leaving the country next week. I don't think she'd be above trying to get him into a bit of trouble by spreading the rumour that he wasn't where he claimed to be that night. And we do need to know for certain.'

'You've found out quite a lot today,' Betsy said in admiration.

'More than you know, my dear,' Mrs Jeffries replied. She then went on to tell them about her meeting with Inspector Witherspoon in front of the Hodges home. She told them about Miss Marsden's disappearance and about both the girl and Leonard Hodges being the sole beneficiaries to Abigail Hodges's will.

'Then it's got to be Miss Marsden that done it,' Mrs Goodge said. 'She were the one that buried that gun, she's the one that's gettin' the money and she's the one that's disappeared.'

'Mr Hodges inherits half the estate,' Mrs Jeffries reminded them. 'And with Abigail Hodges gone, Thomasina Trotter will learn the whereabouts of the child she gave up and Jonathan Felcher will gain control of his own property. So Miss Marsden isn't the only one with a motive.'

'My money's on Thomasina Trotter,' Luty declared. 'I think that findin' out about that letter finally pushed her mind too far. She decided she didn't want to wait any more, so she killed the old girl.'

'I reckon it were that Mr Felcher,' Mrs Goodge said. 'Drinkin' and gamblin', they always lead to trouble. Besides, makin' it look like a robbery is the kind of silly theatrics a man would come up with. Women's got more sense.'

'Truth is,' Smythe added, 'we don't know who done it. Mr Hodges has got just as much motive as the rest of them.'

'But he's a nice man,' Betsy protested. 'I'm sure he's not the killer. Why, today he took a bundle of clothes over to St James's Church to give to the vicar. They was newish things too, a good coat and hat that look like they'd never been worn. I know 'cause I followed him. Besides, 'e's the only one who couldn't have done it – he's the only one with an alibi.'

'I thought you were going to make contact with someone from the Popejoy household,' Mrs Jeffries asked Betsy.

'Oh, I did,' she replied. 'But after I finished, I thought I'd nip over to the Hodges house and see if I could find out anythin'. Mr Hodges was comin' out the front door when I got there, so I followed him. Didn't have much else to do, the only thing I heard over at the Popejoy house was that some old admirer of Mrs Popejoy's was pesterin' her again. But I reckoned that didn't have nothin' to do with the murder. Mrs Popejoy stopped seein' this Mr Phipps months ago.' Betsy shrugged and laughed. 'From what Peter tells me, Mrs Popejoy's a bit of a flirt, always has been. She kept this poor Mr Phipps dancin' to her tune for months before she got tired of him.'

'We know it weren't her,' Mrs Goodge said impatiently. 'What I want to know is how come this Mr Felcher's up and leavin' the country all of a sudden.'

''Cause his aunt's dead, that's why,' Luty said tartly. 'I think one of us ought to keep watch on Mrs Trotter. No tellin' what she'll do next.'

They all began arguing for their various candidates in the role of murderer. Hoping the free flow of ideas would spark something in her own mind, Mrs Jeffries didn't interrupt. She listened. But after a few moments she realized they were doing nothing but going over every detail they'd already learned. She glanced up at the window and noticed that night was falling even though it was barely five o'clock.

'I say,' Mrs Jeffries said loudly, 'did Wiggins happen to mention precisely what he would be doing this afternoon?'

'I can't think what's keepin' the boy,' Mrs Goodge said, 'but I'll save him a bit of cake. He'll be hungry when he gets home.'

'I'd hoped he'd be here by now,' Mrs Jeffries murmured. 'For you see, there's something else we must do and we must do it quickly. We've got to locate Felicity Marsden before the police do.'

'Why?' Betsy asked.

'Because I don't think she's guilty. If the police find her and Mr Vogel, they'll arrest them. You've all forgotten one of the most important clues in this investigation. The note. Someone wrote that note to Constable Griffith ordering him to search the Hodges home. That someone is probably the person who planned and executed the plot to murder Mrs Hodges.'

'How can we find the girl?' Mrs Goodge asked cautiously.

'Come now, Mrs Goodge,' Mrs Jeffries said. 'With your sources of information, you can probably find anyone in London. But for the rest of us, we'll have to rely on our feet and our good sense.'

'You mean you want us to wander the streets searchin' for the lass?' Smythe asked. He looked horrified. 'But we don't even know what she looks like.'

'Besides, if the girl's got any sense, she's long gone by now. What if she's left the city?' Luty added.

'It'll take days,' Betsy complained.

'Of course it won't,' Mrs Jeffries declared. 'You're all forgetting yourselves. You're all forgetting just how good you are once you set your mind to a task. Betsy, you can easily keep an eye on Miss Plimpton. She's a friend of Miss Marsden's. She actually lied to protect her, so it's safe to assume that if Miss Marsden is in difficulties, she might try to contact Miss Plimpton. Smythe, you can talk to the liveries and cabbies around the area. Someone must have picked up Miss Marsden and Mr Vogel. Remember, they were in a hurry. They wouldn't have hung about the neighbourhood waiting for a tram or an omnibus. Luty, you've acquaintances all over the city, many of whom travel in the same social circles as Miss Marsden. You can ask about and see if anyone's spotted her.'

There was a general murmur of agreement around the table. Mrs Jeffries leaned back and smiled. 'Good, then it's all settled. Our first priority is to find Felicity Marsden.'

'You don't have to do that,' Wiggins's voice piped in. Everyone turned and looked. Wiggins and a tail-wagging Fred were standing in the doorway.

'It's about time the two of you come home,' Mrs Goodge said. She stood up and headed for the cooling pantry. 'Poor Fred hasn't had a bite to eat all day.'

'What about me, then?' Wiggins exclaimed. 'I haven't 'ad me tea, either.'

Mrs Goodge returned with a plateful of scraps, and Fred, who'd been butting his head against Betsy's knees, deserted her instantly.

'Sit down and have something,' Mrs Jeffries told the

boy. 'And then tell us what on earth you meant by that provocative statement.'

Wiggins poured himself a mug of tea and cut a huge slice of cake. 'Huh?' He stuffed a huge bite into his mouth.

'She means what did you mean when you said we didn't have to do that,' Betsy explained. 'What were you on about?'

'Felicity Marsden.' While they all waited he picked up his mug and downed a mouthful of the strong brew. 'You don't have to go huntin' for her.'

'Oh dear,' Mrs Jeffries said, 'does that mean the police have found her?' She thought perhaps Wiggins had run into the inspector.

Wiggins started to reach for his fork, but Luty snatched it out from under his fingers. 'Boy,' she said tartly, 'some of us ain't as young as you are. I'd sure as shootin' like to know what you was talkin' about before I die of old age.'

'I'm trying to tell you I've found Felicity Marsden.' Wiggins grinned triumphantly. 'You'll never guess where she is. Me and Fred were ever so clever. I told you I'd find out she weren't guilty. I just knew a pretty lass like her couldn't have done such a terrible thing.'

As the footman rambled on, Luty rolled her eyes, Mrs Goodge sighed, Smythe scowled and even Hatchet pursed his lips together.

Wiggins's cocky grin faded as he stared at the faces surrounding him. 'She's staying at Jonathan Felcher's lodging house,' he blurted. 'And so is Mr Vogel.'

CHAPTER NINE

'How on earth did you manage to find out where Felicity Marsden went?' Luty exclaimed. 'We only jes' found out she'd flown the coop.'

'I followed the lass,' Wiggins announced. 'Fred and me was walkin' in the road round the corner, tryin' to suss out who to talk to next. All of a sudden this gate opens and Miss Marsden comes flyin' out like the 'ounds from 'ell was on her 'eels. I could see she had a carpetbag with 'er, so I figured she weren't doing her shoppin'. As soon as she walks past, me and Fred were right behind 'er.'

'Did she see you?' Smythe asked.

Wiggins shook his head. 'No, the lass were in such a state she wouldn't 'ave noticed a bloomin' elephant doggin' her footsteps. She were right upset. White as a sheet she was, movin' so fast she kept trippin' over her own feet. Why she almost ran in front of an omnibus. I trailed her to a lodgin' 'ouse and then she and this bloke come out. There was a boy sweepin' in front of the 'ouse next door, so I asked the lad who the bloke was. He told me it were Benjamin Vogel. So naturally I took off after the two of 'em.'

176

'You've done very well, Wiggins,' Mrs Jeffries said. 'Knowing Miss Marsden's whereabouts will certainly make our investigation easier.'

'What are we going to do, then?' Betsy asked eagerly.

'Tomorrow morning we're going to confront Miss Marsden and Mr Vogel.' Mrs Jeffries stated firmly, 'and then we're going to get to the bottom of this case once and for all.'

'Tatty-lookin' place, isn't it?' Wiggins clucked his tongue. 'Imagine a lady like Miss Marsden hidin' out in a miserable hole like this.'

'Perhaps it's cleaner on the inside than on the outside,' Mrs Jeffries said doubtfully.

'I wouldn't bet on it,' Smythe muttered.

They stood on the pavement outside Mrs Blodgett's lodging house and eyed the place warily. The building had once been white, but was now a uniformly dirty, dingy grey, matching perfectly the leaden dull skies overhead. The walkway leading to the porch was broken and uneven, the windows were dirty and there was black peeling paint on the doors and ledges. A gang of noisy boys ran back and forth across the road, chasing a ball, and in the house next door to Mrs Blodgett's a slovenly man with red, watery eyes watched them apathetically.

'How very sad this place is,' Mrs Jeffries said as she led the way to the house. She pursed her lips, knowing this neighbourhood was actually far better than many areas of London. At least here the children didn't look as though they were starving, the windows weren't broken and the road wasn't littered with rubbish.

Gingerly she banged the green-scaled brass knocker

and then waited. A few moments later the door was opened by a stocky, dark-haired young woman who stared at them with a blank, incurious expression on her face.

Mrs Jeffries was grateful that Elspeth Blodgett hadn't answered the door. She smiled at the girl and said, 'Good morning.'

The girl bobbed a brief curtsy and nodded.

'We'd like to see' – she hesitated for a moment – 'the young couple who arrived yesterday.' She was fairly certain Vogel hadn't given his real name when renting the lodgings.

The maid frowned in confusion.

Mrs Jeffries held up her hand and pointed to her wedding ring. 'Yesterday,' she said slowly, 'the new lodgers. A man and woman.'

'Ah.' A smile crossed the girl's face, transforming her blank features and making her rather pretty. 'The Mr and Mrs Brown. They come. Da, da.' She opened the door and pointed to a narrow, dark staircase. 'Room is at the high of the stairs.'

'Huh?' Wiggins whispered. 'What'd she say?'

'She means the top of the stairs,' Smythe explained. He darted ahead of Mrs Jeffries. 'Let me go first, these stairs don't look all that safe.'

The stairs didn't sound particularly safe either. The banister was rickety and covered in a layer of dust. And the stairs creaked and groaned as the three of them made their way to the top-floor landing.

'Why would someone like Miss Marsden want to come to a place like this?' Wiggins asked again, shaking his head in disgust.

' 'Cause it's the kind of 'ouse where no one asks any questions as long as you can pay the price of a room,' Smythe replied. He looked at Mrs Jeffries. 'You want me to knock?'

She nodded and the coachman rapped lightly against the thin wood.

The door opened a crack. 'Yes, who is it?'

Smythe wedged the toe of his boot into the crack. Mrs Jeffries summoned her most charming smile. 'Mr Vogel, my name is Hepzibah Jeffries and I must speak with you.'

'You've got the wrong man, the name's Brown. I've never heard of this Mr Vogel. Go away and don't bother us.'

He tried to close the door but couldn't. 'Now see here,' he sputtered angrily, glaring at Smythe's toe.

'Listen, Mr Vogel,' Mrs Jeffries said quickly. 'If you don't speak to me, you'll find yourself under arrest. If I could find you so quickly, then the police can't be far behind.'

Slowly the door opened, revealing a grim-faced young man and an equally worried-looking young woman standing behind him.

'Who are you?' Benjamin Vogel said flatly. 'A black-mailer? How much will it take to buy your silence? Be warned, though, we've not much money.'

'I'm afraid you don't understand, Mr Vogel,' Mrs Jeffries said. 'I'm not here to blackmail you, I'm here to help you.'

'Why should you want to help me?' Vogel said sus-piciously. 'I'm nothing to you.'

Mrs Jeffries decided to take a firmer line. Standing

out on the landing trying to convince this young man she was solely interested in justice was simply taking too much time. 'That's correct, I don't know you from Adam. However, I do know that the gun used to kill Abigail Hodges is buried in St John's churchyard, the stolen jewels were found in Miss Marsden's room at the Hodges house and that neither you nor Miss Marsden has an alibi worth two shillings.'

Vogel's jaw dropped and the colour drained from his cheeks.

'Now,' she continued firmly, 'if you'll let me and my friends inside, perhaps we can help you extricate yourselves from this terrible mess.'

Silently Vogel opened the door wider.

Mrs Jeffries, with Smythe and Wiggins right behind her, rushed into the room. 'As I've told you, my name is Mrs Jeffries and this is Smythe and Wiggins.'

'I still don't understand why you should want to help us?' Vogel put his arm protectively around the woman.

'Because if I don't, you're going to be arrested for murder, a murder I'm not all that certain that you or Miss Marsden had anything to do with.'

Felicity stepped forward. 'How do you know who I am? I've never seen you before.'

'But I've seen you,' Mrs Jeffries replied. 'Now, we don't have much time. I suggest you answer my questions as quickly and completely as you can.'

Felicity Marsden looked at Benjamin Vogel and he nodded slightly. 'Would you like to sit down?' he asked. He grimaced as his glance took in the shoddy, scratched table and chairs and the lumpy settee that made up the furniture. 'It's fairly dirty, but Fliss and

I managed to spend the night here without having to fend off anything worse than the cold and damp.' Mrs Jeffries shook her head. 'No, thank you. First of all, I must know where the two of you were on the night Abigail Hodges was murdered. The police already know that neither of you have alibis.'

'We were together,' Felicity Marsden replied. She lifted her chin defiantly. 'And I'll tell the whole world if it's necessary. I don't care what anyone thinks of us or our morals. We were together and no one can prove otherwise.'

'Be careful, Fliss,' Vogel said gently. 'You're making it sound as though we were doing something wrong. But we weren't.' He looked at Mrs Jeffries and said, 'It's not what you think. We weren't doing anything improper. Fliss and I arranged to meet at the theatre, then we spent the next two hours walking about, just talking. That's the only way we've managed to see each other since Abigail started interfering in our lives.'

'So you've been seeing each other all along,' Mrs Jeffries said, confirming what she already knew. 'And breaking off your engagement was merely a pretence. Is that correct?'

Vogel dropped his gaze. 'Yes. We had no choice. Abigail didn't think I was good enough for her niece. She tried buying me off, and when that didn't work, she told Fliss a packet of lies.'

'I never believed her,' Felicity declared. 'Never, not for one moment.'

Mrs Jeffries studied the girl shrewdly. 'But you pretended you did, didn't you?'

'There was no choice.' Felicity shrugged her

shoulders. 'I knew what Abigail was capable of. I knew how very ruthless she could be.'

'Excuse me,' Smythe interrupted, 'beggin' your pardon, miss, but you're of age. Why didn't you just tell Abigail to sod off and marry Mr Vogel. Why sneak about?'

The two lovers exchanged glances. Then Vogel cleared his throat. 'We were trying to wait her out. My company has agreed to send me to Canada. It's a promotion.' He smiled proudly. 'But that's not going to happen till next month. I was going to go on to Toronto and Fliss was going to make arrangements to join me there as soon as possible.'

'But short of tossin' Miss Marsden out on 'er ear,' Wiggins asked, 'what could Mrs Hodges 'ave done to you if she knew you was still seein' each other?'

Vogel laughed bitterly. 'She could have ruined our entire future. My new position will ensure Fliss and I can marry. I'll easily be able to support a wife once I'm in Toronto. But if Abigail had known we were still seeing each other, she'd have got me sacked. She was a rich, powerful woman. I work for Tellcher's, they're a rather conservative merchant bank. If she'd had any idea I was still engaged to Fliss, she'd have been round there like a shot. One word from Abigail Hodges would have been enough to have me tossed in the street with no references and no prospects.'

'But instead Mrs Hodges is dead, you've still got your employment and Miss Marsden stands to inherit a great deal of money,' Mrs Jeffries said thoughtfully.

'But we didn't have anything to do with her murder,' Felicity cried.

'Perhaps,' Mrs Jeffries replied. 'But you can't deny that you both had good reason to wish Abigail Hodges was out of the way.'

Felicity waved her hand impatiently. 'Of course we did, she made our lives miserable. We had to sneak around like two children hiding from their nanny. Wouldn't you loathe having to behave in such an undignified fashion? But we didn't kill her. The night Abigail was murdered we were walking around trying to keep warm. It was a horrid night out, cold and damp and foggy. And that wasn't the first time we'd had to spend what few hours we had together on a public street.' She closed her eyes briefly and shuddered. 'But I didn't mind that part of it so much. I could easily put up with the cold and the wind and the rain. What I hated was the constant worry that someone, some friend of Abigail's, would see us.'

'Well, if you've been sneakin' around for two months without gettin' caught, you've been pretty lucky,' Wiggins said cheerfully.

'Lucky!' Felicity Marsden snapped. 'We weren't in the least bit lucky. We were almost discovered several times.' She turned to her fiancé. 'Remember when we saw Mrs Popejoy? That was a close call. She'd have gone running to Abigail like a shot.'

'Mrs Popejoy,' Mrs Jeffries interrupted quickly. 'What about her? Did she happen to see you that night?'

'Not that night, but one other time we were together. It was a fortnight or so ago.' Felicity laughed nervously. 'And it wasn't just Mrs Popejoy we almost ran into either. We thought Uncle Leonard was with the woman. That would have been utterly disastrous.

Leonard wouldn't have kept silent. He knows what side his bread is buttered on.'

'Now, Fliss, don't upset yourself,' Vogel said gently. 'Everything turned out all right in the end. Mrs Pope-joy didn't see us and the man she was with wasn't your uncle. In the dark and the fog, you just thought he looked like Leonard.'

'I know,' Fliss replied. 'But it was still a very close thing. When I think of how Aunt Abigail could have ruined — would have ruined you without a second thought, it makes my blood run cold.'

'If I was you, Miss Marsden,' Smythe said, 'I'd keep them feelin's to myself when the police start talkin' to you.'

'The police! Why should I talk to the police? We're innocent.' Felicity began wringing her hands together. 'As much as I loathed my aunt's interference in my life, I wouldn't have killed her and neither would Benjamin.'

'Then why did you run?' Mrs Jeffries asked.

'I was scared. First I found that wretched gun and then last night Uncle Leonard told me that Abigail's jewels had been found in my room. Today, when the maid told me that the police were downstairs waiting for me, I couldn't think of what to do, so I tossed a few things in my bag and slipped out the back door. I went straight to Benjamin's.'

'Who, luckily for you, hadn't gone in to work today,' Mrs Jeffries said, turning her attention to Mr Vogel. 'Could you tell me why you didn't go in this morning, please?'

Vogel shifted uneasily. 'I sent a note there, telling them I was ill and that I wouldn't be in for a few days.'

He jerked his chin up defiantly. 'Well, why shouldn't I take some time off? I've an excellent record, and after I saw my gun had been taken, I decided perhaps it would be best to . . . to . . .'

'Be prepared to make a run for it?' Mrs Jeffries finished for him. She felt a wave of sympathy for them, but she had to make sure their flight hadn't been pre-arranged. 'Now, Miss Marsden. Can you tell me where exactly in the house you found the gun, and more importantly, why you didn't give it to the police right away?'

'I found it in my drawer yesterday morning. As soon as I saw it, I knew I couldn't give it to the police. It was Benjamin's.' She swallowed painfully. 'Even worse, the gun had been fired recently. The barrel still smelled of powder. But as God is my witness, I've no idea how it got into my drawer. I was terrified. All I could think of was getting rid of the obscene thing.'

''Ow come you buried it in a bloomin' churchyard?' Smythe asked. 'If I was goin' to get rid of a gun, I'd throw it into the Thames.'

Felicity gave Vogel a shamefaced glance. 'Because it was Benjamin's and I knew he wanted to have it with him when he travels. He couldn't afford to buy another one – and he's going to Canada soon. I didn't dare hide the gun in the house or bury it in the garden. Then I remembered Abigail and Leonard had gone to a funeral at St John's just last week. I knew the earth would still be soft enough to dig in, so I took the gun and buried it there.' She paused and gazed at Mrs Jeffries curiously. 'How did you find out where the gun was?'

'You were followed, Miss Marsden,' Mrs Jeffries

replied honestly. 'But what makes you so certain Mr Vogel's gun is the one that was used to murder your aunt? Are you familiar with weapons – are you absolutely positive it had been fired recently?'

'Yes, I am,' Felicity declared. 'My father taught me how to handle guns when I was a girl. He hunted. And also I'm sure that whoever really did the killing is trying to make it look as though Benjamin and I were responsible. I began to suspect yesterday that someone wants us to take the blame. Benjamin sent me a note telling me his gun had gone missing. Then when the jewels were found in my room, I knew for certain.'

'Mr Vogel,' Mrs Jeffries said, 'assuming it was your gun that murdered Mrs Hodges, how do you explain someone being able to steal it from your room?'

Vogel stroked his chin. 'I think it was stolen on one of those nights that Fliss and I were out together.'

'You leave your rooms unlocked then?' Smythe asked.

'No, of course not. But half the time my landlady is drunk and the lock on my door is so flimsy a child could open it,' Vogel replied earnestly.

'I suppose it's possible,' Mrs Jeffries murmured. She wasn't sure she believed him, but then again, she wasn't sure she didn't either. 'Were you planning on giving up your employment? Surely you realize that the police will be around there fairly quickly.'

Vogel shrugged. 'Losing my job is better than hanging, Mrs Jeffries. You see, the police already knew my gun was gone. Once Fliss told me about the jewels being found in her room, I knew we had to get away. I don't know who was responsible for killing Abigail

Hodges, but I do know that whoever it was is planning on making sure that Felicity and I take the blame.'

'That certainly appears to be the case,' Mrs Jeffries said. 'However, it may not come to that. Miss Marsden, who else had a reason to want your aunt dead?'

'Well, Jonathan, my cousin, wasn't overly fond of her. She's had control of his inheritance for years now.' Felicity tilted her head and looked sadly around the room. 'Abigail's kept him on a pittance of an allowance, otherwise he wouldn't be living in a hovel like this lodging house. She was always trying to get him to move into her house. She liked controlling people. But he refused, preferring instead to eke out a living working for that shipping company and living in a place like this.'

Mrs Jeffries was curious. 'Why did you and Mr Vogel come here? Was it because of your cousin? Were you hoping he'd help you?'

'We came here,' Vogel replied, 'because we knew Jonathan's landlady wouldn't ask any questions. We were afraid to go to a hotel. We thought that would be the first place the police would start looking. We didn't come here to involve Felicity's cousin in our trouble.'

'Besides, Jonathan's gone.' Felicity smiled grimly. 'He's gone to Leicestershire to take care of some business. It appears as though he'll have the last laugh after all, now that he's gained control of his inheritance. I don't think he's even planning on staying for Abigail's funeral or the reading of the will. He told me he's sailing next week for America.'

''Ow come everybody leaves this country?' Wiggins asked.

Much as Mrs Jeffries would have liked to stop and give the footman a short, concise lesson on surplus population, improved opportunities for advancement and a pioneering spirit, she refrained. This was hardly the time or place.

'His property is in America,' Vogel explained, taking Wiggins's question seriously.

'Exactly 'ow much money does Mr Felcher get control over now that Mrs 'odges is gone?' Smythe asked.

'I'm not certain of the exact amount,' Felicity replied, 'but I think it's close to fifty thousand pounds.'

'Cor, that's a lot of money.' Smythe glanced at Mrs Jeffries. 'Lots would kill to get their 'ands on that amount.'

Felicity shook her head impatiently. 'Jonathan's no more capable of murder than I am. I know he drank a little and perhaps gambled more than he should, but he's no murderer.'

Mrs Jeffries heard the shuffle of footsteps on the stairs. She held her breath, hoping it wasn't Inspector Witherspoon. Everyone else heard the noise too, for the room fell silent until the steps faded down the corridor.

Sighing with relief, Mrs Jeffries decided to hurry matters along. Time was getting on. 'Is there anyone else connected with Mrs Hodges who might have reason to wish her dead?'

'Mrs Trotter wasn't overly fond of my aunt,' Felicity admitted. 'I think the woman's half-mad, I don't know why Abigail kept her on or why Mrs Trotter stayed. They quarrelled quite frequently. And Leonard wasn't the best of husbands. I can't prove it, of course, but I suspect that he only married my aunt for her money.'

'Careful, my love,' Vogel said softly. 'People may one day say the same of me.'

'That's ridiculous,' Felicity declared.

'Why do you think that Mr Hodges wasn't in love with his wife?' Mrs Jeffries didn't think this was a particularly fruitful line of enquiry, but she might as well listen.

'Oh, he acted devoted to Abigail whenever they were together. But I used to watch his face when he thought I wasn't looking.' She shivered delicately. 'Sometimes he stared at her as though he hated her and it was so awful. She was besotted with him.'

'How long had they been married?'

'Let me see, not all that long. About eighteen months. Yes, that's right. They were married in July of eighty-five. Abigail was determined they wed, even though it was barely a year to the day from his first wife's death. She even married him against the advice of her solicitors.'

'Goodness, Mr Hodges seems a respectable enough man,' Mrs Jeffries commented. 'Why would Mrs Hodges's solicitors object to him?'

Felicity smiled wryly. 'They weren't keen on his background. Leonard hadn't much money of his own. His investments weren't doing all that well. He had only a small income from some property up north. But I gather it wasn't doing all that well – there were only some tenement flats, a shop or two and a theatre, I believe. But it didn't bring in much, all of the property was in the very poorest part of Leeds. And there was something to do with Leonard's first wife. She died under very mysterious circumstances. Drowned,

I believe, in a boating accident in the Lake District. I can't remember all the details, but Mr Drummond, that's Abigail's solicitor, claimed that Leonard's former father-in-law, a man named Harry Throgmorton, had tried to get the police to bring a case against Leonard after she died.'

'What'd 'e do?' Wiggins asked eagerly. 'Push 'er over the side?'

'No. Leonard wasn't there when the accident happened. He was miles away, but you know how people are, there was some ugly gossip.' Felicity frowned. 'I'm sorry. I simply can't remember any more details. But I do know that Abigail instructed Mr Drummond to threaten Mr Throgmorton with legal action if he said another word about Leonard.'

Mrs Jeffries was very disappointed. 'Well, if you do remember any more details, please let me know at once.' She reached into her cloak and drew out a scrap of paper. 'If you think of anything, anything at all that's pertinent to your late aunt, please send word to this address.'

'You mean, you want us to stay here?' Vogel asked in disbelief.

'Yes, I believe that by the time the police get round to looking for you here, we'll have found out who the real killer is.'

As they'd arranged earlier, they met Hatchet at an ABC Tea Shop. The butler, looking extremely dapper in a formal old-fashioned morning coat and top hat, met them at the entrance and ushered them inside to a waiting table.

'I've taken the liberty of ordering tea, madam,' he announced to Mrs Jeffries. 'And of course' – he glanced at Wiggins and Smythe – 'an assortment of buns and cakes.'

'Thank you, Hatchet,' Mrs Jeffries replied. 'That was most thoughtful. May I ask if your enquiries were successful this morning?'

Hatchet grinned. 'Extremely, madam. So successful that I and my associate had to duck behind a letter box to avoid meeting the landlady of the establishment from which you've just come.'

'In other words,' Smythe said, 'Mrs Blodgett almost caught you.'

'Precisely. However, as you'd clearly surmised earlier, Mrs Blodgett left to do her shopping early, and after your good selves had gone inside in pursuit of your own enquiries, my associate and I were able to make the acquaintance of Miss Kuznetzov.'

'Excellent, Hatchet.' Mrs Jeffries smiled in delight. 'You seem to have developed a real talent for this sort of thing.'

Hatchet acknowledged the compliment with a dignified nod. 'I'm glad you think so, but one isn't sure one really wants to develop this particular skill. Questioning the lower classes and immigrants from the less enlightened nations isn't something one would care to do on a daily basis. Especially this young woman. Miss Kuznetzov has a very suspicious nature.'

She reached over and patted his arm. 'I'm sure it was most difficult.'

'That it was, madam, but we managed.' Hatchet coughed delicately. 'After my friend – speaking in Miss

191

Kuznetzov's native tongue, of course – had convinced her we weren't from Her Majesty's secret police—'

'The what!' Smythe exclaimed. He looked truly shocked.

'The secret police,' Mrs Jeffries explained quickly. 'An institution which is common in other parts of the world. Especially that part which is ruled by the Czar of Russia.'

'Quite, madam,' Hatchet said. 'Now, if I may continue. After we'd convinced the young lady that no such institution existed in this nation—'

'I should bloomin well 'ope not,' Smythe put in.

Hatchet ignored him. 'We, of course, being a free people. She was very cooperative in answering our questions. She told us that Mr Jonathan Felcher had, indeed, been gone the night Mrs Hodges was murdered. She hadn't meant to mislead our police, of course. But Miss Kuznetzov's English isn't very good. She said that whenever one was dealing with a uniformed official, she'd learned to agree to whatever they said. The truth is, the poor girl didn't have a clue what she was being asked. She simply kept hearing Mr Felcher's name, and not wanting to get him into any sort of difficulties, she kept nodding in the affirmative whenever the police asked her a question.'

'Cor, you mean she just kept sayin' yes because she were scared to say no?' Smythe looked really disgusted now. 'That's the daftest thing I ever 'eard.'

Tempted as she was to take this opportunity to further educate Smythe, Wiggins and Hatchet on the evils of unrestricted monarchies and their attendant institutions, Mrs Jeffries forced herself to stick to the matter at hand.

'Gracious. Then Mr Felcher doesn't have an alibi for the night Mrs Hodges was killed,' Mrs Jeffries said softly. 'And neither does Thomasina Trotter, Felicity Marsden or Benjamin Vogel.'

'But Miss Marsden and Mr Vogel were together that night,' Wiggins protested.

'That's what they've said,' Mrs Jeffries replied. 'And they may very well be telling the truth.'

'You think they might have done it, then?' Smythe asked.

'I don't know,' she admitted honestly. 'I'm tempted to believe their story, but I don't know for sure. Not yet at any rate.'

Mrs Jeffries was silent on the trip home. Smythe and Wiggins were still talking about the horrifying conditions one must find in places like Russia, but she'd deliberately stopped listening to them.

She closed her eyes and let her mind wander, trying for that free flow of concentration that seemed to come from nowhere, but that could actually serve to point her rational thoughts in the right direction.

Mrs Trotter might be mad, but was she a murderess? Jonathan Felcher hated his aunt and now had control of fifty thousand pounds. But did the murderer steal Mr Vogel's gun from his bedroom? And why go to such silly lengths to try to make the murder look as though Mrs Hodges had interrupted a robbery and then bungle the job so badly? And who had written the note? Mrs Jeffries sighed and picked up on the conversation.

'I wonder if you could get arrested for arguin' with a tram driver?' Wiggins said. 'They wears uniforms. Or maybe a train conductor or even a vicar. Could you get nicked for arguin' with a vicar in Russia?'

'In Russia they're known as priests,' she murmured. Vicars, priests, Mrs Jeffries thought. Churches. Yes, of course. Why hadn't she considered it before? The footman's last words triggered something in the back of her mind. She sat bolt upright and stared straight ahead as the snippets of information and hard facts came together in her head and formed a true straight course.

As they descended from the omnibus near Holland Park, Mrs Jeffries suddenly turned to Smythe. 'I need you to do something and I need you to do it right away.'

' 'Course, Mrs J,' Smythe said, looking concerned. 'What is it?'

'That driver, the one who drove Mr Hodges and Mrs Popejoy to the train station, do you think you can find him again?'

'Yes, but it may take a bit o' time.'

'We don't have time, Smythe,' she said earnestly. 'You must find him quickly.'

'All right.' The coachman shook his head doubtfully. 'But he's already confirmed he took 'em to the station. I don't know what else 'e can tell us.'

'Find out if the hansom stopped anywhere on the way. If it did, ask the driver to take you to that very spot.' She reached into her cloak and pulled out some coins. 'Give him a guinea if you must, but it's imperative that if they stopped, he must take you to the precise spot.'

Puzzled, Smythe pocketed the coins and pulled his coat tighter against the suddenly chill wind. 'All right, I'll be off then.'

'Can you be back late this afternoon?' Mrs Jeffries's voice stopped him.

He frowned and pulled out his pocket watch. 'It's already gone eleven. But I'll do me best. Would three o'clock do you? There's a few lads that owe me a favour or two. Maybe I ought to get them to give me a 'and on this one. I reckon from the way you're actin' that it's important.'

'Excellent.' She turned to Wiggins. 'And I want you to get over to Luty's. Tell her and Hatchet to come round to see us this afternoon at three. Tell her it's imperative she be there.'

'You want me to go now?' Wiggins wailed. 'But I 'aven't 'ad me lunch.'

'Gracious, Wiggins, you've just had a huge tea. Three currant buns and two tea cakes should be enough to keep even someone of your prodigious appetite from starving to death.'

He gave her a shamefaced smile. 'All right, but while I'm gone, could you look in on Fred?'

'Yes, of course I will,' she promised. Her brows drew together in concern. 'The dog's not ill, I hope.'

' 'E's right as rain, Mrs Jeffries. But 'e gets a bit lonely without me, you see, and I promised him I'd be back by noon.'

CHAPTER TEN

M RS JEFFRIES GLANCED at the clock. It was five past three and there was still no sign of Smythe. 'Oh dear,' she said apologetically, 'perhaps Smythe was unable to accomplish his task.'

'Give him a few more minutes, Hepzibah,' Luty said. She absently reached down and patted Fred on the head.

'Madam,' Hatchet said, 'am I to understand that our presence here implies we won't be attending Mrs Mettlesham's at-home? We're due there at precisely five o'clock. You accepted the invitation last week.'

'Well, we'll jus' have to unaccept it, won't we?' Luty said impatiently. 'I ain't budging from here until I find out what Hepzibah's got up her sleeve. Besides, them at-homes is nothing more than fancy tea parties fer a bunch of gossipin' biddies.'

'Oh Luty,' Mrs Jeffries said, 'I know I told you it was important that you be here, but I certainly didn't mean for you to cancel your engagement. Gracious, I'm afraid I've acted prematurely. Without Smythe's confirmation of a very important piece of information,

I'm afraid—' She broke off at the sound of the back door opening.

''E's 'ere,' Wiggins cried. He sprang to his feet and Fred, who probably thought it was time to go for a walk, leaped up as well.

'Sorry I'm late,' Smythe said, reaching down to pet Fred, 'but it took a bit o' time to track that driver down. I found 'im, though, and I did just like you said, Mrs Jeffries. You was right, you know.'

Mrs Jeffries closed her eyes briefly in relief. This was the first real confirmation of what had been nothing more than a rather farfetched theory on her part. Yet if one looked at the matter rationally, it was the only sequence of events that made sense. 'So the driver did make a stop that night.'

'Yup, I 'ad the bloke take me to the exact spot too,' Smythe explained. 'That's what took us so long, you see. The driver 'ad a bit of trouble backtrackin' the route he took to the train station. It were so foggy that night the poor feller could barely see the backside of his 'orse.'

'But he was able to find the place again?' Betsy asked anxiously.

The coachman grinned. 'He remembered just fine once we were on our way.' His smile faded and his expression sobered as he turned his attention to Mrs Jeffries. 'And he's prepared to swear to it in court too, if that's of any importance.'

'It is, Smythe,' Mrs Jeffries replied fervently. 'It's of the utmost importance. Now tell us all the details.'

'Like I said, it were foggy that night and the driver was thinkin' of haulin' in and quittin' for the evenin' when he gets this fare from Mr Hodges and Mrs Popejoy.

They get in the cab and direct 'im to take them to the railway station, but they hadn't been movin' for more than ten minutes before Mr Hodges is shoutin' at him to go another way. Said he wanted to make a quick stop.' Smythe made a wry face. 'This didn't set too well with the driver, I can tell you that. He was right narked about it. But they was payin' good money, so 'e did as 'e was told. Mr Hodges finally called for him to halt just as they were goin' down Lewis Road. Then Mr Hodges and Mrs Popejoy nips out of the hansom, tells the driver to wait and disappears into the fog. A few minutes later they was back. They climbed in and Mrs Popejoy shouted for 'im to drive on.'

'Let me make sure I've got this correct,' Mrs Jeffries said. 'When they entered the hansom the second time, it was Mrs Popejoy who spoke to the driver, not Mr Hodges.'

'That's what 'e said.'

'Hmmm,' she murmured softly as they all stared at her. 'That certainly makes sense.' Mrs Jeffries gazed at Smythe. 'Now tell me exactly what you saw when the driver took you to the spot he'd stopped at on the night of the murder.'

'Just a minute, Hepzibah,' Luty interjected. 'I've got a question. How long did they stay stopped?'

' 'Course the driver couldn't be too certain about that, 'e weren't lookin' at 'is watch. But as close as 'e can figure, it were about five minutes,' Smythe replied.

'Five minutes isn't enough time for 'im to have nipped 'ome and done in 'is missus,' Wiggins put in. 'Not unless this Lewis Road is just around the corner from the Hodges 'ouse. Was it?'

'No, the road's a good distance away,' Smythe admitted. He turned to Mrs Jeffries. 'Despite the fog bein' thicker than clotted cream, once we was in the neighbourhood, the driver remembered everythin'. He'd stopped in front of a pub, a place called the Red Lion. 'E pulled up right under the sign and waited. Now, next to this pub is a couple of shops—'

'What kind of shops?' Mrs Jeffries asked quickly. She needed details.

'A Frieman's Butcher Shop and the Lewis Road Fishmongers. Across the road is Phipps Chemists, and next to that a small hotel called Billson's.' He tilted his head to one side. 'Funny, though, the name on the chemist's shop was right familiar to me. I know I've 'eard it before.'

'It sounds familiar to me too,' Mrs Goodge muttered.

Smythe frowned. 'I wish I could remember where I'd heard it before.'

'I can,' Mrs Jeffries said. She stood up and pulled a small black purse out of the pocket of her dress. 'But before I explain, you've all got pressing matters to attend to immediately, before the inspector gets home for dinner tonight. If my assumptions about this murder are correct – and after hearing Smythe's information, I'm sure they are – then we'll have this murder solved within the next twenty-four hours.'

'Who done it then?' Luty asked eagerly.

'I'm sorry, I can't tell you, not just yet. I need a bit more evidence. And if everyone is successful with their tasks this evening, I'll know for sure.' Mrs Jeffries wasn't being coy, but before she accused anyone of murder, even here in the privacy of the kitchen, she wanted to make absolutely certain she was right.

Not giving those around the table time to do anything but look surprised, she began issuing instructions.

'Wiggins,' she ordered briskly, 'you've got to get to St James's Church. According to what Betsy told us, Mr Hodges gave a bundle of clothes to the vicar to be distributed to the poor.'

'What now?' Wiggins moaned. 'Ahh. It's bad enough you won't tell us who the killer is, but if I nip all the way over to that church, I'll miss me supper.'

'Stop yer moanin', boy,' Luty said kindly. 'If you're hungry, you kin chew on a bun as you go, but this here's more important than missin' a meal or two.'

Wiggins blushed. 'Sorry,' he mumbled. 'Guess you're right. Now, what do you want me to do, Mrs Jeffries?'

She drew out a pound note and handed it to the footman. 'It's imperative we get our hands on those clothes. If you have to, buy them.' She glanced anxiously towards the window, frowning at the darkening sky, and then looked at Luty. 'I hate to interfere with your plans for this afternoon . . .'

'Don't worry about that, madam,' Hatchet said cheerfully. 'The plans are of no importance. Mrs Crookshank and I are always delighted to be of service to the cause of justice. What do you want us to do?'

'That's mighty good of you, Hatchet,' Luty muttered dryly. 'But I thought you was frettin' over me missin' that tea party.'

'Not at all, madam,' he replied smoothly. 'I was merely reminding you of the engagement. It's hardly my place to interfere in your decisions.'

Luty snorted. 'All right, Hepzibah, give us our orders and we'll get to it.'

'I want you to contact Edmund Kessler,' she said. 'Betsy can give you his address. Supposedly that young man is well known in spiritualist circles. You must get him to arrange a séance at Mrs Popejoy's for tomorrow night.' She started to open the purse again.

'Don't bother reachin' fer any money,' Luty commanded. 'I'll take care of greasin' any palms that's needed to git that woman to see us.'

'Really, Luty,' Mrs Jeffries said, feeling her cheeks turn pink. 'That's not necessary . . .'

'Don't be silly, Hepzibah, I've got more money than I'll ever spend—'

'That she does, madam,' Hatchet interrupted, 'that she does.'

'Pipe down, man,' Luty said, exasperated. 'And I don't mind spendin' some of it to catch a killer. Besides, I owe you all.'

Mrs Jeffries gave in. She knew that Luty Belle Crookshank could be one stubborn woman. 'Thank you, Luty.'

'What if Kessler's full of hot air?' Smythe suggested, carefully avoiding Betsy's eye. 'What if he can't make the arrangements? Didn't we 'ear that this Mrs Popejoy don't just see anybody?'

'Edmund's not full of hot air,' Betsy said defensively. 'You just wait, he'll be able to fix it up.'

Seeing another argument in the making, Mrs Jeffries quickly intervened. 'I'm sure that if Mr Kessler fails us, Luty will be quite able to use her considerable connections to ensure Mrs Popejoy is amenable to our plans.'

'Yup, much as I hate to admit it, money can jus' about buy anything,' Luty said.

'Will you be wantin' me to do anything?' Mrs Goodge asked. She tried to sound unconcerned, but Mrs Jeffries could hear the hopeful note in her voice.

'Of course I do,' the housekeeper assured her. 'But it might be very difficult.'

'You just tell me what you need, I'll take care of it.' The cook's ample bosom swelled with pride. 'I've never run from difficulties in my life and I don't intend to start now.'

'It's rather old gossip, I'm afraid,' Mrs Jeffries began. 'But I'm confident that if anyone can dig up the information we need, you can. Find out exactly how long Mr Hodges and Mrs Popejoy have known each other, and most importantly, find out if Mrs Popejoy was anywhere near the Lake District when the first Mrs Hodges accidentally drowned.'

'Hmmm,' the cook mused, then her broad face broke into a wide grin. 'It won't be easy, but it should be fun. I always did love a bit of a challenge. I'll get you somethin'. How much time have I got?'

'Not much, I'm afraid. If my plan's going to work, I'll need some answers by tomorrow, the earlier in the day, the better.' Mrs Jeffries turned her attention to Betsy. 'I've a task for you, of course, but I'm not certain you can do it this evening.'

'Why couldn't I do it now?' Betsy asked. 'It's not gone four o'clock yet.'

'Yes, but it's getting dark outside. Dreadful, these winter evenings, the night falls so early. I'm not sure it's safe for you to be out and about.'

'Can I go with the lass?' Smythe asked. He carefully avoided looking at Betsy.

Mrs Jeffries shook her head. 'No, I'm afraid I need you for another task.' She glanced uncertainly at the maid. 'Oh dear, I really don't want you out alone . . .'

'Come on, Mrs Jeffries,' Betsy pleaded. 'I know how to take care of myself. I'll be very careful. If Smythe can't go with me, maybe we can get one of his cabbie friends to drive me. Where do you want me to go?'

Mrs Jeffries thought about it for a moment. 'That's a good idea. Now, I want your word of honour that if you aren't successful in getting the information we need by nine o'clock, you'll come right home. Furthermore, you're to use a hansom cab and not be walking about on the streets. Smythe can take you out when he leaves, and make sure he puts you in a cab with someone he trusts.' Mrs Jeffries then spent ten minutes giving Betsy her instructions.

As the housekeeper told the maid what she wanted her to do, Smythe's mouth flattened into a grim, disapproving line. 'Hey, now. I don't rightly think the lass is up to all that,' he objected, when Mrs Jeffries had finished. 'This feller might be in cahoots with the murderers.'

'I quite agree, Smythe. He may well be,' Mrs Jeffries said kindly, 'but if Betsy is driven there by your friend Jeremiah and he keeps her in sight the whole time, I do believe she'll be all right.'

'I will, I promise,' Betsy said. 'And you've said yourself, Smythe, Jeremiah's a good bloke. He'll keep an eye on me.'

'I don't see why I can't take her,' Smythe insisted. He

scowled at Mrs Jeffries. 'Whatever you've got in mind for me, can't it wait till later?'

'I'm afraid not,' Mrs Jeffries answered. 'You need to leave right away. You'll be gone most of the night.'

'Cor, all night?' Smythe's eyebrows drew together. 'Where ya sendin' me? Scotland?'

'Not quite that far,' she said kindly. She knew the coachman wasn't trying to shirk his duty. His objections to going out this evening were solely because he was worried about Betsy. Mrs Jeffries understood his concern. She was worried herself, but she had to have more information. And Betsy was the best person available to obtain it. Smythe's special talents were needed for another purpose.

'Then where am I goin'?' he said impatiently.

'You're going to Southend.'

'I say,' Inspector Witherspoon said as he glanced around the dining room, 'it's jolly quiet tonight. Where is everybody?'

Mrs Jeffries laid a second pork chop on the inspector's plate and put it in front of him. 'Mrs Goodge is where she always is – the kitchen. I didn't think you'd mind, but I sent Betsy over to Mrs Crookshank's for the evening. Everyone's got the flu and they needed an extra hand.'

'Of course I don't mind,' Witherspoon replied. 'I was merely curious. It's not often the house is this quiet. I say, did you tell me this morning that we'd got a dog?'

'Yes, a stray. Wiggins found the poor thing in the street. He's out walking it now. Again' – she smiled brightly – 'knowing how kind-hearted you are and how much you love animals, I didn't think you'd object if we kept the animal. Dogs do help keep the rodents away.'

'That's all right then. Have Wiggins bring the dog in when he gets back. I'd like to meet him. What's his name?'

'Fred,' Mrs Jeffries murmured. 'Now, sir, how is the investigation going?'

'Not well.' He sighed and began cutting his chop. 'As I told you earlier, our chief suspects have disappeared.'

'Miss Marsden and Mr Vogel?' Mrs Jeffries said innocently. She knew perfectly well who the suspects were, but she knew they were innocent. Now she had to concentrate on getting the inspector to learn the same thing. 'You know, sir, this morning you told me about Mrs Trotter.'

'Yes, I remember. What about her?'

'Well, after you left, I heard the most extraordinary gossip about her. I wonder if it has any bearing on your case?'

Witherspoon's fork halted halfway to his mouth.

'You know how I abhor gossip, sir,' Mrs Jeffries continued quickly, 'but I really felt it was my duty to listen, seeing as how you're investigating this terrible crime.'

'By all means, Mrs Jeffries,' he said, hastily putting his fork down next to his plate. 'Do tell.'

'Supposedly Mrs Trotter has been walking the streets of London looking for her daughter.' She gave an embarrassed smile. 'Twenty years ago Mrs Trotter had an illegitimate child. Mrs Hodges helped to adopt the child out. I've heard that Mrs Trotter wanted the child back. But Mrs Hodges refused to tell her where

205

the girl was. She promised Mrs Trotter that upon her death, she'd leave a letter naming the adoptive parents of the child.'

Witherspoon looked shocked. 'How very strange.' He started eating again.

Mrs Jeffries stared at him. 'But, sir,' she finally said, when he continued shoving peas in his mouth, 'don't you see, that means Mrs Trotter had a motive for Mrs Hodges's death.'

'Oh yes,' the inspector replied. 'No doubt Mrs Trotter is a tad peculiar in her habits, but as it happens, we know she had nothing to do with the murder.'

Now it was Mrs Jeffries's turn to be surprised. 'How do you know?'

'Because of her habit of walking the streets.' He smiled knowingly. 'She's known to many of our lads, you see. She was seen on the night of the murder by one of our constables. Mrs Trotter was hanging about Waterloo Bridge for hours that night. She was seen getting into a hansom cab around eleven. Another constable saw her in the area near Miss Bush's house less than half an hour later, so whatever motive she may have had, however odd the woman is, she couldn't have committed the murder. She hadn't time.'

'I see,' Mrs Jeffries commented. 'Your constables have obviously been very busy.' She knew perfectly well Thomasina Trotter wasn't the killer, but she had hoped to muddy the waters a bit and get the inspector's mind off Felicity Marsden and Benjamin Vogel.

'We do our best,' he replied proudly. 'I say, is there any pudding tonight?'

'There's a Royal Victoria.'

'Ah, delightful. Her Majesty's favourite.' He chuckled. 'And mine too. Will you share some with me?'

'No, thank you, I've already eaten.' Mrs Jeffries decided to try a different approach. 'You know, sir, I've been thinking about something you said. You once told me that appearances are often deceiving.'

'Really? I said that?'

'Yes, sir. It was during those horrible Kensington High Street Murders . . .'

The inspector shuddered. 'Please, Mrs Jeffries, not while I'm eating. That case was absolutely dreadful.'

'I know, sir, but you solved it.'

'Of course I solved it,' he said, 'but to be perfectly honest, I can't quite remember how.'

'You did it by not being deceived by appearances, sir,' she replied.

'You've a remarkable memory, Mrs Jeffries.'

'Not as good as yours, sir,' she shot back quickly. 'Well, I was thinking about something else you mentioned about the Hodges case, and naturally the two ideas began to flow into one in my mind.'

He gazed at her quizzically. 'I don't believe I understand what you're getting at. What specifically are you referring to about the Hodges murder?'

Mrs Jeffries knew she had to tread carefully here. 'Appearances, sir. That's what I'm getting at. Mr Hodges and Mrs Popejoy appear to have an alibi . . .'

'But of course they do,' he protested. 'We double-checked with Mrs Popejoy's friend. She saw them together at the train station.'

'Yes, but did she really see them, or did she only think she saw Mr Hodges? You've said it yourself, sir.

Sometimes eyewitness evidence is the least reliable. Ten people will see the same incident, and if you ask them to describe what they saw, they'll each describe something different. And what about Mr Felcher? Was he really in his rooms, or did he only make it look like he was there in order to fool his landlady into saying he was?' She spoke quickly, earnestly; she had to get the inspector to start looking beyond the obvious.

He frowned in confusion. 'I'm not really sure I understand.'

She forced herself to laugh. 'Now, sir, you know very well what I'm doing. You're just up to your old tricks and teasing me a bit. Why I'm repeating your own advice to you and you're sitting there letting me go on and on.'

Witherspoon laughed as well. But she could still see the uncertainty in his eyes. He really had no idea what she was getting at. 'Perhaps I am, Mrs Jeffries. Er, what do you think I'm going to do next?'

'That's an easy one.' She smiled smugly. 'You're going to do what you always do and double-check everyone's alibi. You're going to send some constables out to have a word with the hansom drivers in the area and see what else you can discover. You're going to continue searching for Miss Marsden and Mr Vogel, and once you find them, you're going to ascertain if their flight was caused by panic or by guilt. And last but not least, you're going to confirm that Mr Felcher really was in his rooms.' She sat back and folded her hands in her lap. 'You can't fool me, sir. I know how that brilliant brain of yours works. You've been planning on doing this all along.'

The inspector didn't retire for the night until after 9:30. Mrs Jeffries, who'd been keeping an eye on the clock, hurried down to the kitchen.

She was greatly relieved to see Betsy sitting safely next to Mrs Goodge. 'Thank goodness, you're back. Has Wiggins come back yet?'

'He come in a half hour ago, dropped that bundle of clothes on the floor,' Mrs Goodge replied, pointing to a paper-wrapped parcel lying by the dish cupboard, 'and then he went up to bed.'

'Good.' Mrs Jeffries walked over and picked up the parcel. She came back to the table, sat down and turned to Betsy. 'Were you successful?'

'Everything went right as rain,' Betsy announced. 'I did just like you said. The shop was still open when I got there, so I went in and got a good look at him. Then I waited for him to come out. I saw him wearin' his hat and coat.'

Mrs Jeffries untied the string and pushed the brown paper aside. Standing up, she shook out a man's coat. 'Now, think carefully,' she instructed Betsy, 'was the coat Mr Phipps was wearing like this one?'

'That's it, all right.' Betsy pointed to the slightly flattened bowler. 'And he had on a hat like that one too. I also got friendly with a girl who works for Mr Phipps. She's a right little chatterbox, too. Told me all sorts of things about Mr Phipps.'

''Ere, don't I get a turn?' Mrs Goodge chimed in. 'It's gettin' late and I've got to be up early if I'm going to have a word with the milkman.'

'Let Mrs Goodge go ahead,' Betsy said

magnanimously. 'The rest of what I've found out isn't much more than gossip. It can wait a bit.'

'Thank you,' Mrs Goodge said. 'I found out a bit of what you wanted. I wasn't able to learn if Mrs Popejoy was anywhere near the Lake District when the first Mrs Hodges drowned, but I did find out that she and Mr Hodges have known each other a lot longer than they let on.'

'Peter was right, then,' Betsy interjected.

Mrs Goodge nodded. 'He certainly was.' She gazed at Mrs Jeffries. 'Remember when we heard that Madame Natalia claimed that Mrs Popejoy weren't a real medium and had probably worked in the music halls?'

Mrs Jeffries nodded.

'As luck would have it, my sister's husband's cousin works in one of them music halls, has for years. Knows everyone and everything that goes on. Well, I sent him a note as soon as we were finished this afternoon, and while you and the inspector was at dinner, Ernest – that's the cousin – he dropped round. He told me that Esme Popejoy used to work in a theatre in Leeds. A real ratty place, didn't do much business and had the worst acts you've ever seen. Mrs Popejoy used to do a mind-readin' act. But you'll never guess who owned the theatre.'

'Leonard Hodges?' Mrs Jeffries replied.

'That's right. It were one of his investments.' Mrs Goodge smiled triumphantly. 'Now can you tell us who the killer is?'

'Not yet, Mrs Goodge,' Mrs Jeffries replied. 'I really need to speak to Smythe before I make an accusation. Betsy, did Mr Phipps remind you of anyone?' She wanted to make sure she didn't plant the suggestion in the girl's mind. If her theory was correct, there was only one person that Ashley Phipps could resemble.

Betsy hesitated. Mrs Jeffries's heart plummeted to her toes. Oh dear, what if she was wrong?

'He didn't act like him much; Mr Phipps is a right nervous, rabbity sort of feller, but from a distance he looks an awful lot like Leonard Hodges.'

Mrs Jeffries didn't get much sleep that night. She was absolutely sure she knew what had happened on the night of the murder, but she was having a difficult time thinking of a way to get Inspector Witherspoon to come to the same conclusion. She wasn't so terribly sure that sending Luty Belle to a séance at the Popejoy house was going to accomplish her goal.

By five o'clock, she decided that trying to sleep was pointless. She got up, lit a lamp and walked over to her desk. She might as well write everything out – perhaps putting pen to paper would help her tune the finer points of her plan.

Sitting down, she reached for her letter box. She reached in to get some paper when suddenly her fingers stilled. Of course, she thought, notes. Why, it would fit right in. It would work perfectly if the timing were right. And, of course, if Smythe confirmed the last bit of evidence she had to have.

Luty Belle and Hatchet arrived just after the inspector had left for the morning. Mrs Jeffries hurried them into the kitchen. Smythe, Betsy, Mrs Goodge, Wiggins and Fred were waiting.

Smythe gave them a bleary-eyed glance and then rubbed his hand across the stubble on his cheek. 'Cor, it's been a long night. Let me say my piece so I can get a bit of sleep.'

'By all means, Smythe,' Mrs Jeffries said quickly, 'speak right up. You'll need a bit of rest. We're not through with this case yet and I fear I shall have you running about even more before today's over.'

He yawned. 'Right. I went to Southend, just like you told me. Miss Trainer's 'ouse is just down from a pub, so I tried there first. But I didn't have much luck, none of her servants was in that night and no one knew much about 'er. Spinster lady, keeps to 'erself mostly.'

'Oh dear,' Mrs Jeffries said.

'Don't fret, Mrs J. I didn't let that stop me.' He suddenly grinned. 'There's more than one pub in Southend. The third one I tried, I got lucky. There was a lad in there that does odd jobs for the lady. He knows all about 'er. Said she were a silly, nervous woman it'd be dead easy to fool. He also told me she's very short-sighted, but she won't wear her spectacles.'

'Excellent, Smythe.' Mrs Jeffries turned to Luty. 'Were you able to arrange things for tonight?'

'Edmund's goin' round to see Mrs Popejoy this mornin'. I told him to fix it for seven o'clock.' Luty cocked her head to one side. 'Are you gonna tell us who done it?'

'In good time, madam,' Hatchet interrupted, 'in good time. We haven't heard what Miss Betsy has to say yet.'

'Thank you, Hatchet,' Mrs Jeffries said. She smiled at Betsy. 'I believe it's your turn now.'

'Like I told Mrs Jeffries and Mrs Goodge last night, I saw this Ashley Phipps fellow,' Betsy began. 'And I also did a spot of diggin' about him. He was gone on the night of the murder, and even better, he's been in love with Mrs Esme Popejoy for ages.'

'Mrs Popejoy!' Mrs Goodge snorted. 'Well somehow, I'm not surprised. That one sounds like she's been around the park a few times.'

'Do go on, Betsy,' Mrs Jeffries said.

'What? Oh yes, as I was sayin', about six months ago Mrs Popejoy up and tells Mr Phipps she don't want to see him no more,' Betsy continued. 'He were ever so upset. Went round with a long face for weeks, at least that's what Gertie – that's the girl who cleans for him – told me. Then, less than two weeks ago, he gets a note from Mrs Popejoy saying she wants to see him. Cheered him right up, that did.'

'Why don't you tell everyone who Mr Phipps resembles,' Mrs Jeffries suggested.

Betsy smiled proudly. 'Ashley Phipps looks very much like Leonard Hodges.'

For a moment they all looked puzzled, then one by one, their expressions changed.

'So that's 'ow they did it,' Smythe muttered.

'Clever, wasn't it,' Betsy agreed.

'Diabolical, that's what it was,' Mrs Goodge muttered.

'Brilliant plan,' Hatchet said, 'but rather risky.'

'I'll be danged,' Luty exclaimed. 'If that don't beat all.'

'Huh?' Wiggins scratched his head.

'Now.' Mrs Jeffries reached into her pockets and

drew out the notes she'd written earlier. 'We've much to do today if we're going to bring this case to a successful conclusion.'

'I don't understand,' Wiggins wailed.

'I'll explain it to you later,' Mrs Jeffries said. 'But for right now you must get busy.' She handed him a note. 'I want you to take this note to Phipps Chemists on Lewis Road. Don't let anyone see you, but make sure that Ashley Phipps himself reads it.'

'But 'ow can I do that? What if 'e isn't there?' Wiggins asked.

'If he isn't there,' Mrs Jeffries said patiently, 'then track him down. But it is imperative he receive that note and that he receive it today.' She pulled another note out of her pocket and handed it to Betsy. 'Take this one to Mr Hodges, but make sure he doesn't receive it until six o'clock this evening. Do you understand?'

'I understand,' Betsy replied, reaching for the paper and tucking it carefully into her pocket.

''Ow about me?' Smythe asked.

'Well,' Mrs Jeffries hesitated. 'I know you're awfully tired . . .'

He grinned. 'I ain't that tired. What is it?'

She told him. Then she gave Luty and Hatchet some instructions. 'Be sure and be there right at seven o'clock. Do whatever you must to get Mrs Popejoy to start the séance on time.'

'Do I get to go to this one?' Betsy asked hopefully.

'No, I'll need you with me,' Mrs Jeffries replied. 'Besides, Peter might be there, and if he sees you, it could ruin everything. Mrs Popejoy mustn't suspect.'

She spent the next ten minutes going over the fine

points of her plan and looking for flaws. The others picked at it, but couldn't pull it apart.

'Everything should work perfectly if nothing untoward or unexpected happens,' she said.

'Something unexpected always happens,' Luty warned. 'That's the nature of life. But in this case, if everyone does like they're supposed to, them varmints that murdered Mrs Hodges should be locked up before the day is out.'

CHAPTER ELEVEN

'COME IN. SIT down. Let Madame Natalia help you with your troubles.' She smiled sympathetically and gestured towards a round table covered with a spotless white cloth. A crystal ball rested in the centre of the table.

'Thanks, don't mind if I do.' Luty plopped down in a chair and motioned for Mrs Jeffries to do the same. 'But we didn't come for no séance, not that I didn't enjoy it the last time I was here.'

Mrs Jeffries dragged her gaze from Madame Natalia's 'study' and took the chair next to Luty. The room was most extraordinary. The blinds were drawn and the windows were covered in layers of pale mauve and blue gauzy fabric that seemed to float mysteriously of its own accord, for she couldn't feel a draft. In front of the fireplace was a painted octagonal screen etched with the golden script of some unknown language. Over the mantel, there was a huge black-and-silver drawing of the zodiac and at each end of the mantel stood a brass brazier wafting up delicate-scented smoke rings.

Mrs Jeffries took a deep breath and inhaled the exotic scent of sandalwood. She blinked and fixed her gaze on the portrait of an ethereal young woman with long flowing hair. She blinked again, trying to force her eyes to adjust to the dimness. The only light in the room came from dozens of candles scattered about on the tops of tables and highboys. Then she turned to the medium.

Madame Natalia was staring at Luty. She was dressed in a full bright red skirt with a white sash around the waist. Her blouse was emerald green, high-necked and had wide, flouncy sleeves. On her head was a turban the same colour as her skirt. Tiny black curls escaped from around the top and sides.

'If you are not here for a reading,' Madame Natalia asked archly, 'then I do not understand why you've come.'

'Actually,' Mrs Jeffries replied, 'we're here for a bit of professional advice.'

'Advice?' Madame Natalia laughed. 'But I do not give advice, Mrs Jeffries. The spirits do. I'm merely the channel for the voice from the other side.'

Mrs Jeffries noticed that the more the woman spoke, the thicker and more exotic her accent became. 'Yes, well, I'm sure you're probably quite good at being a channel, but we were thinking of engaging your services for a rather different matter.'

'I do not perform parlour tricks,' the medium replied haughtily.

'We wouldn't dream of asking you to do such a thing,' Mrs Jeffries assured the woman quickly. 'However, you do have certain, er . . .'

'We want to know how you fake that Indian's voice,' Luty stated bluntly.

Madame Natalia swelled with indignation. 'I do not fake this voice. It is real, as real as you or I. How dare you, madam. How dare you insult me and the spirits.'

'Now don't git on yer high horse. You put on a right good show for people,' Luty retorted. She plonked her purse down on the table. 'You do a danged good job. We wouldn't be here if you didn't.'

'I don't know what you're talking about,' Madame Natalia replied. But she seemed to have lost most of her righteous indignation and her eyes were locked on Luty's purse.

'Please, madam,' Mrs Jeffries said quickly. 'We've the highest respect for your abilities and we really do need your help.'

'Let's start talkin' turkey,' Luty interrupted. 'We know you ain't talkin' to the other side, whatever in tarnation that is, but we think you're right good at soundin' like Soarin' Eagle.' She broke off and opened her purse. Taking out a wad of notes big enough to make Madame Natalia's eyes widen, she plonked them on the table right under the madame's nose. 'Now, do we talk business or do I pick up my money and skedaddle?'

The medium hesitated briefly, reached over and snatched the bills. She tucked the money into her sash, grinned and extended her hand. 'The real name's Nessie Spittlesham. The feller out front is my husband, Bert.' She leaned forward on her elbows and pushed the crystal ball to one side. 'Now, as you say, let's talk turkey. Exactly what do you ladies want?'

'Can you teach one of us to do what you do?' Mrs Jeffries wasn't sure how to explain what she wanted. But if her plan were to be successful, she needed this woman's help. 'With your voice, I mean. Luty says that when you're speaking as Soaring Eagle, it sounds very authentic.'

' 'Course it sounds authentic,' Nessie said proudly. 'All my voices sound good. I've been workin' on them for years. Let me see if I've got this right. You want me to show one of you how to sound like Soaring Eagle?'

'Not Soaring Eagle,' Luty said. 'We want you to teach us how to sound like someone else, like someone from the other side, like a ghost.'

Nessie regarded them thoughtfully. She didn't seem overly upset by the unusual request. 'What kind of accent does your ghost have?' she asked.

'Upper-class English,' Mrs Jeffries replied promptly. 'But actually, we'll need you to help us learn to do two separate voices. Oh yes, and we'll need to know how to do this by tonight.'

'Two voices,' Nessie yelped. 'By tonight? That's bloody impossible.' She jerked her chin towards Luty. 'And with that flat twang of hers, it'd take me a bloomin' year to teach 'er to sound like a toff.'

Luty snorted.

'Well, how about me?' Mrs Jeffries asked. 'Could you show me? It's dreadfully important, you see.'

Nessie drummed her fingers on the tabletop. 'How come you two want to learn something like this anyway? You thinkin' of goin' into the business? 'Cause if you are, I can tell you now, it's a bleedin' 'ard way to make a livin'.'

Mrs Jeffries studied the woman for a moment before answering. She decided to tell her the truth. 'We've no wish to go into this professionally,' she explained. 'We only need this particular skill for one night. If you can't teach us, are you available for hire tonight?'

'Lord, Hepzibah,' Luty exclaimed. 'What are you doin'? We can't get her into the Popejoy house. What do you expect me to do, hide her in my muff?'

'Did you say Popejoy?' Nessie snapped.

'Don't be absurd, of course we can get her in,' Mrs Jeffries replied. 'And yes, I did say Popejoy. You see, Nessie, we're trying to catch a murderer. To do that, we're going to need your help.'

'Now, Constable,' Inspector Witherspoon asked for the third time, 'you did say this driver was prepared to testify in court?'

'Yes, sir,' Barnes replied patiently. 'The driver is fully prepared to testify to the truth. The cab stopped on the way to the train station that night. Mr Hodges and Mrs Popejoy both got out. But I don't see what good it's goin' to do us, they were only gone five minutes.'

Witherspoon didn't see what good it was going to do either. But somehow he felt it was important. He sighed. His head ached, he'd missed his lunch, and despite having found the cab driver, he was still no closer to a resolution on this wretched case. On top of that it was starting to rain again.

'Excuse me, sir.' A middle-aged constable stuck his head into the office. 'But there's a Mr Phipps to see you, sir.'

'What about? I don't know any Mr Phipps.'

'He says he's got a note from you, sir. Says it's about the Hodges murder.'

'A note! From me?' Witherspoon couldn't believe his ears. Egads, was there a whole army of people out there sending notes with his name on them? By golly, he was going to get to the bottom of this. 'Send him in.'

A moment later there were impatient footsteps in the hall and a man in a bowler hat and heavy topcoat stepped into the inspector's office.

'Why, it's Mr Hodges, sir,' Barnes began. 'No, it's not. Beggin' your pardon, sir, but you look very much like another gentleman.'

'My name is not Hodges,' the man snapped as he advanced towards Witherspoon's desk. He had a high-pitched, very feminine voice. 'It's Phipps. Ashley Phipps. And I demand to know the meaning of this.' He flung the note onto the inspector's desk.

Witherspoon opened the paper. He scowled as he read its contents. 'Barnes, what do you make of this? "Dear Sir," ' he read. ' "You are in possession of vital information concerning the murder of Mrs Abigail Hodges on the night of January fourth. Kindly come into my office at the Ladbroke Grove Police Station to help us with our enquiries. Signed, Inspector Gerald Witherspoon." '

'Did you write it, sir?' Barnes asked.

'Of course I didn't write it,' the inspector replied.

'Then why does it have your name on it, Inspector?' Phipps said angrily. 'And furthermore, I've no idea what this is all about. I've never even heard of this Abigail Hodges.'

'You didn't read about the murder in the news-papers?' the inspector asked.

'No, I did not,' Phipps retorted. 'Are you claiming you know nothing about this note, sir?'

'I didn't send it, Mr Phipps. I've no idea who did.'

'If this is someone's idea of a joke,' Phipps sputtered, 'well, I must say it's in dreadfully bad taste. If you didn't write this, sir, then I take it I'm free to go?' He began edging towards the door.

'Just a minute, sir,' Barnes said. 'You don't, by any chance, happen to remember what you were doing on the night of the fourth, do you, sir?'

Phipps stopped. 'As a matter of fact, I know precisely what I was doing. I was at home with my mother – we live just over my shop in Lewis Road.' He faltered as he saw the inspector and Barnes exchange glances.

'I was there until half past nine,' he continued. 'Then I escorted a lady friend to the train station. Both ladies will be quite happy to confirm my whereabouts on the night in question, I'm sure.'

'What's the name of your lady friend, sir?' Wither-spoon asked. He held his breath.

'Mrs Popejoy.' Phipps smiled proudly. 'Esme Pope-joy. A lady who I hope will soon do me the honour of consenting to be my wife.'

Betsy pounded on the door knocker and then scurried quickly into the shadows. She saw the door open and the maid appeared. Hilda Brown frowned and stepped outside. She glanced up and down the road.

Betsy held her breath as the girl shrugged her shoulders and turned to go back inside. Suddenly she stopped, knelt down and picked up the envelope that was lying at her feet.

Betsy let her breath out as the maid went back into the house.

It was exactly six o'clock.

Silently Betsy stepped out of the shadows and hurried down the road to the waiting carriage.

'Cor, it took you long enough,' Smythe growled as he opened the door and helped her inside. He climbed in behind her.

'Well, I had to wait and make sure she saw it,' she responded. 'Mr Hodges is due home soon. Let's hope she gives it to him right away. If this is goin' to work, he's got to make his move in the next hour.'

'When you requested a private reading,' Esme Popejoy said, glancing from Luty to Hatchet and then to their heavily veiled companion, 'I assumed you meant you'd be alone.'

Luty waved one diamond-bedecked hand negligently. 'Does it make a difference whether there's one or two of us? I didn't think you'd mind, considerin' what I'm payin'.' She gestured to her companion with her large fur muff. 'This here's my sister, she ain't never been to one of these here séances. But if my bringin' her troubles you, I'll be glad to ante up with a little more cash.'

'That won't be necessary,' Mrs Popejoy said. 'Your sister's presence doesn't bother me, but then, I'm not the one who matters.' She smiled and turned to the table in the centre of the room. 'It's Lady Lucia who occasionally gets temperamental. She doesn't like surprises. Please, come over and sit down.'

'If it's all the same to you, madam,' Hatchet said, edging quietly towards the window behind the table, 'I'd prefer to stand over here, out of harm's way, so to speak.'

Mrs Popejoy raised one delicate eyebrow and cocked her head prettily to one side. Dressed in an elegant peacock-blue evening dress and matching velvet ribbons in her upswept auburn hair, she was the very picture of the lady of the manor.

'I'm afraid that's impossible,' she stated firmly. 'I don't allow anyone to stand away from the circle during my séances. It upsets the balance.'

Hatchet tripped over a footstool and stumbled backwards, catching himself on the window ledge.

'Are you all right?' Luty cried. She grinned at Mrs Popejoy. 'Clumsy feller, always trippin' over his own feet.'

'I'm quite all right, madam,' Hatchet replied tartly. He leaned against the window for a brief moment, his hand resting on the lock. 'Just give me a minute to recover.'

'If you'll be seated,' Mrs Popejoy prompted, 'we'll get started.'

As soon as the butler had sat down, she clapped her hands together and a maid appeared. The girl began turning off the lamps as Mrs Popejoy lit one large white candle and pushed it into the centre of the table.

From outside the window, three people crouched quietly in the bushes. Mrs Jeffries and Betsy stood on one side and Smythe on the other. Keeping low, they all cocked their heads as close as they dared to the small opening. Luckily Hatchet had been able to get the French window cracked enough for them to hear some of what was going on in the room. If they were really lucky, Mrs Jeffries decided as she stared at the narrow opening between the small panes of glass, an unwanted blast of wind wouldn't give them away.

'Please join hands and close your eyes,' Mrs Popejoy ordered. Save for the one flickering candle, the room was now in darkness.

Luty held her breath as she saw the candle flame twist and jump as though it were being chased by the wind, which, she knew, it was. Hatchet's little stumble had accomplished their goal. Now she only hoped that this daring plan would actually work. If it didn't, she was going to end up with a lot of explaining to do.

Luty extended her hands. Hatchet sat to her right and Nessie to her left. Then she waited for the séance to begin.

Mrs Popejoy began to breathe deeply and evenly. Luty saw the flame jump again and she felt like spitting. The medium's chest began to move up and down as she took in long and large breaths of air. Suddenly a low, eerie keening sound issued from the woman's throat.

The keening turned into a moan and then a wail. 'Darkness,' the medium finally whispered, 'darkness everywhere.'

From Luty's left, there was a low groan.

Mrs Popejoy didn't open her eyes, but her mouth moved. 'Death, despair. I must tell you . . . I must warn you.'

'Water,' came a voice from out of nowhere. 'Drowning. No, no, murder!'

Mrs Popejoy's eyes and mouth popped open at the same time.

But the voice continued. 'They killed me. Killed me. Murder, murder.'

'Who the dickens are ya?' Luty blurted when it looked like Mrs Popejoy was going to say something.

'My name is Dorothy.' The voice was a piteous wail.

As instructed, Luty kept her eyes on Mrs Popejoy, who was rapidly turning white. 'What do ya want?'

'Justice,' the voice screeched.

Hatchet jumped and the veiled lady jumped too.

'Is that Lady Lucia?' the butler asked Mrs Popejoy quickly.

Mrs Popejoy blinked in confusion. Luty almost laughed out loud. They had the woman between a rock and a hard place. The medium could hardly admit she hadn't the faintest idea what was going on.

'Dead.' This voice was decidedly different from the first. 'Murder.'

'Who the blazes is this one?' Luty asked. 'Lady Lucia? Yoo-hoo, are you Lady Lucia?'

'Abigail . . .' The voice trailed off. 'Murdered.'

Mrs Popejoy was slowly rising from her chair, her face a mask of shock.

Suddenly the door to the drawing room burst open. Inspector Witherspoon, Constable Barnes and Ashley Phipps entered.

'You can't go in there, sir,' yelled the maid. She rushed after them. 'Mrs Popejoy is having a séance.'

The bright light from the hallway spilled into the

darkened drawing room. Mrs Popejoy, her hand at her throat, her eyes wide with fear, stared at Ashley Phipps as if she'd seen a ghost.

'Dreadfully sorry, Mrs Popejoy,' the inspector began. 'I say, it's awfully dark in here, do you think we could have some light?'

The maid looked at Mrs Popejoy, but the woman wasn't paying any attention to her. Her eyes were fixed on Ashley Phipps. The girl hesitated for a second and then began to light the lamps.

'So sorry to interrupt you, Esme dear,' Phipps said, 'but this police inspector here seems to think I've something to do with some murder.'

'Egads,' the inspector cried as he caught sight of Luty Belle. 'It's Mrs Crookshank. What are you doing here?'

'I've come fer a séance,' she said tartly. 'And we were gettin' a right earful before you interrupted. Some women named Dorothy and Abigail was comin' through from the other side. They claimed they was murdered. Maybe it's a good thing you showed up after all.'

Mrs Popejoy suddenly gasped and they all turned as Leonard Hodges came stalking into the drawing room.

'Leonard,' she yelped, 'what are you doing here?'

He pulled a note out of his pocket. 'You sent me a note, you said it was urgent.'

'I did no such thing,' she said earnestly, glancing quickly at the inspector. 'I think you'd better leave,' she continued in a weak voice. 'We're rather busy right now.'

'Please don't go, Mr Hodges,' the inspector put in hastily. 'It's just as well you dropped in. The constable and I have a few questions for you.'

'Just a minute,' Phipps chimed in. He stared at Hodges. 'Who are you?'

Hodges seemed to notice Phipps for the first time. He started in surprise and then glanced quickly at Mrs Popejoy.

No one spoke. There was only the sound of Hatchet's chair as he quietly got to his feet.

'I don't know what the meaning of this is,' Mrs Popejoy began.

Witherspoon decided to take control of the situation. 'Mr Hodges. You stated that you escorted Mrs Popejoy to the train station on the night your wife was murdered, is that correct?'

'Of course.' Hodges looked nervously from Phipps to Mrs Popejoy.

'But Mr Phipps here claims he was the one who escorted Mrs Popejoy on the night of January fourth.'

'He's mistaken. Tell him, Esme, tell him he's wrong.'

'I most certainly am not mistaken,' Phipps insisted. 'For goodness' sake, Esme. My mother and Mrs Cravit both saw you when you came to the door. This is ridiculous. Just tell this policeman the truth.'

'The truth,' she whispered.

'Don't say another word, Esme,' Hodges ordered.

'Esme,' Phipps exclaimed. 'What on earth is going on here? You know yourself we made arrangements for me to take you to the station weeks ago.'

'Is it Dorothy who got herself murdered?' Luty asked innocently. 'Or was it someone named Abigail?'

The inspector shot Luty a puzzled frown. Constable Barnes cleared his throat and Hatchet moved over to stand by the door.

'Mr Hodges, I'm afraid I'll have to ask you to come down to the station to help with our enquiries,' Witherspoon said.

'Based on what?' Hodges snapped. He pointed at Phipps. 'This man's word. I don't see why you should believe him.'

'It's not just Mr Phipps's word. You see, we've also found the driver of the hansom you and Mrs Popejoy took that night. He's prepared to swear that he stopped in Lewis Road. That's where you obviously slipped off, and Mrs Popejoy then allowed Mr Phipps to accompany her. What we'd like to know, sir, is where did you go when you left Mrs Hodges?'

Hodges looked wild. 'This is absurd. Why, Esme can confirm that I never left her side that evening.'

Witherspoon turned to stare at Mrs Popejoy. 'Is that correct?'

'I – I – I'm not really certain,' Mrs Popejoy muttered.

'Mrs Popejoy,' the inspector said sternly, 'I'm afraid I must insist that you come down to the station also. There's something very much amiss here. I think, perhaps, you know more about Mrs Hodges's death than we've been led to believe.'

'Now see here,' Phipps sputtered. 'The only thing Mrs Popejoy did that night was go to Southend to visit a friend. That's hardly a crime.'

'No, but conspiracy to murder is,' Barnes put in softly.

'Murder!' Mrs Popejoy exclaimed. 'I didn't kill anyone. And I'm not going to take the blame.'

Outside the window, Mrs Jeffries and Betsy huddled closer to the window, straining to hear everything that

229

was being said. The housekeeper felt a surge of relief as she heard the uncertainty in Mrs Popejoy's voice. Their plan was working. Esme Popejoy had become so unhinged during the séance that she didn't realize what she was saying.

'It was his idea, his plan,' Mrs Popejoy insisted. Her voice had a high-pitched hysterical ring to it. 'He killed them both. He bungled the first one and now he's trying to pin this one on me. But I won't have it. I'm not going to face the hangman for the likes of him.'

'Shut up, you stupid fool,' Hodges hissed. He glared at her. 'She doesn't know what she's talking about. She's a silly, hysterical woman and you can't believe a word she says.'

'They'll believe me, all right,' Mrs Popejoy yelled. 'I'm not the one that pulled that trigger. I'm not the one that's going to hang.'

'I think we'd better get to the station,' the inspector said. 'We'll need complete statements from both of you.'

'We're not going to accompany you anywhere,' Hodges stated flatly.

'I'm afraid you are, sir,' Witherspoon began. He broke off suddenly and his eyes widened. Beside him, he heard Constable Barnes's sharp hiss of breath.

Hodges had pulled out a gun.

Witherspoon fought off a surge of panic as he stared down into the barrel of a revolver. 'Now, Mr Hodges, sir. Put that thing away before someone gets hurt.'

'Put this gun down?' Hodges laughed. 'And let you arrest me. I hardly think so, Inspector.'

'But I wasn't going to arrest you,' Witherspoon

replied. He swallowed heavily. 'I was merely going to have you and Mrs Popejoy accompany me to the station.'

'To help with your enquiries.' Hodges sneered and jerked his head towards Mrs Popejoy. 'She wouldn't last an hour under police interrogation. I should never have trusted her. Silly, stupid cow. I should have known how weak she was when she started believing in this spiritualism nonsense. Go to the station with you? Do you think I'm a fool?'

'No, of course you're not a fool,' the inspector said. He forced himself to stay calm. Egads, here he was in a whole roomful of people facing a madman with a gun.

A chill blast of wind slammed into the room, rattling the partially open window. Hodges started and whirled towards the window.

Suddenly a hand sliced down on Hodges's arm and with a cry of rage he dropped the gun. It clattered to the floor and skittered across the room.

Barnes rushed to Hodges, twisted his arms behind his back and slapped him in a pair of handcuffs.

There was a loud commotion in the hallway and everyone turned. Three police constables burst into the room. 'We heard you needed some help, sir,' the first one said.

Witherspoon blinked in confusion. Where the devil had these fellows come from? But he wasn't one to look a gift horse in the mouth. 'Quite right, we can use a hand here.' He pointed to Mrs Popejoy, who was staring blankly into space. 'Please apprehend that lady.' Then he turned to Leonard Hodges. 'I'm arresting you for the murder of Abigail Hodges.'

The inspector cautioned both his prisoners and a moment later they were led away.

Hatchet knelt down and picked the weapon up. He handed it to Witherspoon. 'I believe you should take charge of this, sir.'

'Thank you, er, ah . . . Mister . . .'

'Hatchet, sir. I'm Mrs Crookshank's butler.'

'Well, good work, Mr Hatchet.' Witherspoon stared at him curiously. 'I must say, that was a rather nice trick. Wherever did you learn how to disarm a man in that fashion?'

'Now will someone please tell me 'ow you knew it were Mr Hodges and Mrs Popejoy?' Wiggins pleaded.

They were sitting in the drawing room at Upper Edmonton Gardens, for Mrs Jeffries insisted they might all as well be comfortable. The inspector was likely to be tied up for hours at the police station.

Mrs Goodge had brought in a tray of cocoa and a Battenberg cake. 'You mean you haven't figured it out yet?' she asked as she sliced the cake.

'If I'd figured it out, I wouldn't be askin' now, would I?' Wiggins replied. He nodded his thanks as the cook handed him a plate.

'Well,' Mrs Jeffries began, 'I can't say it all came to me in a blinding flash, but once all of you began bringing in your various items of information and gossip, I realized the murder could only have been committed by the two of them. There were so many little things that didn't add up.' She shrugged. 'And once I began to really examine everyone's motive, the suspect who had the most to gain was Mr Hodges.'

'Excuse me, madam,' Hatchet said. 'But I don't quite follow that line of reasoning. Surely Mr Felcher, Mrs Trotter and Miss Marsden all benefited by Mrs Hodges's death.'

'True. But how much, enough to risk being convicted of murder?' Mrs Jeffries stated. 'You see, Miss Marsden and Mr Vogel had no reason to kill her; they already had made plans to go to Canada.'

'What about Mr Felcher?' Betsy asked.

'True. He gained control of his inheritance, but why kill Mrs Hodges now? He'd been putting up with his aunt for years. Besides, he had no idea what time the séance was going to end that night and he certainly didn't know that Mr Hodges wasn't going to be bringing Mrs Hodges home.' Mrs Jeffries reached for her cocoa. 'The same can be said of Mrs Trotter. No, when you looked at the murder rationally, when you examined all the pieces of the puzzle, there was really only one solution. But of course I didn't begin seeing the pattern until the note.'

'Which note?' Wiggins wiped a cake crumb off his cheek. 'The ones you sent tonight?'

'No, the one instructing the police to search the Hodges house,' she said. 'You see, that was a deliberate attempt to point the finger of guilt at Miss Marsden. Once I realized that, there was only one person who had reason to want Miss Marsden and Mr Vogel convicted of this crime.'

'What reason?' Luty asked. 'I figured whoever sent that note was just tryin' to save his own skin.'

Mrs Jeffries shook her head. 'Oh no, that note led to the discovery of the jewels in Miss Marsden's room.

There was only one person who would benefit if Miss Marsden were convicted of murder. That person was Leonard Hodges. You see, you can't profit from a crime, so if she'd been convicted of murdering her aunt, Mr Hodges would have received the whole of Mrs Hodges's fortune. I think that at first they really tried to make the murder look like a burglary gone bad. But when they bungled it so badly, they had to fall back on another plan. In one sense it was an even better plan. Getting Miss Marsden arrested would have given Mr Hodges the whole of his wife's fortune.'

'But how did they do it?' Wiggins persisted. 'I know it 'ad somethin' to do with that hansom and stoppin' on the way to the station. I know that Mr Hodges got out and nipped off to kill his wife and Mrs Popejoy got that Phipps feller to ride off with her. But didn't the driver notice he were a different bloke than the one she started out with?'

'No, Mr Hodges had deliberately worn the same kind of coat and hat that Mr Phipps habitually wore,' Mrs Jeffries said. 'Remember when Betsy told us that Mrs Hodges had got angry at her husband for buying some cheap clothes from a ready-wear shop in the East End? Well, then when Betsy mentioned that she'd followed Mr Hodges to St James's Church and watched him give an almost new coat and hat away, I realized that Hodges had deliberately tried to disguise himself that night and now he wanted to get rid of the evidence.'

'How do you think he got Vogel's gun?' Smythe asked.

'Probably exactly like Mr Vogel himself said. He stole it.'

234

'Well, it was a fine piece of work, Hepzibah,' Luty said earnestly.

'Oh please, don't give me all the credit.' She gestured around the room. 'All of you deserve to take a bow. Smythe's tracking down that coachman and confirming they'd stopped so the switch could take place, Betsy's information about the coat and hat, Wiggins following Miss Marsden and of course you and Hatchet were invaluable.'

'Do you think Phipps was in on the plot?' Betsy asked.

'No. I think he's an innocent pawn.' Mrs Jeffries took a sip of cocoa. 'Remember, Mrs Popejoy hadn't had a thing to do with the man for months. Until, that is, they were ready to do murder. Then she up and asks him to escort her to the train station. It was really a very simple plot. Mr Hodges and Mrs Popejoy drive off in a hansom, providing the both of them with an ironclad alibi for the murder of his wife. They make a stop, Hodges gets out, goes home, commits murder and then saunters off to his club. Mrs Popejoy lets Mr Phipps escort her to the train station and goes off to visit a friend. Clever, but not quite clever enough.'

'Well, it was jolly clever of you two to take that Madame Natalia along with you tonight.' Mrs Goodge clucked her tongue. 'Imagine bein' able to do all that fancy stuff with her voice.'

Luty chuckled. 'She's good. Her father was a ventriloquist. And it sure helped to move things along. Mrs Popejoy was so rattled by all them voices from the grave she give herself away.'

'Do you think they really did murder his first wife?' Smythe asked, his expression sober.

'Yes,' Mrs Jeffries replied slowly, 'but I'm not sure the police will ever prove it. And, of course, Hodges didn't gain anything. Dorothy Throgmorton's family saw to that. I suspect that's why he married Mrs Hodges. He and Mrs Popejoy planned it from the beginning. We know they've known each other for years. He married Abigail Hodges, acted the devoted husband, introduced her to spiritualism and Mrs Popejoy and then murdered her.'

Hatchet clucked his tongue. 'Disgusting. Murdering innocent women for money.'

Mrs Jeffries nodded and then looked at Hatchet curiously. 'I must say, Hatchet, you certainly saved the day, disarming a man with a gun. You were quite brave tonight.'

'Hatchet's right good at some things,' Luty agreed with a wide grin.

The butler glowered at his mistress. 'Bravery had nothing to do with it. I assure you, I disarmed Mr Hodges for the sole purpose of inhibiting Mrs Crookshank from pulling out her own weapon. The last time she pulled a gun out of her muff, we were repairing holes in the ceilings for weeks.'